Praise for *Freya the Deer*

"An unlikely stunner! *Freya the Deer* comes across as a modern-day Grimm's tale read beneath a strobe light. Richman's self-possessed prose ensures that readers will face only their own judgments/opinions of autistic teens, Jewish ethics, contemporary paganism, and the Black Lives Matter movement in this important work."

—Stacey Levine, author of *Mice 1961*,
American Book Award winner & Pulitzer Prize finalist

"Meg Richman's gorgeous, enticing prose is a siren calling us to a messy intersection of blind love, political righteousness, and uncompromising morality. *Freya the Deer* is a joy to read and a tantalizing knot I'll be untying for a long, long time."

—Patrick Flores-Scott, author of
American Road Trip and *No Going Back*

"Meg Richman's *Freya the Deer* introduces us to the unforgettable Freya, an atypical girl who, while on a quest to discover proof of the soul's existence, experiences the world in unusual and sometimes fantastical ways. A socially-conscious fairytale, Richman's poignant and sometimes heartbreaking coming-of-age novel is a testament to the limitless boundaries of love."

—Zeeva Bukai, author of *The Anatomy of Exile*

"Tragedy and transcendence hover over Richman's evocative narrative… This deeply moving and intellectually challenging novel offers a complex portrait of a singular woman grappling with maturity, love, and the cost of doing what's right."

—*BookLife Reviews*

"A sensitive protagonist anchors this oddball bildungsroman…Freya is a well-developed character…both believable and fairy tale-like. The climax and denouement of the novel, rendered in sharp, poignant prose, are especially affecting."

—*Kirkus Reviews*

FREYA
THE DEER

Meg Richman

Montpelier, VT

Freya the Deer ©2025 Meg Richman

Release Date: March 3, 2026
All Rights Reserved. Printed in the USA.

Paperback ISBN: 978-1-57869-215-6
eBook ISBN: 978-1-57869-224-8
Library of Congress Control Number: 2026900189

Published by Rootstock Publishing
an imprint of Ziggy Media, LLC
Montpelier, VT 05602
info@rootstockpublishing.com
www.rootstockpublishing.com

Book formatting by Eddie Vincent, ENC Graphic Services.
Author photo by Mark White.

Book cover by English or French artist, active in the late 14th century,
The Wilton Diptych, about 1395–9
© The National Gallery, London

No AI training. No part of this book may be reproduced or transmitted in any form or by any means, electronic or mechanical, including photocopying, recording, or by an information storage and retrieval system (except by a journalist or reviewer who may quote brief passages in an academic or editorial review) without permission in writing.

For reprint permissions, or to schedule a book club visit or author reading, contact the author at edengarden@comcast.net.

To my darling Jesse who taught me how another brain works.

Prelude

As her thin fingers separated the strands of colored wire, she noticed how similar this process was to lace-making. Tatting was mostly a lost art, but she had taught herself out of a crafts book and created yards of delicate floral meshwork from old Belgian patterns. These she had sewn onto her curtains, her pillows, her dress hems. The practice meant she was particularly deft at bomb-making, weaving and connecting the copper threads just so. Which she was also doing from instructions, this time found in the library by her partner in crime and copied meticulously into a composition notebook. For his part, he found the library to be a physical version of the internet, with most all information available, absent the memes. He admired her dexterity and attention to detail, and she would do anything for him, with an animal sort of loyalty.

He brought her a glazed vegan donut from her favorite bakery two bus stops away and fed it to her bite by bite lest she get her hands sticky. She barely lost focus on her work as she chewed, and he smiled, watching her. He found her concentration beguiling. She wouldn't allow him to play music or even talk while she worked. Setting up the timer and remote was serious business and required her complete attention. The explosives, though unlikely to go off spontaneously, held the power to blow the entire house to kingdom come.

PART ONE
Atypical

Chapter One

reya wasn't considered an idiot because of her academic performance. Though she was singularly uncompetitive, she did well enough in school through a combination of willingness to do as she was told and good reading skills. The latter came from her parents who were both professors at fancy universities, oft-published and quoted by their peers. Starting in infancy they plied her with stories and books, ballads from every land on earth, and Sesame Street on TV—even a monkey might have learned to read under these circumstances. Her nature was wide-eyed and guileless if unsmiling. Her unrelenting failure to respond to others with the expected facial expression or turn of phrase is why she seemed stupid to many. It was like she wasn't quite there. Freya's idiocy wasn't spoken aloud but was generally agreed upon by many of those she encountered, particularly peers.

As a child she flourished in a world of make-believe. Fairies were more real to her than were the neighborhood children. Each night before trundling into bed, she kissed every one of her many dolls, stuffed animals and figurines, so none felt neglected. They took turns sleeping with her. She refused to choose favorites. Nor did she abandon her clothes to Goodwill when they began to fray and rip with age, but instead carefully embroidered patches over holes or threadbare spots. If pants or skirts became too short as she grew, she sewed borders on the hems, and likewise let out the seams and added fabric when her body expanded in girth. Her raiments were strange, multi-colored affairs, patched with paisley, tattooed with needlework birds and flowers. She was loyal to what she loved, including clothes. Other children avoided her.

Once they gave birth to her, Freya's parents realized how all-consuming parenting was, and made sure not to have another. They adored her, but honestly perhaps not as much as they adored their areas, as they called their studies. Ruth's was quark theory in the Physics Department at MIT. Harold specialized in ethics in the Philosophy Department at Harvard. The parents had met in graduate school at a colloquium on integrated academic curricula held at Yale, and married. They both changed their name to Rubenstein, as his surname was Ruben and hers Stein. They waited until they were nearly forty to have Freya, a name that sounded vaguely Yiddish but wasn't—just right for American Jews. By then the twin Japanese maple saplings they had planted as a mutual housewarming gift had matured in their Cambridge garden and were high as the house, creating a generous canopy of shade in their front yard. Mother, father, and child could sit at dinner, gloaming light drifting softly through the French windows, each lost in his or her own thoughts, perfectly happy and never speaking a word to one another beyond please pass the broccoli. Harold might hum to himself—a kind of soundtrack to his deep musings, and Freya might babble the songs of the characters conversing in her head. But the humming and singing were low volume and for the others at the table the sounds were comforting and subliminal, like the purr of the refrigerator's motor.

If Freya were odd she came by it hereditarily, whether by nature or by nurture, because so were Ruth and Harold, truth be told. Ensconced in their respective ivory towers, they put the absent in absent-minded.

On several occasions during her childhood Freya brought home furry strays, cats or dogs, once a field mouse, and asked her parents to let her keep them. Some were probably not so much stray as they were lured. The parents always explained that it was impossible to give them their home, because animals entailed too much responsibility and what would become of them when they went on summer vacation. Every summer they went to Rome or Paris or the Cape for a few weeks. A cat or dog could not take care of itself. And so Freya would walk the animal back to where she initially met it, sending it off with tears and returning home in a state of melancholy that her parents barely registered, although once when she was particularly sad they bought her a goldfish. If it died while they were away for the summer, they thought, it wouldn't be such a big deal. Rapunzel, that was the name Freya gave it, went belly up in the spring, before they had a chance to abandon it. Freya put her golden orange friend in a velvet-lined box and buried it under the forsythia bush beneath her window. She decorated the grave with an altar of smooth stones, pop-beads and glistening costume jewels.

The parents were distracted and messy, so Freya cleaned up after them, taking their abandoned coffee cups to the kitchen sink and the discarded newspapers to the recycling bin. When keys or wallets were lost, she could find them. She had an innate desire for esthetic order—not for the exactitude of Versailles, but for visual romance, composed bounty, like Monet's Giverny. She didn't like extraneous objects like junk mail or wine-smudged goblets to obscure the simple beauty of the den or dining room. Unlike all the other kids at her school, she did not devour TV or computer games. The buzzy electric pixilation of the screens repelled her. It sounded like insect swarms. Her lack of interest in contemporary culture proved strong evidence of her dimness to the other kids whose references she never recognized. She liked to sit in the alcove and read her mother's childhood books, *The Secret Garden*, *The Little Princess*, *The Witch of Blackbird Pond*.

In high school she attended a magnet program devoted to the Arts, so her patchwork clothes and dreamy mien struck her fellows as less extraordinary than they might have in a more traditional school. Still, her social skills were underdeveloped from many years of minimal use, and she didn't make friends. Some of her peers were even a little frightened of her, because she didn't smile or show interest in normal things like TikTok or celebrities. At that age she graduated to reading *Wuthering Heights* and *Tess of the D'Urbervilles* and the complete works of George Eliot. She spent many hours in the ceramics room and painting studio, creating works heavy in symbolism and maybe just a little creepy in an Alice-in-Wonderland sort of way.

Her creative writing teacher took a liking to her, or at least to her poetry. Reading as much as she did, Freya's vocabulary was large and she strayed from the often trite adolescent themes of love and confused identity as neither were relevant to her. Less obvious were the actual themes of her work. There were obscure phrases and juicy metaphors; a reader could get lost in the jungle of the words and images. Tom (they called the teachers by their first names at this school) found himself dizzied and dazzled in her tangled literary rainforest. Vulnerable due to a recent breakup by which he was surprised and humiliated, he began to fantasize about what he imagined was in his student's mind. Just the sight of her would not have aroused his lust; she was a wisp of a human with mere suggestions of flesh where hips or breasts would be on an average girl her age. Yes she had rich black ringlets and rosy lips, but these latter did not hide her overbite, nor the former her rather large ears.

Tom showed some examples of the poetry he was falling in love with to his sister.

"Are you kidding me?" she said. "This is drivel. It's absolute sophomoric bullshit, Tom."

"What do you mean?" He felt as if she had stabbed him. He was shocked. And he thought to himself in her defense, that Freya *was* a sophomore.

"Tommy, this writing makes no sense. It pretends to, but it doesn't. It enjoys its own obscurity. It's silly. You don't actually like it?" His sister was an English Literature teacher too, at a tony private school, and a striving poet herself.

He quickly gathered the pages back and hid his hurt. "I just found them interesting. You know, coming from a high school student . . ."

"The drawings are pretty," the sister said by way of apology. Freya had doodled all over the margins of her poems—rabbits and curling flower vines and peacocks, as if they were medieval manuscripts. Tom nodded and stuffed the papers back into his folder, and the folder into his backpack. He changed the subject to this morning's conversation with their mother, who was losing her memory and grip on reality.

But his fascination with Freya persisted. His obsessive remembering of her enigmatic poetry lines was in inverse relation to his mother's increasing forgetfulness about just about everything. Yes, not only had his girlfriend left him, his own mother could not distinguish him from the orderly who fed her with a spoon. Tom was really at a low point. Some would argue that this in no way excused the behavior that followed during that snowy winter.

The blizzards were relentless. The city's plows created huge banks along the curbs. As soon as these crusted over with sooty ice, another storm came until the drifts were heads higher than the pedestrians who slid, cursing, along the sidewalks, shoveled slick by their neighbors. Freya borrowed her father's ski boots, stuffed with several extra pairs of wool socks, and shuffled her way to school, falling only three times. The size of the boots made her look like a clown, in keeping with her image as an individual not to be taken seriously. When she reached the somber brick building, its eaves jaggedly serrated with a row of dangerous looking icicles, she went inside and immediately took off the boots. For the rest of the day she glided around the halls in her multiple layers of socks, which did nothing to enhance her reputation.

When a new blizzard began after lunch, most of the student body took it as permission to leave early, but Freya was not one to jump on an excuse for anything or shirk a perceived responsibility. The day was dark, and in the dim ceramics room she watched the thick snow fall through the glass before turning back to the wheel and the slimy clay. Aside from the teacher, who kept looking anxiously out the window, wondering if she would ever see her home and Akita again, Freya was the only person in the studio. Finally the teacher gave in to her own worry, and asked that Freya clean up now, as she was going to call in absent for the rest of the day.

After that Freya wandered around the nearly empty school, until she found Tom and two of his acolytes in his classroom where her next period was scheduled. Freya heard them talking at his desk over the wonders of anime, about which she had only vague notions. She skated on her socks to her desk and sat down, happy to have some time to daydream while she waited for the start of class. When the dismissal bell rang, the other two students left, and Tom also went out, probably for a bathroom break. Freya rested her cheek on her arms, staring out at the snow.

Tom came back in, wiping his damp hands on his black jeans. In the darkness of the storm, Freya's white skin shone like alabaster, he thought, which was kind as another might describe it as pale or ashen. He also thought she looked a little like Snow White—the Disney version. The black hair and the heart-shaped mouth. "Dolphin chatter the calliope of the sea." For some reason a line from one of her poems popped into his head.

The starting bell rang. No other students had yet arrived. "We'll wait a few more minutes to see if anyone else comes," he told her. No one did. Tom cleared his throat. Freya sat up straight and twined her hands together resting on the desk. Often energy zinged through her fingers when she was anxious and she would try to shake it out, but she avoided doing it in front of other people if she could help herself.

"I'm curious where your poetry comes from?" he asked her.

She furrowed one eyebrow. "I write it," she said. *Did he think she plagiarized it?*

"Yes, of course you write it, but what inspires it? What are your influences?"

She wrinkled her nose. Her nose was a fairly large one, large like her ears. He was glad to notice this, as the prominence of her nose somehow elevated her above the simpering Disney character he had unconsciously assigned her. She wasn't just cute as a button. Her nose gave her gravitas. "Um," she said. "I mean, everything is an influence. Doesn't a person just kind of drink in everything around them? I do. And then I just kind of write it down." She pulled her hands apart and waved them around in front of her. "Scrambled. Synthesized." She quickly put her hands under her rear to rein them in just in case they were tempted to take off in flight.

He nodded. He certainly didn't think her an idiot as he knew some of her classmates did—he thought her wise for her age. Maybe a genius. "Do you want some hot chocolate?" He pointed to the electric kettle on the table behind his desk. "It's hot chocolate weather."

He had some instant in a packet which he pulled out of a drawer. The kind with the miniature marshmallows.

"No thanks."

"Tea?"

"No thanks." She wanted to get back to poetry. "Do you write?" she asked him.

"Me? No. My sister does. We're twins." He tossed the cocoa mix back into his desk.

"That would be so interesting. To have a twin of the opposite sex. You could maybe have a chance of really being a whole person when you were put together."

"You don't think you're a whole person?"

"Well. I'm one sided."

"Do you think males and females are so different?"

She laughed a little. "Just look at us."

"But inside?" he asked. "Are we different inside?"

"I assume so. But how can I ever really know."

He shifted his head left to right and left again, acknowledging her point. "Maybe communication."

"Yeah, I'm not much of a communicator."

"Why is that?"

"I don't know. Never have been."

"You could learn."

"It's OK. I like it in here."

"In here?"

"Inside myself."

"Well, poetry is a way to share, right? To get outside yourself."

She shrugged, as if to say, you don't get me and I don't care that you don't. That's certainly not why she wrote. She looked out the window. The world was filled with snow. There was no negative space which was not snow. Tom's eyes followed hers. "Man," he said. "I wonder if we'll be able to get home." Just then the principal came over the loudspeaker to advise any students or staff still remaining in the building that the school was closing and everyone should head out immediately. He would be sending robo-phone calls, texts, and emails to parents and guardians. Tom looked at Freya, enlarging his eyes in mock surprise. "Yikes. How are we supposed to navigate through this?"

Freya actually felt scared. She wondered if the snow would smother her. Outside it looked like there was no air. "I'm not going out there," she said.

Tom smiled, as if she were kidding, but then realized she wasn't. He could feel his heart in his chest as its rate sped up.

"OK," he said. He said it smiling, as if they were playing a game together. "I'll stay too, then. But we'll have to hide until everyone is gone because they won't want us to stay. Are you good at hiding?"

"I'm not going out into a blizzard."

"OK."

He turned off the lights and locked the door from the outside, as he would do if there were a school shooter.

"Can I call my parents?" She was probably the only student at the school who didn't carry a phone in her pocket.

"Of course." He gestured toward the phone hanging on the wall.

Freya dialed home. She told them she was going to stay at school overnight because she didn't want to brave the storm. Apparently there was no objection, because after saying yes several times in answer to questions, she hung up without drama. After that they sat in silence for half an hour. Tom was interacting with his phone, scrolling through news and stand-up comics and tweets, while Freya watched the snow accumulate outside. When enough time had passed that he thought the coast had to be clear Tom looked up.

"Let's move to the teachers' lounge. It's more comfortable there."

She followed him down the hallway. Her mood had darkened, so she no longer slid along on her nubby socks, instead walking, one foot after the other, heel toe, heel toe. The teachers' lounge door was locked but Tom had the key. Freya hadn't been inside before. She noted several couches, which boded well for sleep that night. She hugged her woolen coat around her thinking it would do for a blanket. Then she took it off and put it down as a place saver on the couch farthest from the door.

"Do you want to play Scrabble?" asked Tom.

"Yes. I know how to play that game. We have it at the cottage we rent on the Cape."

Three times she used all seven tiles, and rarely didn't take advantage of a triple letter or triple word score. Her victory was lopsided. "That's a little embarrassing," Tom said.

"Why?"

"Well, because I'm the teacher and you're the student."

"We all have our different talents."

Everything she said made him like her more. Even the fact that she seemed to have no sense of humor—her lack of irony and cynicism was refreshing. She carefully organized the game pieces back in their box. "I'd like to read now," she said. "If that's all right with you."

"Sure. Of course. What kind of a lit teacher would I be if I didn't want you to read . . ."

She retreated to her couch in the corner and pulled *Anna Karenina* out of her backpack.

He went into the attached kitchen and opened the refrigerator. Across the room he announced to her, "People have left lots of food in here. We'll have plenty to eat." She didn't answer because she was lost in her book.

He was still pretending to himself that this was a completely normal situation. He was still pretending that he was just a good guy, helping out a scared student. He was magnanimous and caring.

He found a few wool blankets folded in a cupboard with the rolled yoga mats and straps—a good thing because the furnace thermostat was set to 60 degrees during the evening and the chill would settle in soon. He took two blankets to Freya over on her couch and sat beside her. She glanced up from her book but went right back to it. She was almost finished with it.

"Do you find that book romantic?" he asked.

"Not so much," she said. "It seems more about morality, and how to live morally to me."

"But what about that charming Count Vronsky?"

She wrinkled her nose. "Yuck."

He realized this was not an entry point, so he backed off the topic. "Do you want me to fix you a sandwich? There are lots of sandwich meats and cheeses."

"I don't eat animals. Or cheese. I'm vegan. I'm OK. I have a granola bar." She patted her backpack.

He waited, snacking, playing Shanghai on the computer compulsively, his anxiety compounding, for the hours until she fell asleep under the scratchy woolen blankets. She snored softly, and he thought it a lovely sound. In her dream she was stringing snowflakes together into a necklace. Magically, they did not melt, but instead shimmered like finely wrought silver filigree, fit for an empress. Freya's breathing was regular and deep.

Tom argued with himself, tried to be better than he actually was, but finally his lust won. He returned to the girl lying so peacefully on the sofa and kissed her softly until she was just barely awake. When she realized where she was and what was happening, she awoke fully, but was paralyzed by the bizarre nature of the situation. He fondled her gently, testing how far she would let him go.

Freya was accustomed to unwanted social advances. Not from peers, who rather veered away from her, and no sexual ones as yet. But she had fielded inquisitive conversations from her parents' friends, insistent hugs from her Grandmother Rachel who smelled too strongly of fried onion and old age. She had learned to enter into a zone of numbness, shutting out the physical and emotional sensations that threatened to overwhelm. It was like holding her breath, but it was her whole being suspended in a jellied aspic of non-feeling. Thus, anesthetized, she did not resist and Tom undressed her, though that subjected her pale skin to the prickles of the wool. Just one more harsh sensation to ignore.

He did not go so far as to take her virginity, though she might have let him, purely out of politeness. With wonder, he touched the bone between her small breasts, her white stomach, her narrow hips. Dizzied, he jacked off kneeling over her, letting out a dragon roar and hosing her with cum.

She looked at the thick and sticky liquid with horrified curiosity. "Yuck," she said. Tom went to the kitchen naked and came back to sheepishly wipe her clean with a dish rag wet with warm water.

Immediately he was overcome by guilt and fear. He almost cried. She was fascinated—he was an amoeba on a slide.

"You can do whatever you want. Of course. But just so you know, if you tell anyone what happened here, I would get in a lot of trouble. I would get fired."

"Do you think you deserve to get in trouble? Do you think it was wrong?"

He looked at her, but she didn't make eye contact. She rarely did, even in less fraught conversation.

"Well, I didn't want to hurt you." He was struggling. "But, maybe from some perspectives . . ."

"Hmm," she said.

His heart was misfiring. What if she told? His life would be over.

"Are you going to tell?"

"Who would I tell?"

"I don't know. A friend . . . Your parents . . ."

"I don't have a friend, not in real life. And ick. I wouldn't tell my parents. Ick."

"OK," he said. He pushed a black ringlet behind her ear. The large lobe held it in place easily. "Thank you so much."

She shook off his revolting touch. She wanted to sleep and be done with him.

"Do you feel OK about it?" he asked timidly.

"So far so good," she said. She gave him a thumbs up. "But I'm really tired."

"Ok, I'll let you get some sleep. Thank you." He retreated sheepishly to a sofa across the room.

Freya put her patchworked clothes back on to protect her skin from the harsh texture of the blankets. She lay back down on the couch. Curled on her side she could see the streetlamp out the window. The snow was no longer a flurry, but rather large, discreet flakes swirling slowly down. She watched them make their sad, graceful way to the ground until she fell back asleep.

In the morning the sun came out glaring off the banks of snow. The sky was a silky robin's egg. In such an excess of brightness, Freya's fear of suffocation dissolved, and she felt able to scrape her way across the icy blocks to her home. Tom left the building a few minutes after she did in case anyone was watching; the school was closed for the day.

On her route home, in the snow-packed entryway of a dentist's office, Freya first heard moaning and hacking, and then saw a woman in rags. The woman was as close to the doorway as she could curl her body. She looked like a dying pigeon. Freya was amazed that she was alive—if she slept there all night she ought to have frozen to death. Perhaps she was recently released from a shelter that kicked its guests out in the morning. But Freya worried for possible frostbite in the bitter weather. The sun, which was bright but not warming, had not yet reached the shaded alcove where the bird-like woman lay. Freya hovered over her for a moment, wondering what she should do. All she could think was to warm her, so she lay down next to her and wrapped her own relatively warm body around the lady. The woman stopped her whimpering and gradually relaxed into Freya's heat, emerging from sleep just long enough to say thank you.

"You're welcome," said Freya.

The icy cement was brutally hard, and Freya wondered if there wasn't a better softer nest somewhere, but then figured the woman was more experienced at this lifestyle than she. The vagabond smelled of urine and other aromas that had accumulated over time in her clothes. But she was used to her own odors, and when she woke again she said to Freya, without complaint, "You smell like sex."

"That would be Tom."

"Named after the cat no doubt."

Freya lay there with her, hugging, for maybe ten minutes, until she heard the woman breathing heavily, having returned to a deep slumber.

Then Freya took off her wool overcoat and placed it atop the sleeping lady. She gently put her striped mittens (she had knit these herself) on the woman's bluish hands. From her backpack she took her last granola bar, leaving it within the woman's reach. Then Freya hurried home, shivering in the raw morning without her coat, but certain that the dove lady needed it more than she did.

The backdoor of her house was swollen with the cold. Freya had to push with her shoulder to get in. Her mother was at the kitchen table, drinking coffee. "Oh, hello, dear."

"Hi Mom."

"Where's your coat?"

"I left it somewhere." Freya rarely even stretched the truth, but she feared her mother would frown on her rash act of charity. So she told the truth while implying a lie. It was the closest she could come.

"Oh no. Well, we'll find something in the attic. Grandma's old camel hair is up there, I think. How was the slumber party?"

"Slumber party?"

"Sleepover."

"Fine."

"You slept well?"

"Pretty well." Freya managed to tug her father's ski boots off.

"That's good, Hon. My university is closed today for the snow, so we can have a family day." Her mom was grading exams and went back to the papers with her red pen. Her mother meant they could work in the same room together, as long as no one talked too much. Freya went up the staircase to take a bath and see if she could thaw her frozen innards. The tub was an antique club footed affair. She poured in hot water and added bubbles that foamed into rainbow-tinged orbs as they caught the morning light. She was transported by their luminescence. She barely thought of her strange night with Tom—his needs seemed pathetically mortal to her, his behavior juvenile. Not worthy of her time.

A few days later her head began to itch like crazy, and she realized her hair was teeming with lice. Harold used a comb intended for the purpose, a remnant of Freya's elementary school days still in the medicine cabinet, carefully picking every nit from her glossy black hair. The eggs were easy to see by contrast. "Where on earth?" wondered Harold aloud. "I haven't had to do this since you were in second grade. Remember when your whole class kept trading the little rascals back and forth all winter?"

Freya did remember. Her father used the same bergamot aftershave then that she could smell now, and as she had done as a child, she cherished the feel of her father's large, soft, and clumsy hands tugging the comb through her hair, affording the nits every bit of his oft-times far away attention.

Chapter Two

reya wended her solitary way through high school. Tom continued to obsess about her for at least a year—she morphed in his imagination from Snow White to some sort of pre-Raphaelite Ophelia. There was truth to both, as she was the kind of person who would befriend a cadre of dwarves or surround herself with flower blossoms and fragrant herbs with medicinal powers. But he didn't dare to touch her again, as there was never again an opportunity served to him on a silver tray. Also, as his heart healed from his breakup a stronger sense of self-preservation returned. He began to date the algebra teacher.

People tried to pin Freya down—her counselor, her guitar teacher, very occasionally her father—about what she might want to do with her life. What college. What area of study. Live where. Do what. Her answers were wildly quixotic. Create a refuge for elephants. Man the space station. Work the levers from the gothic tower on a drawbridge. Give tours at Louisa May Alcott's childhood house. Aside from that last, which might be a possibility, it was all very *trip the light fantastic* and they worried about her tenuous connection to reality. When Harold expressed his concern to Ruth she attributed it to Freya's being an only child and having spent so much time with imaginary friends. Perhaps true, but not helpful. Luckily for Ruth's anxiety, she could only focus on family matters for a few minutes at a time, and Harold had about a fifteen-minute limit, so it was the school counselor who continued to press Freya. With erudite parents like hers, no one even considered the possibility of her not going to University. Her grades and scores were strong enough for most any place, though she paid no attention whatsoever and continued to live in her dreamworld. She would do whatever the counselor and parents thought best. So the counselor made her a list of small liberal arts colleges where a person like Freya might survive, if not thrive, and assigned her the prescribed essay prompts. Freya dutifully wrote them, fastidiously obeying the word limits. Though her answers were a bit eccentric, the counselor thought they might just work to garner the attention of a bored admissions officer. And indeed Freya was accepted everywhere she applied. Looking at all the photos of the schools, she chose the one that struck her as most magical: a college in the woods of Western Washington, the state, where one designed one's own curriculum. Harold and Ruth briefly tried to talk her into going someplace nearer, someplace more prestigious, but their attention was soon pulled away by all-consuming scholastic thought, and Freya was left to her own devices. As a graduation present, her parents bought her a smart phone and a dark green Subaru Forester, thinking that would be an appropriate car for the rugged region where she was going.

Instead of her usual retreat to the Cape, Ruth took a week off from quarks to drive across the country with Freya. They exchanged turns at the wheel. Having had a revelation that she was soon to lose her daughter to adulthood, Ruth promised herself she would take advantage of this time, put Physics aside, and focus on Freya. The car was packed up with the girl's clothes, bedding, arts and crafts supplies, her guitar, and her sewing machine. Across New York, Ohio, Indiana, Wisconsin. Mother and daughter would drive for eight hours and then stop at a motel with a swimming pool, where they could cool off and splash around. It was a long time since Freya had seen her mother so playful. Since she'd seen her this much at all. In the car they would sing along to Ruth's favorite CDs, Springsteen, Blondie, The Pretenders, or play twenty questions. For Ruth it was the first time she'd actually paid such concentrated attention to Freya since she started kindergarten.

Freya expressed little curiosity about others, and didn't ask her mother questions, but Ruth found herself reminiscing aloud about her own college experience, as they drove across the tidy farm-strewn state of Minnesota dotted with white silos and red barns, and then the unkempt fend-for-itself highway of North Dakota.

"I had lots of boyfriends before your dad," Ruth informed her daughter, coyly.

Freya looked at her blandly.

"I was a little sex-crazed," said her mom. "I think I liked the flattery of being desired. You know, growing up such a nerd, it was exciting. Probably more than sex itself."

Freya had never relished attention of any kind from other people, really, so she pondered this alien concept

"It was a phase. You'll probably want to experiment, too. All I ask is that you be safe. Do you have any condoms?"

Freya shook her head no. Ruth saw this in her peripheral vision.

"Well I'll stock you up at a drug store before I get on a plane home. And if anything gets serious you should go on the pill." Ruth glanced over at her expressionless daughter. "No need to be embarrassed."

Freya felt no embarrassment or shame but it was impossible to imagine using condoms with some strange male classmate. Her experience with Tom was all the experimentation she ever needed. She had an unwelcome memory of his sticky cum on her stomach. It had smelled eggy and sour. It had been years since she thought of it, but a whiff passed through her brain. She thought about how her neurons worked. Her mom said condom, but Tom hadn't used one. She did see his penis in her mind's eye, that was not a pretty thing, it was fungal. Condom, penis, connection. Synapses synapsing. And then they actually reprised the odor from long ago. Not the odor really, but the sensation of the odor. The memory of it as if she were smelling in the present. Fascinating, the thought that the reality no longer existed, but the memory of reality was locked there in the neurons and could re-create itself.

Meanwhile her mother continued to talk about her early exploits and assured Freya that she was a late bloomer but would come into her own. Freya thought to herself that she would remain in the bud if flowering meant stinky sticky men with sad needs. She took comfort in her mother's voice though. Going deep into the forest as she was about to do was an adventure but there could be a witch's house made of gingerbread, and she didn't pretend to herself that she wasn't scared. There would be no familiar Cambridge house to come home to, with its nooks and crannies and soups and curries and her father's Beethoven symphonies wafting through the air. She was well accustomed to creating imaginary worlds, but now it would be up to her to create a physical one to surround herself. Driving westward, if she only knew the tiny size of the dorm room she was about to encounter, she would have been less anxious. Once she laid out her quilts and hung up her clothes and set up her computer at the built-in desk there would only really be wall space for a poster or two. She would not have to furnish a palace or even a woodsman's cottage. Just a cement room ten by twelve.

They were in Montana, called Big Sky country for a reason. As they drove further west, the world seemed to decompress. The narrow sidewalks and charming Colonials of Massachusetts, all clenched tightly together, opened up like Japanese paper flowers that unfurl on the surface of water in a bowl. The mountains and the prairies and the sky—they expanded into much larger versions of themselves with vast spaces in between. Here there was room for bison to roam. Hard to imagine in New England. The tap water in Butte tasted like sulfur so they had to buy bottled, though there was something primordial and lovely about tasting the actual minerals of the earth. But then you had to spit it out again because honestly it was not a nice flavor. After that you had to eat a mint to rearrange your mouth.

The Rocky Mountains made her laugh. "Why are you laughing?" asked her mother.

"Because they're so big. Craggy. Snowy even in August. Like Heidi and the Grandfather." She had read the book many times, but also seen the Shirley Temple movie version. They had a DVD. The monkey grinder's monkey throwing chandelier crystals at the cruel governess character was still funny to her.

Ruth nodded, vaguely understanding that her daughter was amused by the monumental quality of the range. "Can you imagine crossing in a covered wagon?"

This took Freya aback. "How could they even?"

"There must have been a pass. Or maybe they didn't take a route this far north. Maybe they bypassed the mountains via a more southern route." Her mother switched the CD to REM as Freya downshifted to power up the slope. "Remember how you were obsessed with the Donner Party when you were a kid?"

Freya shivered. When she had run out of Donner Party books at the public library, her father had taken her to the Harvard Library. She had read every book there about the unfortunate cannibals. Her mother asked if they had been stuck in the Rockies.

"No, they were in the Sierras. In California."

"Why were you so interested in them? So morbid."

"I don't know. It was a feeling I got from the story. A sort of delicious horror. I liked to think about the moment they decided to actually take the plunge and eat someone. That moment of going over the edge beyond what they thought possible. I also wondered what it tasted like."

"Probably chicken."

Freya didn't get her mother's joke, but Ruth didn't mind because she amused herself.

Freya had stopped eating meat when she was five or six but she remembered the taste, and thought human flesh was probably more like beef than chicken. But by the time the Donners finally gave in to cannibalism, they were so thin their meat would have been sinewy and tough as gristle. A vegan herself, she thought she couldn't have done it, and would have offered herself as a human sacrifice. The settlers had eaten the horses first, and even that she couldn't have done. She would have been the first to starve. Just after she braided the horse manes into blankets to warm the smallest children.

They slept that night in Missoula. The rustic hotel they found was a little moldy and a line of ants striped the bathroom door. They went to dinner and Freya told her mother that some of the Donner Party had survived and opened an inn with a restaurant where they settled in San Juan Bautista.

"Ironic," said Ruth. "Don't think I would eat there."

Freya knew from literature class that irony was when the opposite of what you might expect happens. Her teacher Tom had used examples like "a lifeguard drowns" or "the firehouse burns to the ground." Other kids had laughed but she didn't see why irony was funny. The cannibals had a restaurant. OK. Ironic but not funny. They were probably eternally traumatized and hungry after that wretched winter trapped in the deep snow and having stews and soups on the stove was undoubtedly a comfort. You just had to put yourself in their position.

It wasn't easy to eat vegan in Montana. Freya had salad, a side of spinach, no butter, and fries. Ruth had ribs and enjoyed them very much, licking the sticky sweet sauce from her fingers.

When they finally arrived in Olympia, Washington, it was a different story. It was as if the whole town was vegetarian, if not vegan. Soy, lentils, and speltz abounded. The fruits and vegetables were organic and non-GMO. The sky was overcast and the towering firs and pines threatened to take over the place like an advancing army. To Ruth the small state capital nested in the woods was a little eerie and very provincial. Freya, on the other hand, thought she would like it a lot. Fairy tale forest that it seemed, it was more her speed than Cambridge which was so overly civilized. Nature had a toe-hold here. She could imagine it retaking the place.

Freya's dorm room window looked out into the trees. After she drove her mother to the airport to send her home, she came back and stared out the panes. The wind swept through the branches and crows rode the limbs, cawing. It was early September but it seemed fall was coming early. She didn't mind. The drama was compelling. There was a week left before school started. Other students began to gather in the hallways and cafeteria, reaching out tentatively for friendships, but Freya was used to a solitary existence. She practiced her guitar. She found her way to a fabric store and bought a pattern and some red wool. She sewed herself a cape with a hood, thinking those woods behind her dorm might be full of diabolical wolves and she ought to dress appropriately.

PART TWO
The Honeymoon

Chapter Three

ach student was assigned a faculty mentor, and Freya's was Mimi Katz. Mimi gathered her group the week before classes would begin. "Look at my beautiful little chickens," she said to the group of twelve generally scraggly eighteen-year-olds. It was the kind of college that attracted counter-culture kids who didn't buy into societal norms like haircuts and expensive sneakers. In this regard Freya fit right in, with her hand-sewn patchy clothes and long black hair. She was surprised to have herself described as a little chicken, though Mimi Katz did somewhat resemble a hen with her outsized bust and the wattle of her neck. Freya found herself going around the circle trying to see which animal each of her peers most closely resembled. Straight across from her an afro made a young man look like a lion. Next to him the large cheeks and narrow forehead of a girl with a shaved head made Freya think of a hippo. A sharp nose and long neck gave another girl a definite egret look. Suddenly she realized she was being asked a question by Mimi.

"What?" she asked, taken by surprise. First introduction to her classmates.

Gently Mimi reposed her query. "Just tell us a little about yourself. Your name, where you're from, your biggest passion?"

"Freya Rubenstein. Cambridge. Massachusetts. At the moment it's animals."

Mimi expected her to say more, but Freya felt she answered the questions. Next to the bird girl was a boy who looked like a puppy. He saw her staring at him and smiled a lopsided grin at her. She didn't smile, but nodded, because he had validated her initial impression of his dogginess. Freya realized Mimi was talking to her again.

"What?" She was not making the best impression on the others in the circle.

"I'm wondering if you can expand on either of those answers. For instance, what does your family do in Cambridge? Or, do you want to have a career with animals or do you like them as pets?"

"The parents teach. Mom Physics. Dad Philosophy. I want to have an animal refuge." This idea had just come to her. Freya was expressionless.

"OK, thank you." Mimi saw that Freya was going to be a hard nut, probably on the spectrum, and she'd better leave her alone for the time being. She moved on to Freya's neighbor in the circle who was from just up north in Seattle and expressed a passion for marine biology. JoJo loved to explore tide pools and hoped to do research in ocean sustainability. Her family had a summer house on San Juan Island and that's where she learned her love of the seashore. Freya looked at this girl beside her and tried to discern if she had any resemblance to a fish or octopus. One might think JoJo would be a great potential friend for Freya with their mutual love of animals, but JoJo thought Freya put off a prickly vibe and seemed slow witted. And for her part, friendship simply didn't occur to Freya.

After class the Dog Boy tried to start a conversation with Freya, but she didn't take him up on it, and left as quickly as she could. It was one of the last days of sun—she didn't know that yet, in fact, no one did, since the weather west of the Cascades in Washington was unpredictable and meteorologists who had to provide forecasts struggled for credibility. But she did go for a walk in the woods, kicking through the fallen leaves. The rot of autumn was different here than on the east coast—damper and treacly. The forest smelled like honey as summer relented and began the business of dissolving back into the earth. She sat down against a cedar tree and listened to the birds. So many different tones and she didn't yet know which song belonged to whom. High and chipper, percussive, low and harsh, melodic—an entire gamelan orchestra.

When she was back in her room and opened up her laptop, she found that Mimi Katz had emailed her, requesting a meeting the next afternoon. Freya was used to counselors and teachers looking after her so she was not alarmed, and agreed to a three o'clock meeting. This gave her time in the morning to go to the local animal shelter to adopt a kitten.

The next day when she got to the Humane Society she was almost overwhelmed by the cages full of cats and dogs who needed homes.

She wished she could take them all, but her room was small, and pets weren't actually allowed, so she thought one would be her maximum. Of course the soft silly babies who tumbled clumsily all over each other were adorable, but in the end it was a thirteen-year-old gray cat named Wren who won her heart. The way the cat pushed the orb of her head into Freya's palm. Wren's eyes were green and lined with black like Cleopatra's. The shelter worker told Freya that the cat's previous owner had died and it was unlikely such an old plain-looking cat would be adopted by anyone. Freya thought the shelter worker should look again; Wren was not plain, but she didn't argue and filled out the necessary papers. She bought a litter box and litter, crate, and cans of food which she lugged through downtown to her dorm, Wren swinging in her metal cage. Freya didn't bother to hide the cat as she went back into the building, and though a few passing students in the hallway stared, no one said a thing. In the room, freed from her crate, Wren immediately staked out the window seat, and surveyed the forest view. So many birds to dream of. And who knew how much time remained for a thirteen-year-old cat; she was facing her own mortality.

Freya met Mimi in her office. Mimi had dozens of photographs of young people on her desk and on the walls—they couldn't all be her children. To Freya it seemed like a kaleidoscope of people and she had to look away to avoid a dizzy spell. Too many eyes. Mimi greeted her warmly. Freya focused on a shell on Mimi's desk. She wondered if she could hear the sound her mother used to call the ocean. What caused that muffled sound? Was it the engine of one's own body, caught in a cone and then mirrored back? Mimi had to call Freya's name a couple times to get her attention. Freya shifted her focus to Mimi's face, as she had been trained to do, while avoiding her actual eyes.

"How are you doing with the transition to Olympia so far?"

"So far so good." She gave Mimi a thumbs up.

"Not homesick?"

Freya thought about this for a minute. "Not really. I like the view out my window. It feels like the home I always imagined."

"The forest?"

"Yes."

"Have you made any friends in the dorm yet?"

"No."

"Would you like some hints on how to make friends?"

"That's OK. I'm not that into friends."

Mimi nodded. She felt she was starting to get a fuller picture of this strange girl.

"OK. Well, you know that you will be the creator of your own program here after your first year of introductory courses. Have you thought about what you want to explore?"

"Yes. I want to know if animals have souls. If people have souls. I want to know what the soul is."

"Very philosophical."

"I think it's scientific also. Or can be viewed scientifically. I want to study some neuro-biology. And philosophy. Religious history."

"That sounds fantastic. Really." Mimi was genuinely impressed. She would have liked to know herself. What was the soul? Does one persist after death? "I imagine literature and other arts might have something to add."

"Yes. Maybe."

"How did you get interested in this topic?"

"I don't know. Things leap into my mind and stay there. No choice."

Mimi nodded. She was pretty sure this kid was autistic. "OK. Well I see you are self-directed and that's a very good thing here. Self-directed students are the most successful. But I want you to know that you can come see me anytime to talk. About anything. Academics or social life." She smiled warmly. "I'm your Evergreen mom."

No you're not, thought Freya. She could tell that Mimi had a good heart, but she resented exaggeration. Pretending you cared more than you actually did was just as bad as not caring. Freya was anti care-claiming. Just do what a person who cares does. No need to wrap words around what was real. Hence her love of animals who didn't talk about their feelings. She smiled, thinking of Wren, whom she anticipated would sleep against her at night. Mimi took the smile as a sign of Freya warming to her and ended the meeting on that happy note.

Wren did indeed sleep conformed to any crook that Freya's body position provided. Freya cleaned the cat's litter daily as she was very sensitive to smell and there wasn't much air circulation in her small room, even with the window pushed open. She was embroidering patterns on her red cloak; various reds on red. Oak leaves and berry vines. She listened to the Brandenburg Concertos one through six, trying to understand why Bach ordered them in that progression, and if there was a meaning in it. She knew them all by heart, every chord, every trill.

Craving something chocolate, she went out to the vegan bakery a few blocks into town, wearing her cape. As she passed the gas station by the Seven Eleven a sinewy long-haired man with several missing teeth and a suspicious beverage in a paper bag began to sing to her, calling her Little Red Riding Hood, and warning her not to walk in the dark spooky woods alone.

And then he cackled. But Freya just kept walking, spurred on by the thought of cake. She had experienced drunks on the streets of Cambridge before and knew to ignore them. It was her instinct with most people, but she had seen that there were no social repercussions for ignoring men who cat-called. Once inside the bakery she was delighted to see they even had croissants made with a butter substitute, and they looked beautiful. Crisp and Parisian. She bought two croissants, a strawberry tart, and a piece of chocolate devil's food. As she was leaving the store with her pink-boxed confections, she passed JoJo coming in. JoJo the marine-biology fan from her advisory peer group. Though it was probably impossible not to notice Freya's embroidered red cloak, JoJo seemed not to recognize Freya as she hurried toward the eclairs.

Traipsing into the early autumnal forest with her treats, Freya thought it was a nearly perfect day.

Chapter Four

he Freshmen all took a general Humanities class that addressed community, anti-racism, and critical thinking. Freya's teacher's name was Jake. He wasn't much older than his students and like most teachers at this untraditional college, had a strongly leftist point of view. His sense of critical thinking was more about criticizing the powers that be and inherited assumptions than the more abstract concept of generally interrogating logic and sources and prejudices. For him the two were conflated. So the students got a somewhat polemical education, though definitely relevant and exciting for most eighteen-year-olds. No members of the Young Republicans had chosen this college.

Both JoJo and the Dog Boy from Freya's advisory were in her Humanities section. It turned out his name was Caleb. It was apparent that he and JoJo had hooked up in the intervening week, because they couldn't keep their hands off each other in class. Freya observed how they scooted their chairs right next to each other, often intertwined their fingers, pressed their shoulders and thighs together, and even kissed a couple times when she happened to be looking their way. She felt the slightest pang of something or other which she didn't recognize. She did not ask herself if it was jealousy because she was not self-reflective in that way. But certainly she had appreciated, even though she ignored, his previous attention to her. Maybe she wished she could have what they had. Would she ever have such a thing? Whatever her yearning was, it was unarticulated. It was just an unnoticed tone rumbling through. She was listening as Jake discussed settler colonialism and was finding herself confused by his declaration that Israel was an apartheid state. She had done a report on South Africa and Nelson Mandela in high school, so she knew about that version of apartheid. On last year's summer jaunt, she and her parents had actually gone to Israel for two weeks, and she was obviously going to have to do further research into apartheid because she hadn't noticed when she was there. How could she miss such a thing? She had seen magical ancient ruins, and in Jerusalem it was like walking into some alternative universe, as everyone seemed to be in costume. Greek Orthodox in black Cossacks, veiled women, bewigged women, embroidered Bedouin gowns, men in prayer shawls, men in keffiyehs—it was a glorious mix and unlike anywhere they had been before. The Old City was a labyrinth where they had gotten lost several times. Arab men sat at outside cafes enjoying thick coffee and sharing hookahs. In the market skinned lambs hung in rows ready to be butchered. She expected Ali Baba to appear around any corner.

On Shabbat, when the Jewish section of the city all but closed down, they went to a temple near their hotel for the experience. She loved to hear the worshippers chanting and singing the ancient songs passed down through generations. Songs resonant as the relics at the Met that she would wonder over, trying to imagine the living who used them millennia ago. Haunting and deep in the bone.

Afterwards the rabbi invited the visitors to his house for dinner, and they went, which would not have been her choice, as anonymity would be difficult. She and her mother sat at a long table with the other women, decidedly more demure than the men who were getting drunker and drunker on sweet grape wine as the evening advanced. There was barely anything Freya would eat—challah was full of eggs, of course, the matzoh balls were in chicken broth, the main course was roast chicken and the potatoes were roasted in the chicken fat. She ate tzimmes. The tzimmes probably had chicken broth in it too, but she didn't know that. When the Rebbetzin noticed the girl had so little on her plate, she tried to feed Freya hard boiled eggs; there are many Jewish vegetarians because of the kashrut laws. But vegans, not so many. Freya insisted she was fine with the stewed carrots, but the rabbi's wife was at least momentarily despondent at being unable to feed her.

As the men finished eating they began to sing and bang out rhythms on the table. The women merely murmured along, but the men were full throated and joyous. Freya watched her father among the dark coated men with their long sidelocks, trying to join in. He patted the table in time to the song, Od yishama, Be'are Yehudah, U'vchutzot, Veudchutzot

Yerushalayeem ... All of the men were clapping or beating out the rhythm as they sang, looking toward heaven. The wine sloshed merrily in their glasses.

Ruth was tired and not as charitable to this sect that still believed Joshua actually made the sun stand still as it was written in the Torah. Harold grew up with his religious grandparents nearby, so was more open to the charms of nostalgia. Ruth tried to signal to him with her eyes that it was time to go back to the hotel, but he just nodded happily to the song and smiled at her. After two more songs, which each lasted about fifteen minutes thanks to the ebullient harmonies, drumming, and repetition of choruses, Ruth whispered to Freya and they both stood up. This time Ruth's look was not ambiguous, and Harold meekly rose so they could say their thanks and good-byes.

On their way back to the hotel they stopped at a lonely falafel stand still open on Shabbat, and finally Freya was able to eat. The spicy fried chickpeas and salad inside a pita seemed like manna from heaven.

"Why they chose that particular moment in Polish fashion history to stop everything and canonize their dress code is beyond me," said Ruth.

"That's when their founder lived. But the singing is transcendent, no?" countered Harold.

Ruth rolled her eyes, but Harold was undaunted. "It was Ukraine, by the way, not Poland. Though point taken—the fashion all over the Pale of Settlement was probably similar."

"Haute couture, in any case."

"What did you think, Freya?" asked her dad.

"Nice," she said as she devoured the messy food. "It was like a history soundtrack right in front of me. But I was hungry." Her mother handed her an extra napkin.

"So, Freya, what do YOU think," asked her teacher Jake. Jerusalem disappeared and her mind went utterly blank.

"I have no idea what we're talking about," she said.

Once again, she besmirched her own reputation. Around her the faces of her classmates registered mild disgust or amusement or pity. Only Dog Boy, Caleb, seemed to be slightly animated by intrigue. Who was this girl who dared not to listen or participate? Almost as if she sensed Caleb's distraction, JoJo ran her finger up his forearm, bringing his attention back to the possibility of sex as soon as class was over.

"Well then we'll move on," said Jake.

Freya realized that she had irritated the teacher by failing to listen to him, but his voice annoyed her just as much. Hard to pinpoint, but maybe there was a swagger in it that he hadn't earned. It was only the first day, after all. She took out a notebook and pen because when she wrote things down, she generally could stay focused, or at least read it over later to see if there was anything worth remembering. She was good at automatic writing. She thought of Branwell Brontë, the brother of the famous writing sisters. She had read that he could write two different things at the same time, going from left to right with one hand, and from right to left with the other. She saw him in the dark house where they all grew up and the sisters in their cheerless bonnets and gloomy colored cloaks walking out among the moors. Charlotte and Emily and Anne, gathering heather nosegays under the glowering sky. There they talk about their brother—how he is ruining his own life, how he is wasting his talents, how he is petulant and reckless. "But he is so clever," insists the gentle Anne, who can't bear to criticize anyone.

"So are you with us or against us, Freya?" asked Jake, amusement in his voice. Again, she was caught off guard, but this time she could look at her fastidious notes. She scanned them fast, and summed them up.

"You said that late-stage capitalism was failing and that our way of life is bound to implode."

"And what is your hit on that?"

"Scary if true."

"You're skeptical?" He seemed a little irritated, again, this time by her doubt.

She shrugged. "I don't know enough about economics to posit an opinion."

Dog Boy and a couple others noticed that even though she was kind of mentally AWOL this girl sounded like a miniature professor. Posit an opinion. Who talks like that?

Jake nodded. "Well buckle up. We're going to learn." Jake was ruggedly handsome, with a two-day beard and a thick head of unruly chestnut hair. If satyrs were real, he would have been a satyr, but Freya quickly skipped over that notion and realized he was a mountain goat. Already his confidence and rebel stance were winning him a gang of fans among the students. And most of them quickly internalized his subtle disdain for Freya without even realizing it.

A girl named Coraline raised her hand. "Personally, I *want* our way of life to implode. Our way of life is only good for the privileged."

"Interesting," said Jake.

Dog Boy raised his hand next. "But even the privileged suffer. They just don't know it. They're also living in a dog-eat-dog world, and that's not a world where anybody is living their best life."

"Can you take that idea a little further?"

Caleb shrugged as if it were too obvious to have to explain. "Well, I mean, capitalism. Most people work too hard, at mundane jobs, and for what? The rich get richer and, well, fuck the poor. But if your wealth comes through injustice then there is no peace. Like, your soul is rotting. And you have to play this sick game all the time to maintain your position."

The girl who looked like a hippo added, "Like Thoreau said, 'The mass of men lead lives of quiet desperation.'"

"And there WILL be an uprising," said Coraline, whose thick eyeliner reached all the way across her temples. "Their days are numbered."

"I don't know about that," said Caleb. "The elites have armies on their side. They have a nuclear arsenal. I don't think physical force is going to be the ticket."

"So you'll continue to support neo-liberals at the ballot box, and nothing will ever change." Coraline's voice bit like acid. "Pacifism is passivism."

"I didn't say I was a pacifist. I didn't say I would never use violence. I'm just being realistic about its limits."

Jake watched them argue with glee, almost licking his lips, his role as a shaker of young minds fulfilling itself on Day One of class.

JoJo pointed out that they were all pretty privileged and she for one didn't want everything to change. Just the injustice stuff.

At that point Jake noted that the hour was up, undoubtedly saving JoJo from a sarcastic response from Coraline about the injustice stuff. Obviously this discussion would be continued throughout the semester, since they had not yet achieved a satisfying conclusion.

As Freya organized her notebook and pen inside her backpack she saw JoJo hurry after Caleb out the door. Coraline lingered to speak to the professor. Freya didn't like this class, everyone so opinionated already before they'd even looked at the material. She felt behind. If Coraline weren't talking to Jake the Mountain Goat she would ask him what she should read to catch up. He hadn't given out a syllabus or book list.

Next she had an Ecology Intro class. They would learn that the planet was being swiftly destroyed. Conceivably, there were technologies that could address the disaster. They would learn about those. The teacher, who was not a complete pessimist, hoped that some of the students would explore, through their studies, means to combat climate changes and the sociological devastation that would ensue from them. Freya knew this would not be her role, but there were others who expressed an eagerness to take up the challenge. That was surely a good thing. Freya had a strong urge to pet her cat. She wiggled her long fingers in anticipation.

Her final class was a media arts lab where students would learn to use computers to communicate. So many creative programs to learn. So many platforms to choose from. By the end of the class Freya's brain was popping out of her skull. Coraline was in that class too. She already knew how to use Adobe and Photoshop and everything else the teacher seemed to mention. Again, Freya felt she had been living in an oyster at the bottom of the sea. And at that moment, she wished to return there. To be a pearl. Luminescent. No. Pearlescent, she corrected herself.

Chapter Five

s Freya punched in the numbers to unlock her dorm room door she could hear Wren calling to her from inside. "I'm here," she said, as she went in. "Just let me . . ." She shut the door and pulled her arms out of her backpack, dropping it to the floor. "Come here, You." She sat on the bed and the cat jumped into her lap. Freya rubbed her face back and forth across Wren's head, tickling her cheeks with the pet's gray fur. The Lady had told her touching soft things might soothe her when she was feeling too much. It didn't work with socks or a blanket or a feather duster. But the cat, yes. It wasn't the softness per se; it was the cat itself. The Lady had told her so many things that weren't true, and some that were—to believe was like trusting the lottery. Her mother had thought Freya unhappy because she didn't have many friends, so she took her to see the Lady. Freya was about eight at the time. The Lady had a dollhouse and lots of toys. The dollhouse fascinated Freya, as she loved anything made miniature. The Lady watched her play, taking notes in a journal. She waited for Freya to talk, so she waited a long time. After a while Freya forgot the Lady was there and the stuffed creatures on the shelves began to have conversations. There was little the Lady could discern from these, other than that Freya had a good imagination and could speak in a variety of accents. The content of the discussions, however, was mostly about tea and who would serve whom what. Blueberry jam was popular but symbolized nothing obvious. After the sessions Ruth and the Lady would speak in hushed and serious tones in the office, while Freya sat in the waiting room, swinging her legs underneath her chair and wishing she were home.

Wren stretched her front legs and her pink paw pads looked like flower petals. "But you don't smell like a flower. You smell like oatmeal." Freya's phone signaled her that her father was calling with its electronic toned bars of a Chopin étude. Wren jumped down as Freya reached for her bookbag and dragged it to her, fishing out the phone. "Hiya Kiddo," said Harold.

"Hi."

"We're both on," said Ruth. Suddenly Freya felt a pang of longing for the cluttered living room in Cambridge. She examined the feeling as she might a bolt of jagged summer lightning. She rarely felt a strong emotion not attached to an animal. Curious. Then she realized her parents were talking to her. She knew enough about how conversations generally go to assume she would be safe jumping in with news of the day's events. That is what they probably requested.

"I went to all my classes," she said. "Two of the teachers are good. I don't like the other one. He thinks he's smart."

"He isn't smart?"

"Not as smart as he thinks."

"Have you made any friends?" Fortunately, Freya didn't pick up the sad, nervous hope in her mother's voice.

"No."

"Not yet. It's too soon for that, Ruth," said Harold. "It takes time."

Just then, someone knocked tentatively on Freya's door. The sound startled her. Her heart raced.

"There's someone here," she told her parents. "I need to go." Without further niceties, she hung up the phone and opened the door. Standing in the hall was a small-boned Asian girl. Freya saw that the girl looked like a frightened rabbit, and her heart calmed. She was not afraid of rabbits. She adored them.

"Hi. My name is Mei, and I live at the end of the hall. You're in my Ecology class." Wren scraped against Freya's ankles. Mei clapped her hands together into a prayer position. "You have a cat," she said with glee.

"Don't go out," Freya warned Wren. She looked at Mei. "Do you want to come in? I can't leave the door open."

"Sure." Mei stepped in and began to look around. "It's cozy in here. I love your quilt."

Freya picked up Wren and sat on the desk chair.

"Can I sit?" asked Mei. Freya nodded. Mei sat on the edge of the bed. "So you have a cat. I thought we can't have pets."

"I broke the rules."

Mei giggled nervously. "That was brave."

"I just really wanted a cat."

Mei nodded, not wishing to offend and afraid she had already because Freya had yet to crack a smile.

"I'd give anything to have a pet," said Mei. Freya saw the lower rims of the girl's eyes fill with liquid, but no tears passed the dams. "I haven't made any friends yet."

"I haven't either. But I don't mind."

"Maybe because you have a kitty." Mei reached across the narrow room and patted Wren, curled in Freya's lap. On Mei's outstretched inner arm Freya saw a delicate crosshatching of scars, a spectrum from a fresher red to faded pink.

"Where are you from?" Mei asked. When she looked up from Wren into Freya's face, she saw her classmate's eyes focused on her arm. She instantly withdrew it and pulled her sleeve down to her wrist.

"Massachusetts," said Freya.

"I'm from Everett."

"Where's that?"

"North of Seattle."

"Close to Canada?"

"Not that close. Just like half an hour north of Seattle. If there isn't too much traffic." Mei sat upright, consciously straightening her spine. "I was thinking maybe we could be friends."

"What would that entail?"

Mei, who already felt vulnerable asking, wished she could just leave the room at this point. She cleared her throat gently. "Well. I mean, we could sit next to each other in class. We could do our homework together. We could tell each other what we were thinking about."

Freya stroked Wren thoughtfully. "OK."

Again Mei clapped her hands together, just once. "Really? That would be so great." She was confused because Freya still didn't smile, but desperate enough to rejoice in this lukewarm agreement. For her part, Freya couldn't help noticing how Mei had so many bunny mannerisms. Particularly the way she wrinkled her small, round nose. That was endearing. Freya didn't feel a strong need to talk about things, but she realized that others did, and she knew her parents would be happy when she told them she had made a friend.

"Do you like Demon Slayer? BTS?" asked Mei. "What are you into?"

"I don't know what those are."

"Anime. K-Pop?" Mei ventured. Freya shook her head. "Well what do you do besides school?"

"Animals," said Freya. "Embroidery. Reading. Music."

"But not K-Pop."

"I don't know what that is."

"Korean pop." Mei pulled out her phone and found her favorite Boy Band on YouTube. She brought it over to share the wonder with Freya.

"They're very androgynous," said Freya.

"I'm in love," said Mei. Freya looked at her face to see if she was exaggerating or if she really meant it. It seemed like she meant it. Their voices rang out from the YouTube app on Mei's phone.

"Their harmonies sound like the Beatles," noted Freya. "Or REM. Pleasant."

"Which one do you think is cutest?"

Freya looked at the image of the boys dancing on the tiny screen. She was not drawn to any one of them more than another. She was not drawn to them at all. She was not drawn to anyone really. Definitely not since high school and Tom. Whom she also wasn't drawn to, but before that she had not been a negative magnet facing a world of negative magnets, physically repelled by humans in general.

"Wow," said Freya. "I just realized something."

"What?"

"Something that happened a long time ago. I thought it meant nothing, didn't affect me, but I think it marked me. Wow."

"What was it?"

"Nothing. Just interesting that I am not impervious to the actions of others."

"Is anyone?"

"Sometimes I think I am."

"Wow." That possibility impressed Mei.

Freya looked at the dancers on the phone screen. "Are you Korean too?"

"Me, no, I'm Vietnamese. Vietnamese American. I was born here. My parents came before I was born."

"My grandparents came when they were children."
"Where from?"
"Belarus. Lithuania. Poland. And Russia."
"But they all met here?"

Freya nodded. The BTS song ended and Mei began scrolling through acres of Insta pics and Tik Toks. Even peripherally the images dizzied Freya. She looked away. Mei got the hint and put her phone back in her pocket. "So. What are you thinking about?" Mei asked.

"I was thinking about being marked by things that happen to us."

"Totally. We totally are. We're even marked by the stuff that happens to our families. Even our ancestors."

Freya considered. "Do you mean because of the way they behave in response? I mean, it's not genetic."

"No, it is, it's both. My high school teacher had us read this article about genetic trauma."

"Elaborate, please."

"Well, like they did studies on Cambodians after the genocide there. People who had moved to America. And well, I can't remember exactly, but the conclusion was that people carry trauma in their genes and their children inherit it."

Freya said nothing. Mei fidgeted. Freya's silences and lack of facial expression left Mei in a void, unable to latch on to a response to which she could respond in turn. Conversation, in other words. Instead she swam in an unsure sea.

But out of nowhere, Freya asked: "Do you believe in such a thing as a soul?" Mei jumped slightly. She took just a moment to compose herself.

"Like a life-after-death soul? A separate entity?"

"I guess. Yeah."

"No. I'm a science person."

"As a science person wouldn't you be open to the possibility?"

"Well, sure, I don't not believe in it, but I would only believe in what I could test with my five senses."

"What if there are more than five?"

"Senses? Like ESP or something?"

Freya nodded her head. Mei couldn't say if her odd new friend was pretty or not. Her coloring was dramatic—white skin, black hair, red lips.

All her features were large. Large eyes and lips were nice, but a big nose and big ears—off. And why didn't her parents get her braces? Were they financially challenged like her family?

She wanted to be positive with her new friend, not put the kibosh on her ideas or this potential relationship. "Well someone could do scientific research on paranormal energy, or whatever. Maybe you should!"

For a moment it seemed like the best idea ever to Freya. "Maybe I will. Maybe that's what I'll do when I grow up." A life played out in front of her. In it she was wearing a white lab coat.

"It would be interesting."

"Mei?"

"Yes."

"I'm tired now and I'm wondering if you would leave." Freya wanted to dream about paranormal research in comfort.

"Oh. OK." Mei nervously rose and hurried to the door. "Sorry if I wore out my welcome."

"But we'll be friends again tomorrow," said Freya. Mei pulled the door closed and Freya breathed more easily. It was so exhausting to be in the vicinity of others. Even a person as soft as a rabbit.

For her part Mei walked down the hallway towards her room, past three girls sitting against the wall and laughing hard at something. Mei nodded at them and they barely acknowledged her, but she comforted herself with the thought she had now made a friend.

Chapter Six

t some point after a month or so it was clear that JoJo and Caleb had broken up. They stopped coming to class together, and they sat on opposite sides of the room when they did arrive. JoJo maintained a cheerful patina, smiling often with her matte lipstick lips, and laughing aloud at Jake's sarcastic jokes. On the other hand, Caleb seemed to be wrapped in a thick gray cloud of gloom. He was a beaten dog, head bowed, tail between his legs. One would assume he had been cruelly dumped. But Mei overheard another story and reported it to Freya, who was resigned to listening to her friend even if she herself was not equally enthralled by gossip.

It seemed that Caleb and JoJo had been bickering more and more recently over little things—what restaurant to eat at, what movie to watch, who was the first one to tell a certain joke. They were competitive. They sparred about who would be ruler of their union. Until finally there was an all-out public melee in the dining room of their dorm.

At the time of this re-telling, Freya and Mei were in Freya's room. Freya was crocheting a woolen beanie cap and Mei dramatically played out the roles, actually using higher and lower tones to indicate the characters. Mei had a flair for dialogue writing.

JoJo (exaggerated Valley Girl voice): The food here sucks.

Caleb (surly basso): Well don't eat it then.

JoJo: What, do you want me to starve?

Caleb: No, I want you to stop whining.

JoJo: That's, like, typical of a male. Every complaint by a woman is a whine. Our very voices annoy you.

Caleb: It's not a fucking feminist issue. You just complain too much. About everything.

JoJo: But it is a fucking feminist issue. You're trying to suppress my voice.

Caleb: Fucking high school students complain about cafeteria food. We're not in high school. You can go to Taco Bell if you don't like it here.
JoJo: Taco Bell?
Caleb: For example.
JoJo: You know I hate Mexican food.
Caleb: For fuck's sake. Fuck OFF.
JoJo: You want me to go?
Caleb: Honestly? Yeah. I do.
JoJo: If I leave, I'm not coming back, Caleb.
Caleb: I'll live.

Mei switched back to her own voice. "And then she stormed off, and he just sat there and ate his dinner and apparently they haven't talked since."

"What was for dinner?" asked Freya.

"I don't know." Mei furrowed her eyebrows. She thought this was weirdly irrelevant to the story. Meanwhile, Freya thought—*rabbit face*. She was almost tempted to pet her friend. Instead she put aside her crocheting and reached for the cat, pulling her up into her lap. As Freya stroked her, Wren wiggled with delight and mewed. "But what do you think about it?" asked Mei, who was gradually training Freya to converse in a more traditional way.

"I think he is a dog and she is a sea horse and it was destined to fail."

"Dog. Sea horse. I know I'm a rabbit, but what are you?"

Freya smiled a very rare smile. "What do you think?"

"I have no idea. My mind does not work that way. I have a STEM brain. Tell me."

"No. You have to figure it out." Freya put the partially finished cap on Wren's head.

"I know! A cat?"

Freya looked at her like she was crazy. "No."

Mei was bewildered—she seemed to have offended Freya. To herself she vowed not to guess again. Also Wren did not appreciate modeling the beanie and squirmed away from Freya, jumping to the floor. "I'd better go do my homework," said Mei.

After Mei left Freya looked out the window for a while. The leaves on the deciduous trees had all shaken loose, so there were stark black limbs among the evergreens. A Steller's jay glided onto one of the dark boughs, a flash of Prussian blue. Dusk came so early once daylight savings time ended the week before. By four it would be dark; it was 3:45. Freya was stabbed by a sudden sadness. A contraction of the lungs. Usually her emotions were not physical and flew beneath her consciousness. But this one called out. This one insisted upon itself. "What?" she asked. Obviously there was no response. She considered possibilities—homesickness, loneliness, a lack of purpose? Maybe that last. Her classes were OK. The advisory with Mimi was a bit like an Alcoholic's Anonymous meeting. They went around the circle and shared. The big challenge for Freya was to come up with things to say that would satisfy Mimi that she was unloading enough, without actually revealing anything she cared about. In Jake's class the conversations were heated and interesting, though she never said a word there because it felt like a dangerous free-for-all. In Ecology she was bored witless. The only class she really liked was Media Communication, because she could basically do art there on all of the different platforms and the teacher was perfectly happy. But were any of these classes taking her anywhere? None of them focused on the soul, much less anything else she truly cared about. She imagined herself in a rowboat tossed in a tumultuous ocean. No oars. Seasick.

Out the window she could see someone walking in the woods. Dog Boy. She could just make him out, silhouetted against the forest. He picked up a fallen branch and started hitting it against a tree. Not as if he were angry, but more experimentally. It splintered, and he walked on into the woods, disappearing into the deepening night.

Freya noticed that her emotional vertigo had passed. She picked up her crocheting—she was almost done with the hat. The needle moved in and out like a piston, round in concentric circles. Into her mind wandered the old adage: Idle hands are the devil's playthings. When she was done with the hat she planned to knit a sweater from a complex pattern based on a Bedouin motif.

Chapter Seven

reya flew home for Christmas. Not that her family celebrated. They did have a Hanukkah bush, an evergreen shrub in a tub that they hung with cookies in the shapes of dreidels and menorahs. There were presents wrapped in silver and blue paper and they ate latkes at least once over the course of the holiday. Most nights they remembered to light the candles and say the blessing. Outside the streets were lightly powdered with snow, like sifted confectioners' sugar. On actual Christmas Day, they had Chinese food which was a jokey Jewish tradition, and then they went to the movies. They saw *Little Women* and Freya was absolutely enraptured, even though she thought they got Amy all wrong. When she got home she made a drawing of what Amy really looked like.

The next day she took a walk thinking to go to the yarn store with her Hanukkah money and then maybe buy a new book. She found a lovely orchid hued angora wool and decided to purchase enough to make a scarf for Mei as it was her favorite color. At the bookstore she bought a collection of Tolstoy's short stories. Next she went into a coffee shop to get a soy mocha and read. As she carried her steaming mug to a table, she realized that her old teacher, Tom, was sitting just behind her chosen seat with the Algebra teacher whom he married across from him. Her name was Marian, and she smiled broadly when she recognized her former student.

"Freya!" she said. "Come sit with us."

Freya was not enthusiastic about this idea but didn't know how to excuse herself; she saw no escape. Trapped, she calculated whether she would be less comfortable sitting next to Tom or facing him. Neither appealed but she opted to sit next to Marian. Tom looked down at his latte but Marian was oblivious and cheerful.

"Are you at college now? Where did you end up?" Freya filled her in, answering all her questions in her usual minimalist style. It came out that Freya hoped to study the existence of the soul, and perhaps explore paranormal powers. This made Marian, who was of a nonmystical turn of mind, remonstrate. "Oh come on. Not really?"

Freya was confused by her skepticism. "Why shouldn't I? It's so interesting."

"Well because," she stammered, "because it's not real!"

"There are a lot of things that we can't see but are real." Freya said this factually, not defensively. She didn't really care what Marian thought about her future plans. She just needed to make it through this conversation and then hurry home to safety.

Marian looked at Tom. "Help me out here, Hon!" Freya noticed Marian spoke with many exclamation marks. Tom was still peering sheepishly into his coffee, but he now looked up.

"Freya has always been creative. I wouldn't expect her to be a mathematician."

"That is so rude," said Marian.

Freya was bewildered, not understanding what triggered this response. Why was it rude?

"Marian," warned Tom.

"Don't Marian me. Math is creative too."

It had nothing to do with this conversation, at least not its content. Maybe something in the tone of Tom's voice, though Freya certainly didn't identify what. But suddenly her body went red hot. She was completely unaccustomed to the feeling and didn't recognize that she was angry. She couldn't even decipher the vicious but quiet words that were passing back and forth between Tom and Marian as their fight continued. She found herself panting, trying to take in enough oxygen, unable to fill her lungs. A snake, exotic, like something charmed and forbidden, was unfurling inside her body, from her diaphragm up through her right arm. Standing up, she picked up her cocoa and poured it over Tom's head. He yelped—though it wasn't hot enough to scald him. "You shouldn't have done what you did," said Freya. "You knew you shouldn't but you did it anyway."

Marian looked at Tom as if he were a monster. "What did you do?"

"Don't lie to her," said Freya. Tom wiped the drink from his face and neck with a napkin. As quickly as it had risen, the snake recoiled into

Freya's belly and her temperature returned to normal. Now she just wanted to see what would happen.

Tom hesitated, apparently considering his options.

"What?!" asked Marian. "Tell me."

Tom wiped the front of his sweater with the shredded napkin, stalling for time. He spoke, just barely audibly, staring at the front of his wet fisherman's turtleneck, now studded with ragged bits of torn paper. "Nothing happened," he said.

"Hah," said Freya.

"What?" said Marian.

"Tell her."

"Nothing happened. It was the night of the snowstorm that closed the school a couple of years ago? Freya was freaking out, she was afraid to go out in the blizzard. So I stayed at the school with her."

"Tell her."

"That's it," said Tom.

"What do you mean, you stayed at the school with her? How long?"

"We stayed over in the teachers' lounge. Her parents knew. I was babysitting."

Marian looked to Freya for confirmation.

"He took off my clothes and masturbated on top of me."

Marian looked at Tom. She wanted him to deny it.

"It's not true," he obliged. But it so obviously was. "She's fantasizing."

At this point Marian vomited her coffee and partially digested breakfast burrito all over the table. Freya scooted away as the grotesque mixture spread across the lacquered wood and dripped over the edge. The alarmed busgirl hurried to the table with a terry cloth towel, trying to stem the tide. She absorbed what she could. "I'll be back."

"Are you OK?" Tom asked Marian. She looked at him but was too stunned to speak. She was considering who would keep their apartment and where she would go today after they were through here. And through forever. She didn't even bother to wash the residual bile off her chin.

"I'm going to go now," said Freya.

"No, wait!" said Marian. "Who knew about this? Did you report it?" Freya shook her head.

"At the time it didn't seem like a big deal. And he seemed so...pathetic."

Marian glanced briefly at Tom, who did indeed look pathetic. Her face showed no signs of pity. Freya added, "I'm still a virgin, by the way. So it could have been worse."

Marian was shaking her head. "I'm so sorry that happened to you . . ."

"The worst part was the goop. It stank."

"I was in such a bad place then. I—" Tom pleaded.

"Just shut up!" said Marian. She rose. "Freya, do you want a ride somewhere? I have my car."

"No," said Freya, also rising. "I want to walk."

"But," said Marian, desperate for more information. Freya was undeterred and headed toward the door.

Tom grabbed Marian's wrist. "Don't leave. We need to talk."

She pulled away violently. "The fuck we do."

That was the last Freya heard of their conversation as she exited the cafe. Outside, light flakes of snow touched her face soft as fairy wings. She felt like a sprite herself. She wondered if what she was sensing was her soul. Something was fluttering inside her. Something alive and celebratory. Or was it just an emotion? Maybe it was happiness. She took a mental note for her upcoming research. How were emotions connected to the soul? Were they?

When she got home she decided to read in bed, maybe nap. Her bedroom was on the third floor under the rafters, the beadboard walls white, the carpet Persian, shelves filled with books and beloved stuffed animals. She turned on the electric radiator—without it the room was cold, and she crawled under her down comforter. It took a moment for her body to warm the duvet and then for it in turn to warm her. She lay there, snow drifting down outside, a soporific contentment spreading through her. She had a sense of achievement, even pride, for having avenged herself on Tom. But then, to her utter surprise, that serpent that had retreated back to her belly after the cocoa incident, reawakened. She felt it rippling. But instead of moving upwards, into her lungs and heart, into her arm, as it had before, it moved downward. It moved into her groin. She had not felt it there before, and it shocked her. Was she getting her period? Impossible—it was the middle of her cycle. Yet the snake was rattling.

She felt herself with her fingers, moving inside the petals of her flesh into the wet region that was calling to her. There she stroked the snake. Its head rose to her touch and she stroked and stroked. She stroked until there was a hot sensation that almost hurt. It was asking for something so avidly and she didn't know what. She rubbed it harder. And then suddenly it was as if the snake hissed and struck. Freya's whole body convulsed. A nova of honeyed energy burst and sent its rays to every single cell in her body.

When Freya had reported to her mother, at the age of thirteen, that her first menstruation had come, Ruth, tongue-in-cheek, had said, "Ah, today you are a woman!" Ironically, it was the same month as Freya's bat mitzvah, so it seemed like a conspiracy on the part of the Universe to push her into an early adulthood. She did not accept the mantle. But on the day that she discovered how to give herself an orgasm, things really changed.

Chapter Eight

ei had kindly taken Wren the kitty home with her for winter break while her friend was home in Massachusetts. Freya drove her Subaru up to the small city north of Seattle where Mei's family lived to retrieve the cat and girl and bring them back to the dorm. Mei's house was a drab single story built in the '40s after the war. The parents, who were home on a rare day off, welcomed Freya in but did not speak much English so they ushered her with their arms and a cascade of Vietnamese. Wren came running across the tile floor and skidded to a stop at Freya's ankles, massaging them with her furry head. The parents laughed. The mother called, "Mei! Mei!"

Mei appeared from down the hallway. She had two pigtails originating high on her head, their tips dyed pink. Flipping her hair, she giggled. "What do you think?"

"Nice."

Her mother shook her head as if Mei were crazy, but she was smiling indulgently. Then she turned to Freya and addressed her with what seemed to be a question. Mei translated. "She asked if you're hungry."

"Oh. No," said Freya.

"They won't let us leave until you eat, so you might as well just give in now."

"But I'm . . ."

"It's no use," said Mei.

So they sat at the yellow Formica table with chrome legs in the kitchen and ate homemade pho. The broth was beef but Mei ignored that and simply told her mother to leave the meat out of Freya's. This struck the parents as out of the ordinary and unhealthy, but her mother obliged. The fragrance of star anise filled the room and the four of them slurped the noodles without discussion. Wren sat on Freya's feet.

At one point the mother said to Freya, "Good?"

"Good," nodded Freya.

Fully fed, they finally loaded Mei's suitcase and the cat in her carrier into the Forester. The mother wiped tears off her broad cheeks as the girls drove off. Freya was oblivious to Mei's insecurity having exposed her home and parents to a white friend. All she said was, "Thank you for taking care of Wren."

"Did you have fun back east?"

Freya merged onto the freeway and didn't answer right away. She thought about whether it was fun. "I wouldn't say fun," she said. "But I'm definitely inspired for a new year."

Mei pulled on her pink pigtails. "New year, new girl."

Freya thought to herself what a new girl she herself was.

It was an hour and a half to campus from Mei's house, but the time passed quickly as the wipers cleared the rainy window with the rhythm of a metronome. It put Mei to sleep, and she awoke with some shock as Freya pulled the car into a curb spot near the dorm. "Oh, we're here," said Mei, as if she had expected to land elsewhere. She grabbed her suitcase from the way-back, and Freya took Wren in her carrier. As they were heading into the building they passed Caleb.

"Cute hair," he said to Mei. He passed down the sidewalk.

His own short curly hair was the same Middle Eastern gold brown of his skin, Israeli brown, though he wasn't. Israeli. His hazel eyes were the same dark/light value as his skin, so he was almost monochrome. Freya wondered what it meant that he always seemed to show up everywhere at random times. Was it some kind of a sign? She wanted to try sex with a boy. Was he the one?

Mei kissed her goodbye on both cheeks and went down the hall towards her own room while Freya took Wren into theirs. She let the cat out of the carrier and filled the litter box and food bowl. She went down the hall to get water for the bowl. She cuddled the much-missed Wren for twenty minutes, until the cat pulled away and took up her post on the windowsill. Freya wondered what she should do. Read? Knit? Embroider more oak leaves on her red cloak? She decided to go for a walk and wear it instead. The rain was coming down even harder now so she put on a plastic poncho as an outer layer.

Freya took a path that went down to the beach on Puget Sound. She longed to see the slate gray water where sometimes there were seals, their bowling ball round heads poking up above the surface as they swam along. The seagulls would strafe them for fun, kee kee keeing. The trail down to the shore was muddy and her rubber boots were soon smothered in muck, making a satisfying sucking sound as she walked. A banana slug the size of a bratwurst oozed through the goo. She slipped and held on to the tall salal undergrowth to keep from falling. Finally she came out into the clearing of the beach. The rain had stopped a few minutes ago, and there were sun rays straining through the thick clouds. The rocks that covered the shore were layered with seaweed and not easy to navigate. Down by the water she saw a figure—Caleb again—skipping stones. She was pulled toward him by a force she did not recognize.

He heard her and turned. "Hi," he said.

He went back to searching the ground for a good rock. He found a sufficiently flat one and skipped it. Freya watched. "Seven," she said.

"What?"

"It skimmed the surface seven times."

"My hidden talent."

"It's not hidden anymore."

"You gonna post it? Make me go viral?"

"No. I don't do that stuff."

He threw another side-arm pitch. This time the stone only skipped three times. He immediately started looking for another stone.

"What quality makes a good skipping stone," she asked.

"Flat."

She started to look too. She found a perfect gray disc. She made her way over the slippery bed to hand it to him.

"Thanks," he said as he took it from her. He looked into her eyes briefly—she consciously tried to maintain his gaze—and then turned to throw the rock. But before he did he asked her, "Don't you know how?"

She was wondering about sex again, so his question struck her as perhaps overly forward. "How what?"

"To skip a rock?"

"Oh. I see. No. I don't."

"Do you want me to teach you?"

"OK." She was thinking there were things she'd far rather learn as he handed the disc stone back to her.

"So you want to throw underhand, sideways, like this." He demonstrated with his body. "And you want the rock to angle parallel to the water surface, on a horizontal plane."

Freya gave it a try. The rock sank. "Try again," he said. He picked up another stone and handed it to her.

"I don't want to. I don't like to be bad at things." He smiled at her quizzically, maybe because she admitted this so outright. "I'll just watch you."

"I'm kinda done here really. I was gonna walk down the beach. Wanna come?"

She nodded, and they started south along the shoreline, she filing behind him. They had to watch their feet to keep their balance on the slippery stones. A quarter mile down the beach there was a big driftwood log and he gestured to it. "Wanna sit?" They did. "I saw an orca here last week."

"I've never seen one in the wild. Or elsewhere."

"It didn't breach or anything, but I saw its fin."

"You didn't go home over break?"

"I did for a few days but I kinda wanted out. My mom and dad are getting a divorce and it isn't pretty. Whichever house I stay at they try to take down the other parent. I'm just Switzerland around here." He held up his hands in a gesture of innocence.

He wasn't really Switzerland, because he wasn't neutral and he didn't make chocolate. He was more like the United Nations. Not long before they filed for divorce one Saturday his dad had gotten so mad over who should do what chores that Caleb thought he was going to hit his mom, and Caleb had thrown his body between them, yelling at them to stop. Stop fighting. He was begging. His father's eyes were huge and his face red and sweaty. But Caleb knew his mother had been at fault too; she had baited his father, as she often did in her snarky clever way. He himself was the peacekeeping force.

In truth his parents weren't really fighting over chores—they were fighting over their personhood which is what fights between couples are mostly really about. Am I important here? Do you see me?

As it turned out, that particular dramatic incident was the catalyst for the parental split. To his father Dan's credit, he didn't ever want to be that angry again. He was horrified that he had been close to violence. He was generally a very civilized man. And Regina, the mother, knew that this was the last straw. A woman could not allow herself to remain in a risky situation, particularly with a child at home. It would be undignified.

Freya didn't say anything. She just stared out at the water. Maybe looking for orcas. There weren't any.

"You remind me of a deer or something," he said. "The way you're kind of quiet and not interested in the ways of man."

"Yes. I am a deer." She was pleased that he saw the truth.

He shook his head. He couldn't quite figure her out. At all.

"I noticed you staring at me in class before," she said. This embarrassed him completely. It was probably true. She was pretty.

"I'm sorry. Staring is rude. I might have just been staring into space in your direction."

"I don't think so. You looked away when I caught your eye."

He ducked his head and chuckled. "You go hard in the paint."

She didn't really understand what he was saying. "Maybe you were curious about me."

He looked at her profile. She was looking out at the water. "Maybe."

"You can kiss me if you want," she said.

A surprise, certainly, though he had thought about it more than once across from her in class; honestly he tested the idea in his imagination with most girls. Her bluntness frightened him a little, but he leaned over to kiss her lips lightly. They tasted like they were sprinkled with salt, maybe from the mist coming off the Sound. He pulled away to watch her. She put her fingers up to her mouth where the tingling sensation lingered. She did look like a deer, unreadable, gentle, otherworldly. "Again?" he asked.

She nodded again. This time he really went for it, holding the back of her head in the palm of his hand, and exploring the inside of mouth with his tongue. Here in the wet cave beyond her lips it was no longer salty, but rather sweet, like some kind of tropical melon yet to be discovered. She took to it as she got the hang of it. The snake in her gut rattled gently.

"Mmmm," she said when the kiss ended.

He laughed gently. She was so strange and beautiful. They held hands as they walked back across the beach to the trail. Thin layers of kelp stretched over the rocks like green cellophane. Was he starting a new relationship with this girl? He liked having a girlfriend. All through high school he had one—not the same one—but he went from one to the next easily. Girls found him handsome and easy to talk to. He wasn't very sexist, his mom had made sure of that, and he had good manners. Both his parents made sure of that. He liked having someone to watch sports and movies with, to cheer his frisbee moves, to take with him to parties. Of course he liked sex, but he wasn't a beast about it. He was respectful, and sometimes the high school girls only wanted to make out which was fine too. He couldn't say he had ever been in love, except maybe with Patty Alvarado in the fifth grade. She already had breasts and was the karaoke queen, a little girl with a growling alto, but she wouldn't have him. She was a heartbreaker. Patty Alvarado.

It was the fact that he was honest about his less than wildly romantic feelings that had ended most of his relationships; girls didn't like to feel unappreciated, and he didn't mind breaking up, because he wasn't in love. Not that he wouldn't want to be. But it hadn't ever happened. Maybe because his mom and dad had that seething relationship. His heart had a husk.

The wind, like feathers, whooshed softly through the air. It carried briny mist. Freya and Caleb both secured their hoods.

"What happens now?" she asked.

"Well. What do you want to happen?"

"More kissing. Kissing without end."

"OK. But you know my name, right?"

"Caleb." She didn't tell him she really thought of him as Dog Boy.

"Just wanted to make sure."

"Do you know mine?"

"Freya. I know it because Jake says it so often to wake you up."

"I'm not asleep."

"Where are you, actually?"

She shrugged. "Here, there and everywhere."

They reached the opening to the trail where they had to release each other's hands to walk single file. He let her go ahead of him. The rain began pattering again but in the forest the heavy branches of the firs and cedars shielded them from most of the drops. Nonetheless, dankness was everywhere and it chilled their bones. The cold walk gave Freya time to become anxious about what would happen next. Would they have sex? The thick ferns slashed at her poncho above her rubber boots. Her cape needed more buttons down the front. Was this going to be a relationship? Behind her Caleb tripped on a root and then slipped in the mud, but managed not to fall.

"I'm OK," he said, though she had never doubted it. He registered her lack of response. So different from how girls were usually solicitous and eager at this point. How JoJo had cooed over him like he was her helpless baby, until she started hating him. Or he started hating her. He did start hating her. She was shallow as a pizza pan.

"Are you hungry?" he asked Freya. "Wanna get a pizza?"

"I am hungry, but I'm vegan and vegan cheese is inedible and thus pizza is inedible."

"Well, do you want to get something?"

"Yes."

He waited for a few moments, but that was the end of what she had to say. "Do you want to give me a clue?" His irony was lost on her.

"Well, I would like Ethiopian food or Vietnamese food."

"If we get Ethiopian, can I get chicken or lamb, or will that offend you?"

"As long as I don't have to eat it it's OK. My parents always ate meat no matter how much I begged them not to. I'm used to it."

He pondered the long-term implications of having a girlfriend who didn't eat eggs. He wanted to sleep with her. But what would they eat for breakfast if they spent the night together? He liked to cook and he knew that pancakes had eggs and milk, smoothies, omelets—all these specialties off the table. Not that he'd be cooking in the dorm. But long term. The wind shuddered through the trees and as the boughs tilted, the rain their needles had been holding at bay cascaded onto the hikers. They both had on hoods but anywhere that was not fully protected by Gore-Tex or polyester was drenched. The gusts of cold cut through the wet like an axe.

"Fuuuck," said Caleb. The water had spilled inside his boots.

Freya said they had to stop at her dorm room so she could change into warm clothes. Nervous, he stood beside her in the hall while she punched in the code. A pair of girls walked by and took them in and then exchanged an incredulous look: Caleb was a young Paul Newman, and Freya was, well, far from a starlet.

"Don't let the cat out," Freya warned Caleb. She gently shoved Wren back into the room with her boot. He followed them in. Freya quickly started to drop her outer layers, as he leaned down to pet Wren, who nuzzled his hiking boot despite its wet and muddy state.

Caleb watched Freya take off her sweater, her back turned to him. She had on a long-sleeved T underneath. The fabric was thin enough that he could see the knobby bones of her spine. He moved towards her and wrapped his arms around her. "No. You're too cold," she said. Because his lust was aroused, he didn't take this as an utter rejection, but backed off in deference to her warning. He resorted to stripping off his wet jacket and shirt, which could have been just because he was soaking and not because he wanted to be naked with her. When she didn't offer further resistance, he took off his boots and pants too. At which point she was happy to press her body into his. And he led her to the bed.

"Shit, I don't have a condom," he said.

"I do." Mother Ruth had supplied her before returning to Cambridge, good to her word, and Freya had put the package in the drawer by her bed, in the off chance that something like this ever came to pass. Thus she and Caleb were able to make love, if clumsily. Afterwards, that is, after Caleb came, he shyly asked if she enjoyed it.

"It was interesting," she said. Though she was a virgin, it didn't hurt; clearly her hymen had been opened on a horse, in a ballet class, or somewhere sometime. "But I don't think I had an orgasm."

Caleb was mortified. He sat in silence with his chagrin. Freya sat up and moved to the edge of the bed.

"Let me try again," he pleaded.

"Another time. I'm starving." She got up and put on warm clean clothes.

Caleb stared at his wet garments dropped on the floor. He glumly picked them up. "Wanna dry sweater?" Freya asked. He nodded, and she handed him a black cable knit she had purloined from home. "It's my father's." When she wore it, it hung on her skinny frame like a tent, but hugged Caleb's form as it did Harold's.

"Do I look like your dad? Are you going to get some kind of complex?"

"No."

He was beginning to see her answers were always blunt and literal. She was holding her cat and kissing its mouth. "Goodbye Wren."

Across the table from each other at the Ethiopian restaurant, they scooped their food with sour injera and gradually looked into each other's eyes for longer sustained periods. His eyes had little flecks of gold and green like a mandala around the pupil. Her eyes were a deep, deep brown that pulled him into a pool where he had never been before. A grotto. He thought of mermaids. He had no idea how rare it was for her to maintain eye contact.

"What about JoJo," Freya asked.

"What about her?"

"Do you still have feelings for her?"

"Feelings of disgust maybe."

"Will that be me? In a few months?"

He stopped himself from the reflexive reaction that began on his tongue, and actually thought about the question.

"You aren't like her."

"We don't know each other yet. You don't know what I'm like."

He tore off another piece of spongy bread and pinched a piece of lamb with it. He chewed slowly, giving himself a chance to consider what to say. Finally, after swallowing he allowed, "You're right. I guess we can't make a lifelong commitment to each other yet." He gave her a half smile. It was hard to read. Was he making fun of the idea?

"No," she agreed. "Not yet."

Chapter Nine

he taught him how to give her an orgasm. Her teaching style was so direct and unjudgmental that he flourished under her tutelage. This alone was opposite to JoJo, who faked smiles and moods and probably orgasms as well. He loved Freya's honesty. He was all in for it. There was a safety he had never experienced before, ever, in the company of this girl he could trust to always tell the truth. He had grown with parents who sheltered him from the cruel world, and thus lied at least by omission, constantly. And even when he was little there had been a growing war between his mother and father which he sensed but could neither identify nor explain. They didn't yell or fight aloud but attacked each other with stealth missiles. Any questions he asked trying to understand the tensions raging in the household were shot down with denial. Wallpapered over with a mythology of happiness. Until it all went up in flames and burned to the ground.

If honesty were her only trait it might have been enough. Dayenu. But she was also willing and eager to experiment sexually; her drive was strong and she felt no shame. So they played; he couldn't get enough of her body or her mind. She was smart as hell—she could write a paper with clarion logic and perfect grammar in an hour, without need for revision. She had great compassion for animals, including people whom she tended to like pets she had to tame. She stroked him in their sleep and made sure he was fed and watered. This didn't threaten his dignity because she honored animals as equals.

Unlike other girls he had known, she was utterly unshy about her own appetites, including for food. She ate a lot, though no amount of food seemed to flesh out her wisp of a body. (He didn't yet know that some days she would forget to eat altogether.) Her breasts were just slight mounds with solid nipples like pencil erasers. He was fascinated by them. She had no hips or ass to speak of, but inside her pelvis was all the flowering that the outside lacked. Her thick long black hair, like Scheherazade. Thinking of her gave him erections, even in class, even walking down the street.

Of course he recognized that she was not typical. Her responses, her behavior, her thought processes were all off the beaten track. But this he relished. If there was one thing he hated about himself it was his normalcy. It embarrassed him. His good health, his good looks, his decent, normal brain, his upper middle-class upbringing, his lack of risk-taking. Some might see Freya as an odd excuse for a trophy bride but being with her, choosing her, gave him an edginess he couldn't hope to produce on his own. He was cool and unique enough to get her. She was not Barbie, and therefore he was not Ken.

As for Freya. She was obsessed. All her life she had had fanatical and specific passions, dragons, ancient wonders of the world, Renaissance fashion—it was part of her make-up to go all in. A serial monogamy of deep interests. Now it was Caleb. Every thought of his, every emotion, every kink, every pore in his skin. If he only went into the men's room down the hall from their classroom, she ached for him. Though in public she refused to participate in any displays of affection—she didn't know why but it would have horrified her to share their love with others—in private she wanted her body to meld with his. Permanently if possible. Siamese twins would have been just alright with her. She fantasized about which internal organs they would share.

They sat together and listened to music for hours, each introducing every other song or piece as they tried to intertwine their toes. He exposed her to emo and hip hop. She acquainted him with classical and folk music from every corner of the world. Each felt infinitely enriched by the other as the universe expanded. Exploded. She called him Dog Boy. He called her Deer Girl. He licked her body everywhere, as if he could digest her. She swallowed his cum and felt like a magic potion was enlivening the molecules of her flesh. If they had died then, it would have been just fine. They had found paradise. All of January was like this.

One night it snowed and they went outside to dance a dervish. Under the streetlamp outside the dorm they could see the flakes in their whole unique splendor before they melted on their clothes. Perfect lace hexagrams: "Stars of David," said Caleb.

"Baruch Hashem!" said Freya.

She twirled and twirled until she was dizzy. He caught her in his arms, laughing and then they went back inside, into the warm, into the bed where they consummated their love for the hundredth time.

In Jake's class they sat side by side but did not touch. For one, neither of them wanted to rub their relationship in JoJo's face, but also, for Freya at least, she didn't want their Eden contaminated by the mundane world. Their love was of a different order, made of the stuff of her childhood dreams. Of flying horses, rose petals, dolls who came alive in the nighttime. It was pretty clear by then that Coraline was sleeping with Jake, and that brought back bad memories for her. The smell of Tom's cum, the scratch of wool blanket. What she and Caleb had could not be sullied by comparison to any sort of inappropriate liaison.

Jake was now teaching them about White Fragility and Coraline would accuse pretty much anyone who disagreed with her teacher lover as suffering from that affliction. Only Lion Boy, who was Black, could question a Jake theory with her impunity. Coraline demurred to his lived wisdom, at least early on. For his part Lion Boy, who was thought of by his name Trey by everyone but Freya, bristled at Jake's speaking on behalf of Black folk. Even if Jake's analysis may have been correct, his intense self-assurance felt like a micro-aggression in itself. But Trey couldn't put his finger on what was bothering him, so he would nit-pick the ideas rather than the attitude. Jake would usually win the argument, because Trey was arguing about the wrong thing. Lion Boy had come to hate Jake over the course of the semester and he couldn't hide it. In private Jake and Coraline agreed that it was possible for a person of color to side with the oppressor—a sort of Stockholm syndrome of internalized racism—and they came to the conclusion this was the case for Trey.

Freya and Caleb had their first argument in February. It was about Israel. Their college was an ultra-progressive isle in the progressive Western Washington sea. Though Freya had been unaware of it when she enrolled, students had voted to join the Boycott Divest Sanction movement against all things Israel years before. The assumed wisdom was that, as Jake had mentioned in his first lecture, the Jewish homeland was the last colonial outpost, an apartheid state that engaged in ethnic cleansing, a veritable human rights monster. Therefore the student body had decided to have nothing to do with Israel in any form, to apply the sort of pressure the world had placed on South Africa to end its racist government. This included clearing the dorm kitchen refrigerators of Sabra Hummus. Sabra Hummus was actually made in America, but "sabra" was the name given to describe native Israelis, so needless to say a boycott of the dip was necessary.

Freya didn't follow politics closely. They seemed strangely abstract, like an arboretum drained of bark texture and humus scent. Theories made of words that hardly connected to the real-world situations they were meant to describe and improve. Skeletons without flesh or veins or tendons. People warred with slogans, misnaming reality and calling it truth. And these wars of propaganda could turn into actual wars. Better just to get on with life, she thought. Farm and cook and make things, have pets and children, sing songs, engineer traffic. She had argued about this with her parents, ardent liberals, and they insisted that without political organization the world would run amok, fall into the most fascist, top-dog hands, and that voting and activism for good candidates and laws were the most effective means of bettering the planet. They put signs for their favorite causes in the yard, watched the news together, and truly suffered over Trump and his policies. But Freya's brain could not contain it.

So when Caleb began to parrot some of Jake's ideas about Palestine and Israel it didn't sit right with her. She smelled the pardes, the citrus orchards, outside Tel Aviv, the overpowering fragrance of the blossoming orange groves. Felt the sun-hot stones of the fortress ruins at Masada. The sun-browned young soldiers in khaki, men and women, on every urban corner. The hunched gray-haired holocaust survivors with numbers on their creped forearms. The shocking turquoise of the Mediterranean against the blue sky, almost periwinkle by comparison. A carnival of sensory reality. She tried to describe it.

"Yeah, but did you go to Gaza and the West Bank?" he challenged her.

"We went to Bethlehem. And Hebron. That's the West Bank."

"And . . . ?"

"Beautiful. Mysterious.""

"But the people. Under occupation."

"For the most part people seemed to be going about their lives."

"How did you go there?"

"In a van. On a tour."

"And you don't think they might have shown you what they wanted you to see?"

"It's a possibility. It's also a possibility that you want to make it seem worse than it is because you have some idea you want to prove."

"Believe me. I don't want Israel to be the bad guy—I'm Jewish. I don't want to be ashamed of the Jewish state. But I am."

"It isn't our state to be proud of or ashamed of. Being Jewish doesn't make us Israeli."

"Don't you feel a connection, though?"

"Yes." She remembered jewel blue Lake Kinneret with the brown hills of Galilee rising behind it, its history in her blood.

"Well."

"But we don't vote there. We aren't morally responsible for what they do. And beyond that, I think there are reasons for the way things are that are more complicated than Jake ever addresses. Two, no four thousand years of history. Vulnerability. They're surrounded by countries who hate them and wish they would disappear."

"Doesn't give them the right to oppress others."

Freya suddenly felt overwhelmed. She did something which she never did, probably hadn't done since she was seven years old and wasn't allowed to keep a stray dog she had carried home in her willowy arms. She cried.

Caleb said her tears looked like a string of beads falling down her cheeks. He held her tenderly.

"My brain and heart were short circuiting," she said. "I couldn't defend my point but I felt it so strongly.

"It's OK. It's OK." He pet her as if she were Wren. They were at his dorm room and she missed her cat badly. As Caleb stroked her she felt herself mutating into a fur-covered feline. She let out a meow. He chuckled gently but she wasn't pretending, and his mirth was bewildering to her.

"Meow?" she inquired.

"We don't need to argue about it. We can research more together and find out the real deal."

She nestled into his arms, and as usual they had sex before going to sleep. If only the Israelis and Palestinians would slide beneath the covers together and pleasure one another, exploring every inch of enemy skin, the sweet smell of pheromones and sweat, the riotous release of tensions held in muscles and in memories . . . but they would be the quintessential strange bedfellows.

Chapter Ten

Feeling guilty for leaving Wren alone all night, Freya hurried back to her own dorm before dawn. She was no longer a cat. As usual she was a deer. Lithe and silent.

As she entered her hallway she saw Mei at the far end returning to her own room from the bathroom. "Hey there," Freya called.

Mei looked at her but very pointedly did not answer and disappeared through her door. Bemused, Freya went in to tend to Wren. The cat needed food and her litter box changed. Kitty was playing it cool, punishing Freya for being gone all night. Usually Caleb slept over there (which was bad enough, according to Wren) but to have Freya gone so long was something of an outrage. It evoked horrible kitty memories of Freya's trip east in December.

"It seems everyone is mad at me." Freya raked the aqua litter until it was free of waste and caked areas, which she bagged and put by the door. She didn't think it wise to leave Wren so soon to go outside to the garbage bin under the hood of firs that sheltered the back of their building. She sat down on the bed while Wren continued to ignore her from the desktop.

Freya pulled out her guitar and began to sing. It was a song about a calf riding in a wagon on its way to slaughter. And how it would be a better option to choose the freedom of a flying swallow. As if the baby cow had a choice about its fate. Wren jumped off the desk but stopped on the throw rug to lick her paws in a show of nonchalance. "How the winds are laughing," sang Freya. The cat couldn't help herself any longer, crossed the floor and jumped into Freya's lap, displacing the guitar.

Freya continued a cappella. The chorus was a host of "dona donas" and by the end Wren was pressing her smooth gray head into Freya's palm for just the right level of petting pressure. "I wonder if Mei would like me to sing to her, too." But Freya had homework to do and thought she'd better get to it. For Hanukkah/Christmas her parents had given her a new electric water kettle, so she made herself a cup of tea and settled in with her books and laptop for a study session. It wasn't until lunchtime that she realized she hadn't eaten and made her way over to the dining hall to grab a salad and some fruit. Mei was sitting at a table by the window, this one with a view of a red cedar the size of the Statue of Liberty.

Freya took her food over and sat down across from Mei. "Hey," she tried again. Mei clenched her teeth and avoided eye contact. This was OK with Freya, as eye contact was something she had to work at anyway. She peeled her navel orange in one continuous curlicue, as was her habit. She pulled off a section and ate it. "Sweet," she said. "Want some?" She held out a quarter of the orange towards Mei. Mei looked at it and shook her head.

"Is something wrong?" asked Freya.

Mei shrugged her shoulders. This made Freya think she didn't want to talk about it, whatever it was, so she started in on another subject, describing the reading she had done that morning for her class with Jake, and wondering aloud at the thesis of the author. This in turn infuriated Mei more, who had a serious axe to grind and felt Freya was oblivious, which, indeed, she was.

"I don't really care," said Mei.

"Oh. OK." Freya knew that sometimes she had a habit of wearing out a topic that fascinated her but was less interesting to others—so she thought this was that, but it wasn't. "What would you like to talk about?"

Mei's face turned a strange shade of ruddy and her entire body tensed. She was not used to expressing her rage. She nearly hissed through her teeth. "How you missed my birthday yesterday and have totally tossed me aside since you started dating Caleb. If you actually want to have a conversation."

By the time they were eighteen, many young women had already worked through the issues of friends versus boyfriends, but both Freya and Mei were late bloomers and had no experience navigating these waters.

"But I'm obsessed with him," said Freya. "I can't help it."

This was clearly a breach of the girl code, which ought to have been written on Freya's DNA but wasn't. Mei wagged her head back and forth in a mocking gesture, but again, Freya didn't get it.

"When was your birthday?

"Yesterday."

"I didn't know."

"I've mentioned it like a hundred times."

"Well, I'm not sentimental about stuff like that. Are you?"

Mei didn't even know how to respond. She had bought a small vegan cake decorated in iced roses to share with Freya. It was still in its pink box in her minifridge. She had waited up for her friend to come home until midnight and then cried herself to sleep. College was not that fun, not what she had been expecting. She had hoped to escape from the stifling expectations of her provincial parents, but the demands were tattooed inside her. She had hoped for parties, for late nights and jubilation, none of which had materialized. So to have the only friend she'd made abandon her—it was too much.

"Do you want a present? I could knit you a sweater."

Mei looked at her as if she were a stranger. "You're so weird."

Freya was accustomed to acquaintances finding her weird, but not family. Not a friend. She flinched. Mei saw her advantage.

"You like animals and you like sex, but you don't like people."

Freya stopped to think. Was this true? In general, maybe, but she did like her mother and father. With Caleb was it just the sex? She wasn't sure, since that was always there and she couldn't separate the two. She certainly liked him for that. What about Mei? She thought about how Mei colored her fingernails delightful different shades, and her pink hair, and her Hello Kitty bedspread and BTS posters. She smelled like hard candy, and was such a rabbit.

"I like you."

Mei felt this as a slight victory. She invited Freya back to her room to eat the cake. In the hallway of their dorm were some of the usual girls who leaned against the wall and gossiped. Freya saw them as snakes, like one Medusa with many serpent heads. As she and Mei walked by one of them said, "Where's Caleb?"

Freya looked at Mei as if she might know what to say, but Mei just looked blank. "At his dorm, I think," said Freya earnestly. The girls giggled.

When they got inside Mei's room, Freya needed some translation. "Why were they laughing?"

Mei was almost as naïve as Freya, but sometimes things were more obvious to her. "Maybe they think they're clever because they know you and Caleb are together."

"But why is that funny? I don't get it."

"Sometimes people don't laugh because something is funny. Sometimes they laugh because they're mean."

"Oh. But I don't get that either. What were they mean about?"

"It's hard to explain. Knowledge is power—so they feel like they have something over you because they know something important about you. And maybe they're friends with JoJo or something. Or maybe they find you and Caleb an odd pairing." Mei hesitated on this last sentence. She didn't want to hurt Freya's feelings by calling her odd after she had already called her weird earlier. She was odd, of course, but Mei didn't want to overemphasize that.

"But why would they want to have power over me? Why would they care about me and Caleb?"

"Did you ever see the movie *Mean Girls*?" Freya hadn't.

"Well that's what we're doing this afternoon then. Eating cake and watching a movie."

"OK, but we have to do it in my room because I can't leave Wren alone again."

They watched the movie on the computer screen. At one point Freya noticed several fresh cuts on Mei's inner arm, red against the pink crosshatch of scars that patterned her soft skin. Again, Mei saw Freya looking and covered the healing slashes with her sleeve.

"What happened?" asked Freya.

"Nothing, just . . ." said Mei, with more authority in her voice than she normally mustered. Freya heard the "back off" and did.

Wren was allowed a pastel rose to lick as the girls shared cake. Freya found it hard to relate to the film in many ways; she didn't understand why these characters in the movie were being mean any more than she understood why the girls in the hall were. She tried to pinpoint what she didn't get to Mei, who decided Freya was just too innocent to be petty. Freya did like the way the protagonist had visions of the other characters as wild animals. In this they were sisters.

After the movie which was an anomalous midday break, they started in on their homework, this time together. Freya lay on her bed and Mei sat at the desk. Mei was taking a class in feminism and rather pointedly read a passage to Freya about the importance of female friendships. It was all news to Freya, to whom friendship in general was a new experiment. "I'm confused. If girls are so mean, why should we be friends with them?"

"Not all girls are mean. We aren't mean. Or we shouldn't be mean, anyway."

"You think I was mean to forget your birthday."

Mei was accustomed to avoiding conflict and ducked her head. But she was inspired by her readings that urged her to speak up. "I think you're mean because you care more about your boyfriend than about me."

Once again Freya paused to reflect. She was already feeling a nagging sense of loss after nine hours of separation from Caleb. He drew her the way gravity pulled objects towards Earth's core. She could feel his touch on her skin, smelled his hair, longed to be in his presence, even though she knew she focused on her studies better when he was not in the room. As for Mei, she was a bright little bunny in her life, but she was no distraction. She did absolutely care more about Caleb than Mei. Yet she knew enough to know she ought not announce this; that it could be hurtful even if it was the truth. She was confused about what to say, as it was her habitual instinct to be honest.

"I'm sorry I ignored your birthday. I care about you." These were true. "Would you like me to sing you a birthday song?" She remembered how a song had soothed Wren.

"OK," said Mei unsurely.

Freya's guitar was leaning in its case against the wall. She pulled it out. Instead of what Mei might have expected, the traditional birthday song, or even Feliz Cumpleaños which they had sung from time to time at Mei's diverse public school, Freya played the Beatles' version: "You say it's your birthday!..." She knew all the chords and carried a tune flawlessly, though it was not quite the same song in her bird-like soprano. By some magic it did in fact placate Mei. She was ready to forgive and forget. She was not prepared to face the rest of the year without a friend. When Freya finished singing and put down the guitar, Mei clapped enthusiastically, and then got up to give Freya a hug, which Freya endured.

Chapter Eleven

reya was looking forward to Caleb's arrival; they had slept together every night for weeks. But he texted her that he was in the middle of a paper, finally, and he was going to stay in that night and finish it. After so much procrastination he needed to take advantage of his rare momentum. Freya was devastated.

Panic set in. Her skin went clammy and her heart rate accelerated. She had not had an attack like this before and the symptoms themselves added to her sense of alarm. Her breathing became shallow. She found herself shivering uncontrollably and though she got into bed and pulled the covers around her, pulling Wren into her chest, she could not get warm. She was hyper aware of the liquid waves of cold pulsing through her. This went on for five minutes or so.

Then she remembered how she had soothed both the kitty and Mei with song. She started to hum to herself, and then to sing the words quietly. It was Hebrew, a verse from a Psalm that translated as I will look up to the hills from whence comes my help. It was one of those songs that repeated over and over like a melodic mantra, and she did stop shivering after twenty some repetitions. She stroked Wren who was nestled into the C curve of her body, purring along to her song, or so it seemed. One more dramatic shiver bolted through Freya from her toes to her head. Wren freaked out and jumped to the floor, staring at her reproachfully. She thought of texting Caleb just for the contact but decided it would be selfish to distract him. What had she become?

Instead she texted Mei. It was the first time she had spontaneously reached out to her friend just to know there was someone at the other end. Hi, she wrote.

Hi, typed Mei. **Whassup?**

Nothing, texted Freya. **Just checking in.** (That was an expression her parents would leave on a voicemail. She tried it out.)

OK. I'm writing a paper? You?
Just had a panic attack.
Is it over?
I think so.
Well I'm just down the hall if you need me.
Am I addicted to Caleb?
Probably.
What should I do?
???

Freya put her phone down and lay on her back. She didn't really know much about addiction or its cures. She had heard of cold turkey. She considered this possibility, but didn't know if she had the stomach for it. Also there were Caleb's feelings to consider. She supposed she could cut back, lower her level of dependence. That was probably the way to go.

The next morning in Advisory she didn't follow custom to sit next to Caleb, who was already in his normal place when she came in the room. He looked at her full of wonder as she chose a seat across the circle. He raised his palms to shoulder height, neck forward, in question, like a young Bernie Sanders. She gave him a friendly wave. Jojo noticed the exchange and smirked, which suggested she would gladly stab either of them dead if she could do it undetected. Freya was oblivious to Jojo's hostility, since thoughts of this sort never crossed her mind. Mimi started class.

Freya held her jaw closed tightly and avoided looking at Caleb. She played piano scales across her knees with her extra energy. For his part, his own left knee refused to stop jiggling up and down, and since he couldn't stop it, he focused on keeping it quiet so it wouldn't draw attention. He couldn't listen well to Mimi, who was leading a discussion on sexual improprieties and power. Freya began to melt into a memory sparked by the conversation. She was in the teacher's lounge at her high school. The windows were opaque with snow. The woolen blanket scratched her skin. Tom's face was red as he frantically yanked at himself, his panting accelerating with his motions. Unaware of her surroundings, she gasped in horror in the present, unlike in the past when she had remained silent and obsequious.

"Freya," said Mimi. "Are you all right?"

The entire class was turned toward her. The attention was unbearable. "I have to go," she said. She got up and hoisted her backpack into position, hurrying out of the classroom. Caleb followed her.

He shouted after her as she rushed down the hall towards the exit. "What the fuck?" he yelled after her. She paused at the door as she turned to his voice which allowed him to catch up. He grabbed hold of her arm. "What is wrong with you?"

"They were all looking at me."

"Because you groaned so loud."

She looked down. "I had a bad memory."

"What was it?"

She glanced up at him again but shook her head. She didn't want to tell him.

"Why didn't you sit with me? What did I do? Are you mad at me for not coming over last night? I had to write that paper."

She grabbed his hand and pulled him outside. The ever-wet air hit her face along with the smell of pines and firs that were whipping around in the wind like Isadora Duncan's arms. Or perhaps the fatal scarf in the speeding coupe. "Let's walk," she said. She led him down a trail towards the forest, where she knew there would be some peace.

When they got deeper into the woods where the trees protected each other and the human pair from the wind, where the evergreens absorbed sound and seemed to hum to themselves with some kind of ancient shamanic song, she stopped and faced him. He thought her face had never looked so beautiful, her cheeks flushed with cold the same rose color of her lips, her black curls framing her white skin, her eyes moist with emotion.

"I was so afraid last night," she admitted.

"What happened?"

"I slept alone."

"Where was Wren?"

"I mean without you. And I thought I was going to die, Dog Boy. My heart was beating so hard I thought it would burst out of my ribcage . . ."

"Like a panic attack?"

"And I realized I just can't need you so much. It isn't safe."

"But, I missed you too, Freya." When he had finally gone to sleep around three, after finishing the paper he had been putting off forever, he did think how strange it felt to get into bed alone. He remembered pulling his pillow close into his body so he had something to hold.

"But this was more than missing. This was insanity. I scared myself. Dog Boy, I couldn't breathe."

"So that's why you wouldn't sit with me? You were trying to separate?"

"I don't want to be insane."

"Maybe it's just love, Freya."

She looked down at the earth, so brown and swollen with the morning's rain. Needles everywhere. There was something she couldn't say aloud.

"What?" he asked.

"All my life I've been the odd one."

"I wouldn't say odd. You're just uniquely you."

"People have always thought I was weird."

He started to object, though he was sure it was true.

"Don't worry. It's OK. I have been very happy in my own world. And I didn't care what other people thought because my own world is where I wanted to be and if they didn't get it it just didn't matter. I didn't want them in it anyway. But now I don't want to be here all by myself anymore." She looked up at him, her face a lovely plea.

"I want to be with you, too, Deer Girl. We don't have to sleep apart again. We don't. We don't, ever."

"You won't tire of me? I never tire of anything I love, but other people do. Other people like novelty. I don't like novelty."

"But you always surprise me." He covered her pretty face with kisses. He couldn't help himself. "I love you, Freya. Forever and ever." Even in the heat of their mutual passion it was too cold and damp to have sex in the February forest, so they went back to her room.

Naked and sated an hour later they stroked each other's smooth skin beneath the quilt. An idea had come into Caleb's head, a wild idea, but more compelling because of its very wildness. A risky idea for a boy who had failed to take many risks beyond a daring skateboard move or Halloween prank in his short life. Manhood itself seemed to mock him for his lifelong caution. "I want to marry you," he said. In that moment he was so sure this was the move that would seal his character. She needed him and he adored her. He felt himself growing hard again.

"We're only eighteen," she pointed out.

"So?"

"Really? It's unexpected. People just don't get married this young anymore."

"Yeah, but we're not like anyone else. Our love is . . ." He searched for the word. He thought, magnificent, unprecedented, pure. All true. He turned sideways towards her and she felt his erection against her thigh, like a needy child birthed by their union. She reached for it to soothe and comfort it.

"My parents would think we were crazy," she said.

"So would mine. But we're adults. We know ourselves better than they do." Ruefully: "It's not like my parents are experts on love." By then his desire was mounting from her splendid touch, and so they fucked again, pausing their verbal conversation as they thrilled one another. As if it were the first time (though they were getting better and better at it). Adam and Eve in the dewy fruit-filled orchard of Eden.

Finished, their bodies glowing, he told her how in Las Vegas you didn't need to wait, it was like a McDonald's drive-thru. They could go first thing Saturday, be there by evening, go to a McChapel, say their vows, return the next day as husband and wife and they wouldn't even have to miss a day of school.

Not only was it a brilliantly romantic confection of a dream, but they were buoyed by the novel excitement of personal agency. Neither of them had ever before made a life-changing decision completely without parental interference. It seemed so right. And so it was decided. They gassed up the Forester and loaded up on snacks. By 5 a.m.. on Saturday they were on the road.

They took turns driving. They told each other stories from their childhoods, they listened to CDs, they sang. Sometimes the one in the passenger seat slept—it was almost eighteen hours to get there.

At one point Freya got a series of texts from Mei: Do you think our whole generation, if we could do it with just the snap of a finger without any pain, would just be happy to disappear? Not like suicide, but just a finger snap?

No. Freya texted back. Are you OK?

Yes I'm fine.

I'm going to get married. We're going to Vegas.

Congratulations!! Mei posted a line of bunny emojis interspersed with daisies.

Over the rivers and through the desert. Driving up and across the rugged Sierra Nevadas was frightening. By then it was dark and salad plate-sized flakes of snow landed on the windshield. In front of them a plow cleared the pass, but the going was slow so they lost an extra hour. By the time they pulled into Vegas, fortunately a city that never sleeps, it was nearly midnight. Neither of them had been there before and the Strip was certainly something to behold; a secular Christmas kingdom alight with the spirit of dopamine addiction and petty greed. No rest for the merry gentlemen inside who were gambling and drinking and leering at cocktail waitress titties. Caleb and Freya hurried to the licensing bureau, which they knew closed at twelve, and got there with ten minutes to spare. They doled out cash for the license (no one was ahead of them in line) and breathed more easily, as they had met their deadline.

Using Google, Freya located an all-night chapel. There were actually several, but they settled on one called the Little Chapel in the Pines, as it sounded the most like them. Unlike the Chapel of Crystals, The Little Neon Chapel, The Elvis Chapel, Bliss with a Kiss, Wee Kirk O'the Heather, or Viva Las Vegas, all of which made Freya feel contaminated just from the sound of them. Using the GPS they arrived at their marriage locale at one in the morning. It was on the outskirts of town and there was in fact a lone Ponderosa Pine standing between the street and the chapel.

They walked up the four steps to the unassuming two-story building. The porch light was on, but it seemed pretty dead inside. They rang the bell, it was an actual bell with a ribbon that activated the clapper, and waited. Nothing. They tried again. After half a minute, a light went on in a window on the second floor. Caleb took Freya's mittened hand in his own, gloved in sleek leather, a Hanukkah present from his dad last year. They looked at each other, the seriousness of the moment keeping at bay any exhaustion they might feel. Applying for the license had felt like registering for class, all information on dotted lines, but this moment, the vows ahead of them, was Shakespearean.

An old balding man with glasses and apple cheeks opened the door. He had thrown on a sports coat over his pajamas. He ushered them in, shuffling deeper into the house in his slippers. "I thought we were done for the night, but here you come," he said, not unkindly. They followed him into a room that was clearly used as the wedding room. There were large bouquets of artificial flowers in urns lining a velvet runner that created the sense of an aisle. It led to a trellis woven with silk wisteria under which the bride and groom were meant to stand. "No witness?" the old man observed, again not unkindly. They shook their heads no. "Wait here," he said.

He walked past them back down the hall and called up a staircase. "Tilly? Tilly, we need you."

He came back into the room with Freya and Caleb. "She won't be but a minute." He asked to see the marriage license, remarking that everything seemed in order.

"You two are mighty young," he said. "Are you sure you're ready for this?"

"We have our IDs," Caleb said.

"That's fine," said the man. "I didn't doubt you were legal, I just meant are you ready? Marriage is a big commitment. Not to be made in haste."

"Isn't haste kind of the hallmark of a Vegas wedding?" asked Caleb. "Couldn't be the first time you saw a quick decision."

"You're right about that. I don't hold out hope for most to last. But you two look kind of sweet and innocent. Like maybe you're really in love."

"We are," said Freya.

"It's often a drug- or alcohol-inspired choice."

"Yeah, no, we're completely sober," said Caleb.

Just then a round woman came into the room wearing a red and green plaid robe over her candy cane festooned flannel nightgown. She had round glasses and a round face, round bosom, round belly. She was smoothing down her hair over the dome of her head as she entered. She could have been Mrs. Claus. The man smiled at her.

"This is my wife Tilly," he said. "And I'm Pastor John."

"I'm Caleb, and this is Freya."

"Tilly and I have been married for fifty years come June. And I'm a lucky man." He turned to Caleb. "I hope you will be so lucky."

"Aren't they beautiful?" said Tilly, beaming at the young couple. "Just a minute." She left for a moment and returned with a blooming narcissus planted in a teapot. "Such a beautiful bride needs a flower." She handed the spouted vessel to Freya. Freya held it awkwardly, both hands clasping the white china orb spotted with green shamrocks as the fragrant blossoms tickled her chin.

"So," asked Pastor John, "Have you written vows, or should I use the traditional ones?" Freya and Caleb looked at each other. This event had happened so suddenly they hadn't thought to write their own vows, though it's something they might have liked to do.

"The traditional ones, I guess," said Caleb, looking at Freya for agreement. She nodded. Pastor John studied the license for a moment, memorizing their names.

He showed them where to stand, and Tilly beamed at them from a spot next to her husband. He took a deep breath and began. "Dearly Beloved. We are gathered here today in the presence of our Lord Jesus Christ—"

Freya giggled at the un-Jewishness of this, and Caleb elbowed her. The pastor had seen many emotions in front of him at this post, from drunken tears to panicked laughter, so a titter barely registered. "—to wed in holy matrimony Freya Reubenstein and Caleb Becker.

Caleb, do you take this young woman to be your wife, to live together in holy matrimony, to love her, to honor her, to comfort her, and to keep her in sickness and in health, forsaking all others, for as long as you both shall live?"

Caleb said he did. When Pastor John repeated the question to Freya, it suddenly became very real, for both her and Caleb. The part about cherishing until the end of all time. They looked into each other's eyes and there saw the length of infinity and the love of God. Time stopped and outside reality blurred, like the scene in the *West Side Story* movies, both versions, where Maria and Tony met at the dance in the gym. But this was their own shared moment of ecstasy, a moment they would each privately refer to in moments of waning faith later on, as proof of the validity of their union, forged by a higher power, however vague, and cemented deep in their flesh.

They had to admit to the old folks there was no ring, yet, but that was just a little glitch. They would get rings in due time. "I now pronounce you man and wife," said the Pastor. And so it was. All the paperwork was in order and the benevolent old man and woman kissed and blessed the youngsters, sending them on their way. It was now nearly 3 a.m., and

Freya and Caleb decided just to sleep in the back of the Subaru under the lonely Ponderosa Pine in the parking lot. It didn't occur to them to make love then. They held each other tightly, like refugee babies in a sea-tossed rowboat. All the rest of the night they slept that way. They were tired enough not to move, despite the cramping, despite the cold creeping in beneath the blanket they shared.

They were woken by a rap on the fogged window. It was Tilly, dressed now, offering them coffee in Styrofoam cups and Safeway cinnamon buns. They blearily accepted, embarrassed to admit they wanted to pee behind the tree. And that Freya couldn't eat the pastries because though they were undoubtedly free of cow's butter, they probably contained eggs. Maybe even lard. Semis whooshed by on the highway. It was 8 a.m. on Sunday, and they had an eighteen-hour drive ahead of them. The Pastor came out and invited them along to church, but they made their excuses—the long drive and school tomorrow—and drove to a nearby gas station, where they relieved themselves in a filthy restroom the size of a phone booth. Outside there were tiny flakes of snow falling, the size of aphids, melting as soon as they hit the oil-stained pavement. But it didn't bode well for their trip over the pass if it was snowing in Las Vegas. They googled it and found out the average snowfall was zero inches, which meant some years there must have been negative snow. This mathematical mystery they discussed on the first leg of their journey. Now in daylight they could see the expanse of high desert around them; Freya had never been to the southwest before and the scale of its desolation was astonishing. She couldn't wait to return to the lush welcoming darkness of Olympia's thick forests. They were taking turns choosing CDs. She put on Gregorian chants because that was the echoing sound of the woods she missed.

Caleb had not been a childhood aficionado of the Donner Party as Freya had been, so as they approached the foothills of the mountains she told him the grim tale of the pioneers trapped in a blizzard, resorting, finally, to cannibalism in their rabid hunger. He was appalled. "Why didn't they teach us this in school?" He felt he had missed an essential part of American history crucial to understanding, what? The spirit of the West? The inhumanity of the colonial mentality? The natural outcome of manifest destiny? For Freya it was not a political story, but something more like a fairy tale with characters adrift in the forest. At the mercy of a wicked witch and her enticing gingerbread trap or a tempting poison apple. A more personal, darkly magical story.

As they climbed toward the pass, pancakes of snow splatted on the windshield and the road, which had been recently plowed, but which was now receiving a new thick white layer. It was collecting quickly. There was enough traffic that so far tire tracks were striping the carpet, but this would prove short lived. Though the heat was on in the Subaru, Freya shivered. It wasn't the temperature; it was more in response to the Donners' plight, the impression of their horror pressed into her memory like an angel scraped into existence by a child on a snowy lawn.

Chapter Twelve

hey climbed. They passed cars along the side of the road which had skidded out and couldn't make it up the mountain. Their car had all-wheel drive, and so far had traction. Caleb introduced Freya to a band who sounded like a circus version of the rock bands her parents had listened to. It was pleasant, dreamy, as the melting stars of snow were swished away by the wiper blades. The sky was a fearsome gray that dissolved into flakes. Ahead of them a Mack truck churned through the sludge its wheels created out of the ice and mud. In the facing lane cars were swooshing down the pass, with a joie de vivre that celebrated their having scaled the other side of the mountain. But all of a sudden an insouciant SUV lost control, skiing madly off course and heading straight for the semi. The truck driver braked, and his cab planed over the ice one way while his cargo bed flew another. The Explorer crashed head-on into the side of the rig which had jack-knifed across the highway.

Caleb stopped the car safely, yards from the wreck. The noise had shattered the sky and was still reverberating eerily in the snow-humid air. "You OK?" he asked Freya. She was shaking visibly. He looked at his own hands and they were trembling. "Jesus."

"We need to help," said Freya. She was already getting out of the car.

"Put on your coat," he called. "Put on your mittens."

She didn't listen, so he put on his own, grabbed hers, and ran after her. They had to climb into the ditch to circle around the truck, and he was still helping her arms through her coat sleeves as they rounded the semi and saw the crushed car. Other descending drivers had stopped and the truck driver had emerged from his cab, apparently unhurt. The windshield of the SUV was blasted out and there was blood and glass everywhere, and more frighteningly two shredded dead bodies strapped into their seats. Caleb saw and pulled Freya backwards. "There's nothing we can do. It's too late." She glanced at him, not absorbing his words, and continued forward.

Freya passed the small crowd that had surrounded the truck driver. Several were on their cell phones, no doubt calling the authorities. She made a beeline for the back of the smashed van. There was a dog. It was alive and whimpering. It had slammed up against the caging that kept him in the way-back, but was now lying on the floor. Again Caleb caught up with Freya, and when he realized her purpose he just said, "Oh."

"We need to get him out."

They tried to open the back, but it was locked. Caleb noticed a bumper sticker on the ravaged car's rear bumper. It read, "How am I driving." Below in smaller type two lines: "How does an engine work, anyway?" And then in a teeny tiny font, "How does a loving God cause such agony?"

Again, Freya moved with intention and speed without communicating with her new husband, who tracked behind her protectively. She went to the driver's side of the smashed SUV. The crushed door didn't open. There was nothing for it but to climb up atop the mangled metal hood and push her arm through the splintered windshield. She ignored the tearing of her coat sleeves and the shard of glass sticking into a rib through layers of clothes. People were calling to her to stop, worried that the car might explode, but it didn't. The engine had just stopped functioning in the crash. Still they had no idea what she was doing as she managed to wiggle on her stomach across the wreck and reach into where the ignition key might be. She couldn't see but she felt around until she found it, meanwhile unintentionally touching the driver's body and smearing herself with blood. Caleb held onto her ankles. She had to think backwards to extract the key, but she did it. She dislodged her arms. "Pull me down."

He did. Others had ventured closer as she didn't blow herself up but averted their eyes from the hideously dead couple in the van. Freya was now pretty bloody herself, and seemed crazy enough that some caution might be in order; strangers kept their distance. But she simply went on with her mission, opening the back of the van. She spoke gently to the dog; it was a springer spaniel with long silky ears. Terrified. Freya climbed in next to him. He let her pet him. She began to feel his body, probing, but he was tender and let out little yips. She feared he might have internal injuries, broken bones. She looked up at Caleb, her eyes moist with pain for the dog. "We need to get him to a vet. We need a gurney."

Caleb told her to stay there while he went and opened their car, cleared a space, and brought the rubberized floor guard from the backseat. They managed to shimmy the mat under the sad dog, and then, each taking two corners, carry him to the Forester. The dog was wearing a collar with a tag on it. "His name is Jimmy."

"That is the wrong name," said Freya, as she pet him and he settled in, still shivering with shock. She put a blanket over him. The police and emergency vehicles were arriving, driving along the shoulders, their colored revolving lights reflecting off the snow like a laser show. Traffic was backed up for a mile on both sides of the highway. Until the smashed car with its grim inhabitants and the truck moved, everyone was stuck.

Caleb wrote his name and contact information on a piece of notebook paper, with Jimmy's dog license number, and while Freya stayed with the spaniel, Caleb approached one of the police officers. All the authorities were understandably distracted by their tasks at hand. Caleb managed to command the attention of a uniformed female and communicate that they had the dog who had survived the crash. And if there was family, or . . . "Where is the dog now?"

He's in our car, with my girlfriend. My wife."

"OK, OK," said the cop. "Thanks." She shoved the information into her pocket, patted Caleb on the shoulder, and headed toward Armageddon.

Back at the car, Caleb checked on Freya and Jimmy in the back. "How's he doing?"

Freya smiled at him. "He's OK. But you know what?"

"What?"

"I'm going to name him Honeymoon."

"That doesn't sound at all like Jimmy. It might be hard for him to adjust."

"That's the least of his problems." The dog was lapping up Freya's affection. As she pet him his eyes gradually closed and he nodded off to sleep. "I never thought about the word before, though. Honeymoon. It's like its own haiku. Honey sweet moody moon . . ." Caleb reached out and pushed one of her curls off her face. Her left cheek was striped maroon with dried blood and the sleeve of her jacket was now a rag. She looked into his face and they each remembered what they had done and how their fates were braided together now.

"I'm freezing. I'm going to turn on the car for a while for some heat." He closed the rear door and got into the passenger seat, turned the car on. The CD that had been on when the crash occurred blared—it was all wrong and Caleb switched it off. He looked through their box but decided he didn't really want to hear anything. "It's gonna be so late by the time we get back."

"I think the vet opens at nine. So we'll have a couple hours of sleep . . ."

"Do you think Wren will like Jimmy?"

"Honeymoon."

He shook his head and smiled at her stubbornness. "OK."

"Honeymoon might have to stay in your room for a while . . ."

"Dogs aren't allowed in my dorm."

"Of course not. Cats aren't allowed either. Not in my dorm either. But animals are more important than rules."

"You sound like Coraline."

"No I don't!" She thought he meant it.

"Yes you do. You're an anarchist. Jake would be so happy."

She looked at him shrewdly. "You're teasing me, aren't you?"

"Yup."

Snow had started falling again, and since the windshield wipers weren't on, the car began to turn furry white, like a caterpillar. The light dimmed. The dog snored. Freya's phone vibrated. "Hello?"

"It's mom and dad!"

"I know. Hi."

"So how are you?" asked her dad with a little too much cheer.

"Well right now we're stuck in the snow in the Sierras like the Donner Party. Except we have snacks."

"What? Who are you with?" It was her mom, anxious.

"I'm with Caleb. We got married. In Vegas."

There was silence for a moment, and then Harold and Ruth erupted simultaneously.

"What?"

"Are you kidding me?"

"Are you out of your mind?"

"Not at all. It's perfect. We're in love," said Freya. She looked up at Caleb in the front of the car, but he was facing forward, listening.

"And you're stuck in the snow? Do we need to come get you?"

"Mom, you'd get stuck in the snow too."

"Well, are you going to die?"

"Not likely. There are tow trucks here now to clear the crash. I saw dead bodies though."

Silence again. Freya can overhear her parents speaking quietly to each other, discussing what they should do. Whether they needed to buy plane tickets. This was in relation to the surprise marriage, not the stuck-in-the-snow issue. She interrupted them. "You'll like Caleb. He's smart. And Jewish."

"We don't care if he's Jewish," said Ruth, annoyed.

"I do," said Harold.

"Why?" said Ruth. "Would you mind if he were Black?"

"Of course not. Not if he were Jewish."

"OK, you guys," said Freya. "I'm gonna get off. Gotta save the phone battery." This wasn't entirely true, as they had a charger that hooked up to the car, but it was very slow. "I'll text you when we're safe." She could imagine the look her mother was giving her father, as if the whole thing were somehow his fault, and in response his helpless, bewildered face.

"My parents are gonna freak too," said Caleb from the front seat. Honeymoon was sprawled across the way-back, still breathing heavily. "I don't even want to tell them."

This brought up some complicated emotions for Freya. She knew she was different and that she had made few friends over the course of her life. She had seen kids look at her funny and heard them talking about her behind her back. "She's a freak," they would say. She hadn't liked them anyway, and was able to comfort herself with that truth, and throw herself into her passions—reading, crafts, dolls, animals. Her parents were so distracted and odd themselves that they just took her ways for granted. But this was different. If Caleb didn't want his parents to know about her because of her strangeness, this was unbearable.

Caleb glimpsed her frowning face in the rear-view mirror. He turned around. "What's wrong, Freya. Besides the obvious."

She looked at him and once again he was struck by her smooth white skin framed by her glossy black curls, her large dark eyes, her red lips. For him, she was the paragon of beauty. Her overbite was adorable. "I can behave in front of your parents," she pleaded.

"What?"

"They don't have to know about me. I can act normal."

He kind of doubted that, doubted that she could completely mask her differences, but now was not the time to say it. "It's not that they won't like you. They'll just think we were crazy to get married so young. And without inviting them." He ducked his head. "Not that they'd want to be in the same room together . . ."

The ambulances gathered their grim cargo and started back down the mountain towards civilization. One tow driver used his winch to move the death car and followed. The truck driver, with support from the tow guys and the emergency personnel, climbed up into his cab and turned on the engine, which wasn't damaged. Together they managed to maneuver the truck until it was once again in one lane rather than across all four, by carefully edging backwards towards the ditch, and forward towards the right, bit by bit. The waiting cars were now backed up several miles going east and west, gathering snow on their roofs, their hoods, their windshields—polar caravans. Many of them had idled the entire time in order to keep the heat on inside their vehicles. Vapor rose from their exhaust pipes. Some feared they would run out of gas.

Once Freya had returned to the passenger seat, Honeymoon whined for her and managed to wiggle his way over seats and sleeping bags and suitcases until he was in her lap. This mobility suggested he had no broken bones. He licked her face.

The very officer to whom Caleb had given their contact info was now using a flashlight to direct traffic on their side of the highway. Caleb took off the parking brake and revved the engine. The tires spun in a threatening gyre, but then the car lurched forward. The policewoman calmly waved them forward up the mountain, and they were on their way. By now it was late afternoon and they had lost hours, so they wouldn't be home until the next morning.

Their tires crunched against the ice. Day was giving way to darkness.

"Husband," Freya whispered into the air, trying out the word.
"My wife," said Caleb.
The dog barked softly. "Jimmy," said Caleb.
"Honeymoon," corrected Freya.

Chapter Thirteen

he spaniel did not last long in Caleb's room. Freya felt she had to be with Wren, and she couldn't be without Caleb, so they left the dog alone for a few hours and went to sleep in her room. Apparently he barked the entire time, and that went over well with no one in his hall. Caleb was reprimanded and read the riot act. He resorted to calling his mother, who was living single now in the large family house, and asked her to keep the spaniel for the time being. Obviously he and Freya would have to rent an apartment together, but they couldn't do that right away—they'd prepaid for their dorms.

By afternoon they had given up on slumber and their Monday classes and instead drove the dog up to Caleb's childhood home in the north end of Seattle. Both of them were in danger of falling asleep as they traveled the freeway, so they didn't discuss strategy—what to tell the Beckers about their marriage. Would Caleb break the news on this visit? Freya was too drowsy to ask. Caleb was biting the insides of his cheeks at the prospect, and to keep his eyes open.

The family house was a large craftsman in a yard designed with layers of shrubs and trees, and planting beds carpeted with chartreuse sprouts that would presumably be flowers soon enough. A brick pathway led from the sidewalk to the house. His mother wasn't home from work yet, but an Airedale barked madly in the window from its perch on a couch. "That's Evelyn," said Caleb. Honeymoon cowered behind Freya.

"Will she hurt him?"

Caleb chuckled. "No."

He had a key and let them into the house. "Hey, hey, hey," he said to Evelyn, who was jumping up on Caleb with unbridled joy. Honeymoon trailed behind Freya, reassessing the situation now that the terrier had stopped barking. He padded toward Evelyn and did a downward dog, to show his willingness to play ball. Evelyn pawed at Honeymoon, indicating her own readiness to romp. "Come on you guys!" Caleb led them through the kitchen and out the sliding backdoor into a large cedar-fenced yard. The dogs zoomed and chased. Caleb laughed, and Freya took his hand.

They left the dogs outside and, finally able to relax, went in to sleep together on the couch. They were awakened only when Caleb's mother, Regina, came home. "Caycay?" she called. "Are you here?" The young people popped up from the sofa. She was taking off her trench coat and hanging it in the closet in the entry.

"Hi Mom." Caleb introduced her to Freya who looked at the woman's chest to avoid her eyes.

"Should I call you Regina or Ms. Becker?"

"Oh. Regina. Please. Where are the dogs?" Evelyn ran in through the doggy door, leaving Honeymoon, who was afraid of the strange passageway, whimpering in the backyard. "*Down!*" said Regina, as Evelyn jumped on her in greeting. Evelyn reluctantly obeyed. Regina didn't have the kind of bearing one would easily disobey. She was tall and thin but large-boned, her shoulders pressed down and back like she practiced a lot of yoga.

"I'll get Honeymoon," said Caleb, leaving Freya standing awkwardly with his mother.

"Did you guys name him that, or was that the name he came with?"

"I named him."

"How did you choose that name?" Her voice was not entirely approving—what a weird thing to call a dog. Evelyn and Honeymoon ran in panting, with Caleb behind.

"Here he is, Mom. Isn't he cute?" Regina pet the relatively quiet springer spaniel, smiling at his droll eyes.

Freya could have used the distraction to ignore Regina's question, but her native thoroughness and honesty wouldn't allow such a ruse. "Because we got him on our honeymoon."

Regina appeared confused, and Caleb looked like he'd just as soon melt into nothingness there and then. On the phone he had told his mom he rescued a dog from a crash on his way back from Vegas. He hadn't told her why he went there. She assumed it was to gamble and drink, but neither of these were legal at his age. Freya felt her question was answered and didn't elaborate. Regina turned to her son with a posture that demanded answers.

"We got married, Mom."

"What?"

"That's what *my* mother said," offered Freya.

"You don't even know this girl," said Regina to her son. At this point the woman wanted nothing to do with Freya and unconsciously backed up from her several steps. "People like us don't get married at eighteen. White trash gets married at eighteen. Hillbillies get married at eighteen."

"Way to stereotype, Mom."

Suddenly something occurred to her and she whirled on Freya. "Are you pregnant?"

"No."

"Mom."

She, incredulous. "Are you telling me you got actually, legally married?"

Caleb nodded. Regina shook her head. She was a well-groomed woman in a well-groomed house. It was very different from the warm, cluttered home from which Freya came, shelves filled with hand-built ceramic pots holding dried flowers, and stacks of dog-eared books. Regina's books were arranged by color. "Maybe we can get it annulled." Evelyn touched Honeymoon on the head with her paw, and he followed her out of the room.

"Mom. We don't want to get it annulled. We are happy. You don't need to fix anything. It's all good."

Regina plunked down on the couch. "I feel like smoking. I haven't felt like smoking in five years. Even during the divorce I didn't jones for a cigarette like this." She stole another look at Freya, who was certainly not making eye contact with this harpy who would rob her of her joy. "Do you smoke, Freya? What are your vices?"

This kind of ironic inquiry was completely out of Freya's wheelhouse. "I'm sorry, I really need to use the bathroom." Caleb pointed her down the hallway to the water closet, which she found carefully wallpapered, a blooming orchid on its shelf.

"She's an odd bird," said Regina to her son, accusingly.

"She's amazing."

"She's odd."

"She's super smart. And creative."

"Do you have any cigarettes?"

"I don't smoke. I haven't ever smoked."

Caleb hadn't shaved all weekend and the stubble on his face made him look less like a boy, you could almost imagine the man, but still. The whole thing had rendered her incredulous. "Jesus Christ, Caleb."

Just then Freya came back in so Regina had to take a different tone. "Sit down," she said. Freya sat down next to Caleb. Freya looked at him to connect, to reassure herself, but then lowered her head. If she met this woman's eyes Regina might zap her and freeze her solid. She thought of Lot's wife, punished, turned into a pillar of sand for looking back at the destruction of Sodom and Gomorrah. Why was her curiosity a crime? Or was it simply disobedience that led to her demise? Freya's brain leapt to Orpheus, who likewise was told by the authorities not to look backwards, but worried when he couldn't hear Eurydice's footsteps behind him. He turned and looked for his beloved. And he was punished for this look by eternal separation. Indeed, looks were dangerous and powerful and no wonder she couldn't always meet others' eyes. And also, what was the relationship between these two ancient stories—did they share a single source, or did one influence the other? Was this like the flood myth, say, that showed up in so many antique cultures?

"So what exactly is your plan now, you two?" The tone, even just the existence, of Regina's voice shocked Freya, pulling her back into the room and the here and now. The horror of her son's stupidity had hit his mother hard again, and she made a sound and shake of head that reminded Freya of a horse whinny. Regina was a horse. A chestnut thoroughbred.

"Mom. Nothing has changed. We're gonna go to school and have careers. We're just gonna be together while we do it. I don't get why you're so upset." Regina licked her lips, maybe still yearning for a smoke. Freya watched her just from the corner of her eye, wary. She wouldn't want to turn into a tower of salt. Caleb continued. "The only thing different is we're going to move out of the dorm when we can and get an apartment."

"Oh you are, are you?" She was thinking since she was the one who paid the bills, it would be nice to be consulted.

"Then we can take Honeymoon home." Just then Evelyn the Airedale came running into the room, actually sliding across the floor. Honeymoon followed, more daintily. Regina held out her hand to him. The dog came and licked her fingers, very gently.

"He's a nice boy," she said.

There was a knock on the front door, and then it opened. A man's voice: "Can I come in?"

"Oh, this will be fun," said Regina. "Your dad is here to take a vacuum." In came a tall man in a suit and tie beneath his trench coat, which he immediately took off.

"Hi all." Clearly this was the father, Dan. He stretched out his hand to Caleb to shake. "My man," he said.

"Bro," said Caleb.

Dan turned to Freya, who looked at his chin. "And who is this lovely creature?"

"This is Freya, Dad."

"His wife," said Regina. And then after his *hunh?* look she started to cackle. She couldn't stop.

"What's with you?" said Dan. He was responding to her strange laughter more than to her words. Since the divorce they had acted civil but testy with each other. Neither of them was sure they had made the right choice, and their ambivalence created static in every interaction. They hadn't been happy together, but they weren't particularly happy apart, either.

Freya observed them with a quick glance. They were probably ten years younger than her parents. And they were professionals, lawyers—more worldly in some way than her academic mother and father. More stylish, more fit, less shabby.

Regina managed to sputter, "They got married. They really did!"

"What? Why?" said Dan. "Are you pregnant?"

"No," insisted Caleb.

Freya found herself unable to hold back; it was so unfair of all the parents, hers and his, to be negative about something so monumentally wonderful. "You act as if we committed some kind of crime making a commitment to each other. What if we just told you the truth?" she asked. "What if we told you we feel that our beings are stitched together, sutured, and if we were to separate, our organs would tear and bleed out until we died? What if I said when I look into his eyes I see the entire heavenly cosmos?"

"Huh. Just like us," said Dan wryly to his ex-wife.

"Right." There was a hint of sadness in her tone.

Meanwhile Evelyn the Airedale danced around Dan until he distractedly patted her head. Honeymoon stood politely at a distance until Dan motioned him over. Dan had plopped himself into a big easy chair and Honeymoon jumped onto his lap. This caused Freya to reassess who this man might be to some extent. More than a suit. If a dog liked him so easily.

"So I'm thinking you're a poetry major?" Dan asked Freya. It wasn't a bad guess.

"No. More like philosophy. I'm interested in the soul."

Dan and Regina exchanged a look. This humorless child was a little scary. A little Wednesday Addams.

"Anyway Mom, thank you for taking the dog," said Caleb. "We're going to look for an apartment together for next year. We can keep him then."

Honeymoon was still settled in Dan's lap, enjoying long strokes from forehead to tail, with an occasional pause at the rump for a scratch. "If I give him back," said Dan. "I might keep him."

"If only you could have pets in your condo." A little dig from Regina. He had moved out and left her. What women did he bring to his new bed?

"If only." Dan let Honeymoon lick his mouth.

"Do I give you a wedding gift?" Regina turned back to Caleb. "Do we send out an announcement?"

"You can do whatever you want, Mom. I mean, I hope you'll still pay for school. And... stuff..." Stuff was room and board. Both he and Freya had it easy when it came to practical matters. For instance, neither of them had to hold down a job to help allay college costs.

Regina looked to Dan. "I'm going to take these guys out to dinner. There's nothing in the house... I wasn't expecting them today... You can come if you want."

So they went to a family favorite bistro where the parents soon learned that Freya was vegan and almost never smiled. They also witnessed the mutual devotion of the young couple and softened. There was a time that they imagined themselves as some version of Romeo and Juliet, and the memory manifested physically before them was both heart-breaking and sweet. Sure, it probably wouldn't last, or at least not last in this version of itself, but what was done was done, and they might as well go with the flow. When Caleb became bored later, in a year or two or five, and decided to leave, or conversely, got his soul crushed, they'd be there for that too. To celebrate the marriage, they ordered dessert and champagne. It wasn't legal for the kids to drink—not until they were twenty-one—but the Beckers, before the divorce, and Regina solo since, had been regulars at this neighborhood restaurant so the owners brought four flutes, winking and then looking the other way. Freya had had wine often, for Shabbat and holidays, but couldn't remember having champagne. The fizziness on her tongue fascinated her. It was like a carnival troupe performing in her mouth. She imagined the tiniest clowns and trained seals cavorting. The alcohol turned her cheeks a vibrant pink and Regina remarked, with some wonder, that they looked like peonies. She was, herself, a decidedly unfloral human being, but she could appreciate the lyric in her son's choice. In the end all was well. And when Dan left to go back to his solo condo with the extra vacuum, he wasn't sure why.

Chapter Fourteen

ut then March arrived. Humans, or at least American humans, tended not to think the worst was coming for them. War, famine, locust infestation, pestilence, all might happen somewhere in the world, on another continent, but not on these shores. In recent years an angry Earth seemed to be exacting some revenge for its ages of mistreatment, via wild fire and flood, drought and hurricane in isolated locales even in the United States. But the unexpected plague arrived in the form of a highly infectious and deadly virus that blanketed the entire world, and America, despite its belief in its own exceptionalism, was not immune.

In the early panic much energy was spent by mothers and teachers disinfecting every possible surface. It wasn't until several weeks later Science deemed this unnecessary as the disease seemed to spread through airborne liquid molecules. Meanwhile, everyone's hands were raw from constant exposure to Formula 409 antibacterial spray along with frequent and thorough handwashing sung to "Twinkle Twinkle Little Star" to assure sufficient time spent soaping up. The administrators at Freya's college put their heads together, and, like many others, decided to send the students home. They would offer classes online and save everyone from contagion. It would be over soon, they were sure, and they would then resume normal routines.

When she heard the closure plan, Freya initially panicked. If she went to her home and Caleb to his they would be three thousand miles apart and she would die. Caleb was quick to assure her that they could stay together. Just calm down and think. Whose parental house would be more welcoming, safer, less complicated. Driving Honeymoon and Wren across the continent would not be easy, and they had already softened Regina's disapproval. Plus, she was banging around in that big house alone. So they got her on the phone. Regina was a bit of a germaphobe, when they called she was scouring the house with disinfectant and scouring the internet for information on this respiratory horror that was spreading at such an alarming rate. As if knowledge could stave it off. Well maybe it could. Ignorance certainly wouldn't help. It wasn't any comfort at all that the first wave of American deaths was in a nursing home less than a mile from her house. She was relieved to hear from Caleb, relieved he would be coming home from the petri dish that college was sure to be. Less enthusiastic about Freya coming with him, but she knew separating them would be a losing battle. And Caleb's safety was paramount. She was a mother, after all. A Jewish mother, however religiously unobservant. Anxious and prone to expect the worst, as history had long correctly taught.

So Caleb and Freya packed the Subaru and drove north the hour and some to Seattle. Evelyn was ding-y Airedale-glad to see them. Honeymoon was his even-keeled self. When they arrived Regina was on the back patio smoking a cigarette—she had restarted the habit. Freya took Wren straight past the dogs in the direction of Caleb's bedroom where she could shut the door. It remained to be seen how the dogs and cat would interact. Caleb, meanwhile, found his mother.

"Don't hate me," she said, referring to the Virginia Slim in her hand.

"I don't hate you. Just ironic that you're so freaked out about a virus that attacks the lungs and yet you're attacking your own lungs." She nodded, accepting the apt criticism. "How's your mental health," he asked her.

"Not great."

"Well we're here. We'll cheer you up."

She held out her cigarette free arm for a hug, and he entered the half circle. "Just don't exhale that skanky smoke on me," he said. He was teasing her, and it was already helping her feel more grounded. "Why aren't you at work?"

"I'm not going back until they cure this thing. I'll quit if I have to." She exhaled a white stream of smoke away from him and then threw the filtered butt down to squash it beneath her shoe. She fastidiously picked it up and went inside to put it into the kitchen garbage. Caleb followed her, and discovered Freya waiting awkwardly in the kitchen. Freya was the opposite of shifty, but she looked shifty because of the eye contact avoidance. Her manner took Regina by surprise again, though she had seen it before.

"Hi Dear," Regina said.

"Hi. Thank you for letting me stay here."

"I'm happy to have you. For everyone's sake I hope it's a short hiatus."

It wasn't in fact a short hiatus. Freya and Caleb began their online classes. In another room Regina lawyered remotely. Only Freya preferred this cloistered arrangement to IRL. What a relief it was to have no external obligations, to basically be forbidden to socialize with outsiders, to drop her tense mask and just live. Sitting cross-legged on her bed, Wren in her lap, she could go to classes on Zoom and both mute herself and turn the camera off. She was merely a circle on the screen with her initials at its center and yet considered present. This was ideal. No extraneous classroom distractions—scraping, coughing, whispers, electronic beeping from phones and laptops, no fluorescent lights, no smells of aftershave or essential oils, no random facial expressions or mysterious behaviors to decipher. Her black screen was a Zen pond.

In Advisory, Mimi Katz was highly concerned about student trauma, and the harrowing nature of this interruption in their education. If in fact it were going to be a harrowing trauma, it hadn't hit Freya and her classmates yet, so they did not respond with the bathos Mimi perhaps expected. More with apathy. For everyone there was something soporific about facing the checkered computer screen, and as hard as she tried, Mimi could not arouse them to share their pain or express any sort of enthusiasm.

For Jake it was different. Whether it was his sheer charisma, or the heat generated by his political views that broke the electronic fourth wall, break it he did. Students shouted over each other, jumped up and down within their rectangles, and used ALL CAPS in the chat. Several times per class Jake would mute everyone and hold forth with his own views. Practiced and well-formulated, they seemed inarguable. Freya still kept her mental distance—Jake rubbed her the wrong way. The fact that she hid behind her initialed square went unnoticed as Jake and most of her classmates had long since dismissed her as a stupid know-nothing, despite her well-written essays.

Caleb, on the other hand, was fully engaged in the class. He took up Jake's reading of political reality with the zealotry of a convert. Caleb's growing anti-corporate, anti-capitalist hostility towards America caused many tense dinners where Regina, a Poli-Sci major, tried to defend the ideals of the Founding Fathers.

"That's why it was called the Enlightenment. Their ideas were amazing, really. They were revolutionary in the deepest sense. Equality for all men?" Regina passed the salad to Freya.

"Exactly. All *men*. Who *owned property*." Caleb served himself a large scoop of lasagna.

"For their *time* they were amazing. History moves forward. They were limited by their time and place, but so are we. Undoubtedly. We can't see what we can't see."

"Anyone can see that slavery is wrong. Anyone can see that raping a person is wrong. A person you own. You don't think Sally Hemings screamed. Or cried? Fuck Thomas Jefferson."

Regina rolled her eyes. He was being obtuse. But she reminded herself he was officially still a teenager. He would mature and stop seeing things in only black and white. Nuance came with age and a fully developed prefrontal cortex.

Freya shivered. All she could eat was the salad and the bread. The lasagna was full of cheese. Regina didn't quite understand the vegan restrictions. But Freya said nothing. She was well aware of her guest status, and that she had no right to make any demands. Or even cause an inconvenience.

"Well, at least in the present, I think we can all agree that Trump and his minions are the devil," offered Regina.

"They're only the logical outcome of America's true values. White supremacy. America's core value."

Regina sighed. "Do you like the lasagna? I slaved over it." She considered Sally Hemmings. "Oops. I mean worked hard."

"It's delicious, Mom," said Caleb. They both turned to Freya, to include her.

"It has cheese," she murmured. She put her hand on Caleb's thigh, because she felt like she had said the wrong thing.

"Oh shit," said Regina. "I forgot that was verboten."

"I'm happy with salad," said Freya. "Really."

"Really Mom, she doesn't eat a lot," said Caleb.

Regina and Caleb returned to politics, and Freya's mind strayed far away. She was imagining the project she was planning for her Media

Class, an animation about goats and their ability to clear blackberries from vacant lots. From there she drifted to the world of the book she was reading, just then the world of Wolsey, Cromwell, More, King Henry, and Anne Boleyn. Her mind was awash in rich reds and velvety greens, seed pearls, a soundtrack of lyres and wood flutes.

"Freya," said Regina. Re-entry to the twenty-first century was startling. Freya felt and looked like she was in trouble for her wandering attention. "Are you a revolutionary like my son?"

"Um," she said. She looked at Caleb for a clue, and then back at Regina's chest, which was as close to her eyes as was comfortable. "Well, I think the world is unkind. There are a lot of people and animals, even trees … ecosystems, that need more love and attention." Caleb was touched anew by her authentic sweetness and stroked her head and then tugged gently on her long curls, weaving his fingers through the tendrils.

"Well, we can all agree about that. Just don't let him become Abbie Hoffman."

"I don't know who that is."

Caleb told her a bit about the yippies and the Democratic Convention and the Chicago Seven. Then for his mother's sake more than hers he said, "Really Abbie Hoffman was the GOAT."

"I need a cigarette," said Regina. "Caleb, clear the table. We can have ice cream for dessert." Regina was not clear on Freya's diet yet, and it was true Freya was just as happy not to eat. She had a pouch of peanuts to nibble on when hunger struck. For Regina not eating meat registered easily, but avoiding cheese and milk and eggs—what was there then to serve? Making dinner every night (well, not every night as they had restaurant take-out several nights a week) was a hellish chore already. To be fair, Freya and Caleb had volunteered to cook, but their menus sounded so unappetizing.

As the weeks went by the world went weirder. Everyone wore masks. Freya set up her sewing machine and supplied the entire household with a variety of prints and solids to wear with any outfit. This as she and Caleb continued their Zoom classes. They rarely left the house other than to roam the quiet neighborhood. Food was delivered from the grocery store, anything anyone may have touched with germy hands washed and dried. When they walked Honeymoon and Evelyn, every time they approached another human being on the sidewalk either they or the other party would take a detour out into the street to avoid breathing each other's potentially infected exhalations. When they finally did venture into a grocery store having run out of something absolutely essential, dog food or chocolate, it was the eeriest feeling in the world, everyone masked and wearing plastic gloves. Their fellow shoppers were frightened, kept their distance; looked like astronauts on a toxic moon.

Jake was eating it up. The disaster was good for his side of the debate. The plague and the government's inability to cope, the over-filling hospitals, the staff wearing garbage bags for lack of appropriate protective gear, the president pretending that all was well, nothing to see here—it all proved that Capitalism was a failed system. No universal healthcare, scientific research starved by short-sighted legislators, no emergency infrastructure. People were lining up for hours in their cars to receive a box of food. Look, he told his students. He drew the connections for them, clear as summer skies, in America you only got what you paid for. And safety for its citizens was not paid for. Caleb was becoming angrier every day. Really he had a soft heart, nearly as soft as Freya's, but his reaction to all this suffering was not deer-like, but dog-like. If only he could tear the system to shreds with his teeth. For her part, Freya sewed more and more masks. She mailed them to old age homes and hospitals with no return address.

She checked in with her parents via Skype every day. So far they were fine. The classes they taught had moved to virtual like hers. Mei, who was terribly lonely at her parents' house—they both were working long hours at the family restaurant selling only take-out—would call sometimes. She seemed to be petering out, becoming a miniaturized version of herself. Her shoulders hunched, her voice weakened. Freya had to remind her every few sentences to speak up in order to hear her at all. Could a human become a feather and blow away?

In the evenings at the Becker household they occasionally played board games. Freya was good at Scrabble, she always won, so Caleb steered them to Monopoly. Here he was the victor every time they played. He had the instincts of a real estate mogul, buying up medium priced properties in a long row that other players couldn't avoid, and populating them with multiple little wooden houses. From the rents he received he turned them into hotels, and this ultimately bankrupted the others as they inevitably landed on one of his pumpkin or grape-colored avenues. His mother teased him hard about his capitalist tendencies, his relishing of money and outsmarting the little guys. Caleb actually sulked about this, and worried that he had been inculcated by American culture with these qualities. Freya shook her head. "Sometimes a game is just a game," she said. But Regina kept on teasing, and Caleb kept on winning and feeling guilty for it.

Late night was different. Freya and Caleb were living in the guest room because the bed in Caleb's bedroom was a twin trundle. In the pale blue covered queen bed in the ample guest room was where they made love. Never was a term so apt. As they explored every part of their bodies together, every pore, every nerve, every flaw, their wonder grew. They found the sources of bodily pleasure, of course. Feet, calves, and sex organs; necks, shoulders, and scalps. But it was far deeper than physical excitement and release. They became wizards of joy. Freya had visions. She saw their souls as clouds of color, whispering secrets as they poured into one another.

Once, weird as it may seem, Mimi Katz appeared in the corner of the room. Though naked, Freya was not embarrassed. After all, she hadn't invited her. Mimi nodded her approval. "You've found your bashert!" Mimi was wearing a surgical mask, but Freya could tell she was smiling broadly behind it from the way her eyes squinted. And then she disappeared.

"Did you see that?" asked Freya.

"What?" asked Caleb. He began to suck on her labia, and her question was subsumed by her pleasure.

Chapter Fifteen

ad things happened all the time, one after another, so if you wanted to bunch them into groups of threes, sure, that was a viable organizational scheme.

First, Freya's grandma, her only living grandparent, died. Rachel had been living in an old folks' home outside of Boston, her cognition not functioning well, dragging an oxygen tank behind her wherever she went like the kid sister who gave her no peace. COVID came roaring through her hall, mowing down the elderly with its cruel theft of breath. Rachel, a fiery old woman, had signed a paper long since that forbade intrusive measures like intubation, so she was a goner as soon as the bug hit. She died an ugly death, with none of her loved ones allowed in to hold her hand. They tried to talk to her on an iPad but it was too hard for her to focus on communication and her breathing at the same time so she turned away from them in order to inhale. This particularly broke Ruth's heart, as if it were her mother's final message to her. Thus did a misreading of reality once again strike a needless blow; the perennial pain of skewed perception. Ruth would carry this wound to the grave. Meanwhile Rachel had simply been trying to catch her breath.

Freya had feared her grandmother. Her smell was sour because of her dentures that were apparently not well-cleaned. And of course the garlic she believed to be a tonic against ill health. The old woman, in queenly manner, would call Freya to her lap for a storybook or a conversation, and Freya obeyed though Grandma's rough woolen sweaters bristled against her skin. Rachel had fierce opinions and had thought a little more discipline might have reined in some of Freya's odder traits. Ruth and Rachel fought. Freya hid in her bedroom humming to her stuffed creatures and dolls. When her grandmother died, Freya felt some relief for herself, but her mother's obvious grief ripped her open. Her mother was a donkey, and who can endure the pain of a sad donkey?

The second bad thing was far far worse, in the hierarchy of the horrible. It had been several weeks since Mei had reached out to Freya—long enough for Freya to start to sense her friend's absence, and consider texting, though she hadn't done it yet. In their shared Zoom class, both of them were mere silent initials in a ring in a section of the screen, so there was no camaraderie to be found there. Freya didn't know that Mei was alone all day every day, trapped in the house by COVID, worried about her parents working too hard, carrying the weight of the bloodline's future on her narrow shoulders as she strove for academic success. But she didn't think she could go much longer studying this way. It was far too abstract, too dull, too drab. And it provided no distraction from the self-loathing that had always riddled her. The desire to be purged from this earth that made her carve into her own tender flesh, seeking its destruction.

It was actually Caleb who found out the news on social media at the very moment Freya was beginning to notice the negative space where Mei had been—she was even toying with the idea of initiating contact at the very moment he came to find her. Freya sat at the sewing machine, pairing two prints to create one more fetching reversible mask. She was listening to Debussy on her phone, swaying her head to the lyrical rhythm. Caleb put his hand on her shoulder, startling her. She looked up into his face and saw there was something wrong. "What?"

"It's hard to say."

She turned her body around so she was facing him fully. "What?"

"It was on Insta. That guy Charles in our class knew her cousin . . ."

"Whose cousin?"

"Mei. Mei passed."

"Passed. You mean died? Is that what you mean?"

"Yes."

"She got COVID?"

"No. It wasn't COVID . . ."

"What?"

"She killed herself."

Freya crumbled.

She slid off her chair onto the floor, pulled her knees in and curled into the smallest possible mass like a potato bug. She rocked. Caleb sat down on the floor beside her. He put his hand on her bony back, noting again the delicate architecture of her spine. She made a low keening sound. Rocked and keened. They sat there like that as the light changed in the sky, first turning golden pink in the magic hour, and then dimming, dimming until Venus appeared in a blue black field.

Regina called from downstairs, "Dinner." Caleb gave Freya a stroke down the gemstone string of bone and got up. He was gone just long enough to tell his mom they weren't going to eat right now, and then he reappeared, a warm and quiet presence hip to hip with Freya. Wren had settled herself on Freya's feet as the girl continued to rock and moan.

When she finally looked up, it was after eight o'clock. Her face was red. Even her eyes were red. Her voice sounded like there were glass shards in her throat.

"How did she do it?"

Caleb looked away. He swallowed the words, as if he hoped to undo what was done by failing to name it. "She hung herself."

"What?"

A little more clearly, "She hung herself."

Still looking toward Caleb, she began her high sharp humming again. Her breathing was shallow and irregular, making the sound percussive. Caleb pulled her up off the floor—she didn't resist—and he led her to the bed, sitting her on the edge. He bent and took off her shoes, and then helped her under the covers, where she furled again and quieted. "Do you want dinner? Some miso soup?" he asked gently. She shook her head. Wren jumped up on the bed and found her place in the cleft of Freya's body. "Is it OK if I go get something to eat? I'll be back soon." She nodded.

Freya saw it all in her mind. There was Mei the rabbit, secret scars lacing her forearms. Alone in her house. Freya had been there. She remembered the white tiled floors throughout, dulled over by wax. The two white vinyl couches in the living room. An altar with electric candles and some oranges in front of a gold-colored statue of Buddha. Plastic indoor plants. The smell of sesame oil and fish sauce lingering in the air like a subtle incense.

And there was Mei the rabbit. Dying her hair a new color and flipping her high pigtails on TikTok. No one cared that on one side of the part her hair was pink, and on the other aqua. No one cared. Listening to beautiful boy bands. They did not love her back. School was on screen. She dared not speak up. Only the opinionated spoke up in Zoom classes, not the bunnies. In her literature class they read dystopian tales that reinforced the sense of doom she already felt. And her parents. Working double shifts at the restaurant to keep it from collapsing. Coming home after midnight, the masks they wore since dawn having carved furrows in their faces. Irritable with each other. With her. Too tired to talk. Too tired to cook. Their only beam of hope was a daughter's success in a crumbling world. She was living on ramen noodles and boiled eggs. The weeks dragged on. Every day like the last. Her roots grew out and she let them. She didn't change out of her Hello Kitty pajamas. Her glasses frames broke—she used duct tape to put them together. She didn't look in the mirror. She let her phone die, so she wouldn't know she received no texts. The charger was lost under the bed, but she didn't look for it. In class she didn't turn on the camera or the mic, nor did she listen. She stopped reading *The Parable of the Sower* on page eighty-six and read nothing more. Not in this lifetime. It rained and rained some more. The windows streamed with angel tears and the neighborhood was gray. She used a rope and did it in the garage, where there was a beam to loop it round.

Caleb had never gotten to know Mei well, but he found the image of her body haunting, swinging from the ceiling, he imagined her in a dress (she was actually wearing her Hello Kitty P.J.'s that she hadn't changed in three weeks), her pale legs dangling like knockers in a bell. He tried to erase the mental picture, but it came back to shock him hourly. For Freya there was no respite. Mei was really the only friend she had ever had. Of course she had family and she had Caleb, and pets, but Mei had created a girl-to-girl relationship between them. It had taken courage and patience on both their parts. Freya knew she herself had not risen to the occasion the way Mei had wished, had needed even, and now there was this. She cried for forgiveness into the vast question mark of space that contained God. Space cried also.

The third thing that happened was the very next day, and there was some causality. If Freya had been herself it never would have happened. But she wasn't herself. She was nearly catatonic.

So she returned from a dazed trip to the bathroom. She closed the door but the latch didn't catch. She didn't notice. She heard the dog's nails clicking down the hall, but the sound didn't register. Honeymoon was running because Evelyn was chasing him. They both skidded into the bedroom. Wren screeched and ran out. Freya shook her head as if waking from sleep, trying to enter the present. Honeymoon came to her for protection from his predator. Instinctively she comforted him, all the while aware she needed to go find Wren.

Meanwhile Wren found her way downstairs and out the sliding door to the patio, which was open because Regina was having a smoke break. Regina did not notice the cat, on her little cat feet, scampering into the shrubbery, where she hid. Having finished her cigarette, Regina came back in, smashed butt in hand. She locked the slider and retreated back into the den, which now served as her home office. When Freya, looking like a wraith, gathered herself enough to descend into the living area, she could find Wren nowhere. Not the kitchen, not the dining room. The den door, where Regina worked, was shut tight. She went back up to see if maybe the cat had found her way into Caleb's childhood bedroom, where he was studying. Caleb joined her in the search. Under every bookshelf, in every cranny a cat might hide they looked but there was no Wren. They looked again. They bothered Regina in the den, but Wren wasn't there either.

It wasn't until some bedeviled hours later that the doorbell rang. Caleb opened to a very repentant masked driver holding the bloody dead cat on a towel and thus the mystery of her location was solved. Caleb asked that the cat be left there on the porch. He shut the door and considered how to tell Freya, who was just now coming down the stairs again after a thirteenth unlucky search of the linen closet. She had put both dogs in the backyard and locked the doggy door so they wouldn't frighten Wren.

Regina came out of her office. "Did someone knock?"

Caleb sighed deeply, still contemplating what words to use. He spoke to Freya. "Wren got out." Gradually he managed to break the news. When Freya understood, she went outside and lay down beside the cat's body on the cold, wet stoop, as if there were something holy about the place where Wren had been placed by the driver. Caleb sat beside her on the step.

"For God's sake," said Regina. "Come inside you two." But they didn't. The wind was blowing the rain under the eaves, and they were getting drenched.

Regina went through the house and out the back sliding doors into the garden shed and pulled out a blue tarp. She came back and tented this over the children and dead cat, then disappeared again. Caleb lay down beside Freya under the heavy plastic and put his arms around her. She was mute. The wind ruffled their uncomfortable makeshift tent. Oxygen was in short supply. Caleb held a flap open to let in air.

After about twenty minutes Regina returned and lifted up one blue plastic corner. At some point in the interim she had put on a hooded coat. "Let's bury the kitty. I dug a grave." She went back into the house to wait. Caleb pulled Freya to her feet. As the tarp dropped to the ground it showered one last cascade of rain onto their shoes. Regina opened the door again. "Don't bring the cat through the house, please." So they went together, Freya and Caleb, Caleb carrying the cat on its now blood burgundy towel, through the side yard, walking on the slate stepping stones slimy with wet moss. In the back they met Regina by the fig tree, where she had indeed dug a hole. Caleb gently placed Wren into the pit. He rubbed his hand down Freya's back to comfort her, and then grabbed the shovel leaning against the tree. Regina, who had never before touched Freya on purpose, moved over and put her arm around the girl's shoulders as Caleb scooped soil back into the grave. "There must be a Jewish thing to say. A prayer," said Regina.

"Do you know it?" asked Caleb.

"Of course not," said Regina. "I don't know anything."

"Yis'ga'dal v'yis'kadash sh'may ra'bbo," murmured Freya, but they didn't hear her.

"We could say Shema," said Caleb. His Jewish education was far inferior to Freya's and in the moment he forgot the existence of the mourner's kaddish, latching onto the most famous prayer he could think of. He started "Shema Yisrael," and then they all joined in, starting over from the beginning, including Freya.

"Shema Yisrael, Adonai Elohenu, Adonai Echad. Baruch shem k'vod malchuto l'olam vaed." Caleb knew it meant that God was One, and that He/She/It should be praised to the end of time. He didn't have strong feelings about God, but he hoped He/She/It would comfort Freya. She was more in contact with the spiritual world than his family. Regina squeezed Freya closer to her, and then let go. As she started back into the house she gave directions to her son.

"When you finish there, help your bride upstairs and take a hot shower together until you're nice and warm."

When the dirt was patted down over the cat, Caleb did take Freya by the hand, leading her back to the house. Up in the guestroom bathroom they showered until the room was filled with steam. He lathered her body and wondered at the snowy whiteness of her skin contrasted against his own permanent Mediterranean tan. She finally began to talk, almost a plea. "Dog Boy," she said. "Dog Boy." His hands sliding along her body aroused her, and they got into bed without drying themselves, making love beneath the feather duvet. If there was a God maybe He/She/It provided sexual connection as a balm. As Marvin Gaye had suggested.

By the time they finished the bedclothes and their activity had dried them, except for Freya's black curls, which would take hours more to dry. They lay on their backs side by side, holding hands. "It's more important than ever," she said.

"What is?"

"The existence of the soul. If. Where is Grandma now? Where is Mei? Where is Wren? I mean, I know their bodies are dead, but can the spirit be dead too? What do you think?"

"I don't know. I mean I hate to say it but the thing we, like, perceive as spirit could just be an expression of like, brain juice. That dies when the brain dies. Or there could be a God and a soul and all that. The jury is totally out."

She turned toward him on her side, stroked his cheek. "I don't see how your being could ever die."

"Yeah. No. I see what you mean. Yours neither. Honestly, I don't see how love can die. It's like sugared air. The air doesn't die."

The next morning, very early, Freya visited the grave alone. She created an altar, decorating a garden rock she moved atop it with acrylics, a rendering of a wren. She placed the cat's favorite toys—a felted ball and a wooden clothespin painted like a soldier—or was it a drum major?—in the shadow of the rock. It was spring so she picked flowers that were sprouting up in the garden: jonquils, forget-me-nots and Spanish bluebells, all still damp from yesterday's rain, and scattered them over the newly turned dirt. Caleb came out the sliding doors from the kitchen in his pajamas, looking sleepy. "You OK?" he asked.

"No."

"Anything I could do to make it better?"

"Make the dead alive."

"We could have a séance." Dark humor.

"Really?"

Of course he hadn't been serious, but when he saw her glimpse of happiness, he turned serious. "We could try."

"I don't really want to see my Grandma. But Mei . . . I want to say I'm sorry. I wasn't a good friend." She saw him about to protest. "Don't pretend I was. I don't even know how. So don't pretend."

"OK." He knew she meant it. Her honesty was so fierce.

"And Wren. Do you think you can reach a cat with a séance?"

"I don't know if you can reach anybody with a séance. But we could try."

They went upstairs and googled: How to hold a séance. There was a lot of material on exorcisms, which was irrelevant to their cause and kind of creepy. Freya had never seen *The Exorcist* but Caleb had, and the way he shivered about it was enough to scare her off. They read up on spiritualists who contacted the dead for sweeter reasons.

That night at midnight, as advised, they gave it a try. In the guest room where they were staying they sat on the floor cross-legged, knee to knee, holding hands. Around them was a circle of burning candles, providing the only light in the room, as recommended by one of the DIY séance sites. The flickering of the flames suggested the presence of spirits. They shut their eyes, as their Google search prescribed, and practiced Yogic deep breathing. Freya felt the air shimmering around her. After five minutes or so, in line with their research, Freya invited Mei to join them, and said they would simply welcome her presence or anything she might like to share with them. They waited, hoping for anything, a chill breeze. At least Freya hoped. Caleb was trying hard to turn off his skepticism, as he knew that if it had any chance of working he had to believe. That was the problem with faith-based practices; they required faith. He really tried. The two of them continued their deep breathing. After another ten minutes, they did find themselves in a state of dreamy serenity—even Caleb. It was like a heavy sleep in that it was otherworldly, but they were still conscious. Though her mind was deeply placid, Freya's senses were on high alert for any message her dead friend might send from the other side. Suddenly something made her open her eyes. It wasn't Mei, as she had hoped, but Grandma Rachel.

The old woman was wearing her old knobby green coat, rubber ankle boots, and one of those pleated plastic rain scarves that fold up into a small packet printed with pink umbrellas over her coarse gray hair. She had a finger up to her lips signaling that Freya shouldn't speak.

"Listen to me, Child," Rachel began. "Everyone dies. You think you won't, but you will. Sooner than you might think. Handsome over there too." She nodded her head toward Caleb. "It's not the end of the world. The dead hover around for a while, in and out, until one day you notice that they're gone and by then you won't even mind so much."

Freya opened her mouth to ask a question. She wanted to know what was on the other side, but Rachel shook her head, demanding silence.

"Your little Oriental friend is fine. She's had a good laugh at herself by now."

Freya squinted. This seemed unlikely.

"You don't believe me? Why would I lie?"

Caleb, still trying to muster faith, his eyes shut, squeezed her hand. Grandma Rachel disappeared.

"Ready to call it?" he asked.

She said OK, and they opened their eyes.

"Did you hear that?"

"What?"

"Grandma Rachel was here. She talked to me."

"Freya . . ." This was simply a bridge too far.

"Don't you believe me?" She pulled her hand away.

He sighed heavily, pulling her hand back into his. "Would you rather I said 'yes' or told the truth?"

"The truth."

"No. I think you imagined it."

Freya looked down into her lap. The news from the great beyond had been good, but his doubt angered her.

"What did she say?" he asked.

"Never mind. It must have been for my ears only." She was used to

keeping secrets. Just not from Caleb.
   That was April, the cruelest month.

Chapter Sixteen

hen came May. The Pacific Northwest exploded as it always did in spring. Azaleas and rhododendrons and lilacs erupted in rococo riot. Trees were frothy with pink bloom—ornamental cherry and then magnolia, and dogwood. It was easier enduring the pandemic since the days were longer and being outside was safer. The light lasted until nine. Talk of potential vaccines on the horizon made it seem possible that the plague would not be endless, as it had been beginning to seem. Freya and Caleb were looking forward to the end of the quarter which was also the end of their freshman stint. In the following three years they were meant to begin the process of creating their own majors. Caleb was thinking about politics and law. He could see himself vying for public office eventually. Not on the national level maybe, but city council, state rep, something like that. And of course all the recent deaths had rendered Freya more committed than ever to study of the soul. Since the séance, since Grandma Rachel's appearance, she had felt the presence of Mei and Wren surrounding her in the ether. She knew it could be a projection of her imagination, even her grandma's ghost could have been an illusion, but she wanted to explore. What was the "ether" anyway, and what was it made of? Maybe it was the stuff of God, of eternity, where time did not exist and all energy was an endless pulsing ocean of gas?

Toward the end of the month everything changed yet again. The whole world flipped on its axis. A teenager named Darnella in Minneapolis witnessed the event and couldn't believe what she was seeing. She filmed it on her phone. The other onlookers pled for mercy for the victim. The policeman, Officer Chauvin, stared with icy eyes as he continued to crush the large Black man beneath his knee. Almost like he was daring the passersby to do something, but he was the cop with the gun in his holster and they were merely mortals. Some shouted at him to stop, some dared to approach, but he had his police buddies with their guns and grim faces, arms folded across their barrel chests, telling them to stand back, and so they did. In wretched slow motion, it was the man below the knee who stopped the heart. Crying into the pavement for his mama, insisting he couldn't breathe, slowly expiring as the witnesses watched in horror. His fleshiness was palpable. His humanity was palpable.

Regina, Caleb, and Freya watched it on the TV. And on their phones. Over and over, everyone watched. Freya saw a lamb taken to the slaughter. It reminded her of the story of Abraham and Isaac, which she had always hated. Why would God test Abraham's loyalty in such a perverse way? Wouldn't it be better to do the right thing, which was obviously not to kill a child, than to be obedient for its own sake? What kind of nasty religion was that? It confused her. And Chauvin ought to have shown mercy, as God finally did, but he didn't. He had no mercy. He was evil incarnate. She mourned. Everyone mourned.

The gross injustice, the obvious wrong of it all, the blatant cruelty and abuse of power hit Caleb as nothing in his life had before. Maybe because Jake had tilled the soil of his consciousness. He would have liked to eviscerate that cop with his own hands. Minneapolis burned. Caleb watched, sure it ought to. Freya saw less of an obvious righteousness in the destruction; the mayhem frightened her. She held Caleb's hand and felt his pulse beating hard for justice. "But non-violence," she reminded him.

"I never said I believe in non-violence," he protested.

He saw her wilt, like a crushed flower. She hated for them to be out of alignment with each other. "There are other principles that are more important than non-violence," he said more gently.

"Well, self-defense, yeah," she allowed. Even that she wasn't sure about. She was impressed by the Jains, who she had read walked with a soft broom to gently clear the dusty path before them of any insect they might harm by stepping on it. She would have liked to be a Jain. She thought of beetles. The various gleaming colors and patterns. Some of them were like iridescent jewels. They came in purples and aquas. Orange and ruby. Any combination you could imagine. She could see a poster with rows and columns filled with gem-like creatures. And then some had polka dots. Lady bugs. So whimsical. She would paint it.

"Not just self-defense." Caleb's impassioned voice brought her back into the present. "Sometimes you have to fight for what's right. You have to fight racism. You have to fight fascism. My grandpa had to fight Hitler." He glanced at the TV which kept showing footage of the police precinct building on fire. "They're fighting for what's right."

Regina was passing behind the couch where they sat watching the television and heard her son's opinion. "That's not fighting. That's rioting. What possible good can that do? It won't bring that poor man back to life."

Secretly Freya was glad Regina said it aloud because it was what she felt.

"It shows the people demand blood. The cops can't get away with murder and suffer no repercussions. They've been getting away with this shit forever. Since America started. There's got to be an end to it. You know the police forces were originally created to go after runaway slaves? That's who they are."

"That doesn't sound right," said Regina. "There were police in Europe. Police pretty much exist everywhere."

"Look it up," said Caleb. He was cock sure. Regina shook her head and let it go. She would wait for his brain to finish developing.

In their morning Zoom class, Jake seemed jubilant. He urged the students to join him at the demonstrations that very afternoon in downtown Seattle. This was history in the making, and they could both participate and observe. He set a meeting place for the class, reminding them to mask up. Even though they'd be outside, it would be a close crowd and the good guys shouldn't risk COVID.

Freya and Caleb and Honeymoon drove towards downtown, parking north of the core so they didn't have to pay downtown parking prices. The streets were full of people moving towards the march site. The avenues were crowded for blocks. It seemed useless to try and find Jake and the others. Freya was beginning to regret having brought the dog. But Honeymoon minded the commotion less than she did. Thank goodness they had left Evelyn at home. Evelyn would have lost her high-strung canine mind.

There were thousands of people. There were swaths of middle-aged women wearing knit pink hats souvenirs from the women's march the day after Trump's inauguration. There were Black activists and their allies behind BLM banners and signs. Tattooed hipsters with man buns. Young moms and dads, with children on shoulders or holding hands. Homemade signs urged defunding of the police, bore stenciled images of George Floyd or a cavalcade of other unarmed victims of racist brutality, insisted I Am a Man, or Hands Up Don't Shoot. There were some less polite: Off the Pig or All Cops Are Bastards. On the edges were dozens of young folks dressed head to toe in black, with balaclava masks. This group always appeared at Seattle demonstrations, and the newspapers usually referred to them, inexplicably, as anarchists from Eugene, as if Oregon somehow nurtured a different sort of radical than its northern neighbor Washington State. Normally their dress was intimidating, but since everyone was now masked against COVID they blended in more easily.

The entire ocean of protestors marched from one end of downtown to the other, chanting the words on their signs, chanting No Justice No Peace, some gray hairs trying to make inroads singing We Shall Overcome, with few takers. A group of First Peoples played ancient drums. A white guy with dreads wove through the crowd on a unicycle. Almost everyone wore a mask to protect against contagion. En masse, ten abreast or so, they walked all the way from the center of downtown to the International District. Here they found some sort of natural end-point: there was a light-rail station and hundreds of marchers swarmed the platforms to find their way home. Others wended their way back through downtown to parking places, or to catch a bus. The demonstration was thinning out. But the young and deeply ardent stayed. Hundreds of them. Caleb finally caught sight of his classmates and teacher, and he and Freya and Honeymoon on his leash joined them.

The crowd remained large enough that the first act of vandalism was hidden from the police. Freya saw the window shatter into a million small aqua-tinted cubes—some kind of safety glass. An appreciative cheer went up from the crowd; it was the Bank of America Chinatown branch. Jake pointed out to his students that this was a violent encroachment on capitalism itself. The antifa army was inspired. More windows were broken. Freya was alarmed.

"We should go," she said to Caleb.

"No way!" he said.

She looked at him, trying to read him. He was flushed. He looked happy, almost like he did when she opened her eyes during sex and caught sight of his glimmering skin, his breathless expression. More windows shattered with violent blasts and gleeful roars from the crowd. Restaurants and small businesses that sold herbs or aquarium fish or Chinese tchotchkes. Asian Mom and Pop shops, some already shuttered from the pandemic, none thriving. Who knew if they were insured against this. There was glass all over the streets. Graffiti appearing on the walls as if the neighborhood were a giant magic Etch-A-Sketch. The police were taken by surprise and made a few arrests, but they were vastly outnumbered.

Honeymoon whimpered and lifted his left front paw. He tried to keep up with Caleb and Freya on three of his legs but he was pulling from behind on the leash. Freya stopped in the middle of the road and checked his paw, with others streaming around them. His black pad was bleeding, punctured by a shard of window. The smaller shops didn't have safety glass. "Oh Baby," she said as she checked the cut. She looked angrily at Caleb, as if it were his fault. He had never seen her glare before. "I'm taking him home. You can come or not." She picked the dog up so Honeymoon wouldn't have to walk.

Caleb looked around for Jake and the other students, already moving many yards ahead of them. Coraline had picked up a piece of metal and was swinging it up and down, looking like Brienne of Tarth with her short blond hair and manlike stature. "OK," he reluctantly agreed. "Let me carry him." She handed the dog to Caleb. Honeymoon put a front paw on each of Caleb's shoulders and sat in the cradle of his arms. Without pressure on his paw, he didn't seem to be in pain. It was a couple miles to the car from where they were. After a few blocks, Freya took a turn. Carrying fifty pounds of canine wasn't nothing.

"Maybe you could take his front legs and I could take the back?" she asked after half a block.

"Just let me rest until the corner and I'll take him again." They soldiered on.

She put Honeymoon down for a moment at the designated trade-off spot. Honeymoon pranced around a bit. "Looks like it stopped hurting," said Caleb.

"Good dog." Freya patted Honeymoon on the head.

"We should go back," said Caleb.

"You can. We're going home." The light changed and with a determined stride she started north through the crosswalk, Honeymoon heeling. Caleb lingered a moment, and then followed.

He caught up with them. "Why don't you wanna go back?"

"I've had enough. Caleb. It's too much for me. I feel like I've been inside a kaleidoscope. I feel like I am one of those pieces of broken glass. In the kaleidoscope. Or maybe on the street. I'm tired and dizzy and dehydrated and I need to be somewhere quiet and still."

"You're not much of a revolutionary."

"Oh is that what that was? A revolution?"

"It might be. The start of one."

They walked the rest of the way in silence. It was just their second fight, and they were mourning separately. Had they cast themselves out of Eden? Once the apple was eaten was there any going back? Right then they both felt too prickly to bother.

They were relieved to be in the car, where they could sit down after all those miles on their feet. This immediately improved their moods, at least a touch. Freya held Honeymoon in her lap and re-examined his paw. There was some remnant of blood in fur around the pad, but whatever had cut him was definitely gone. The Spaniel curled up and quickly fell asleep as Caleb drove them home.

Now they spoke to each other in gentler voices, trying to find their way back to union. "I don't see the point of breaking windows."

"It's just a scream at injustice. It's just a way of saying this system is not working. It's George Floyd but it's everything. All the Black people killed by police. And vigilantes. George Zimmerman. It's Trump and his racism. His anti-Muslim policies. The kids separated from their parents at the border. His lies about COVID. It's all the pain we've been holding in."

"But besides like a primal tension release, does it do any good? Does it change anything?'

"I don't know. We'll see. We'll have to wait and see. I know without pressure nothing changes. Not ever. It's, like, a law of physics. Protestors stopped the war in Viet Nam. They ended Jim Crow."

When they got home there was a vegan dinner left for them by Regina who had already disappeared into her room. Airedale Evelyn of course was ecstatic to see their return and got what was undoubtedly an extra bowl of kibble when they fed Honeymoon his dinner. They watched the eleven o'clock news and saw the coverage of their demonstration, and demonstrations all over the country. George Floyd's parents asked for non-violence, while Minneapolis burned, and the TV station rolled the footage of the murder once again. Derek Chauvin's steely eyes sent a shiver through Freya's body every time she saw them. She imagined Hitler, Mussolini, Stalin. Powerful murderers going back through history. Ivan the Terrible and Nero and Atilla the Hun. All of them swirling in the blue of his cold eyes.

They received a group text from Jake telling them where and when to meet tomorrow.

"You in?" asked Caleb.

"I guess. OK." She couldn't separate herself from Caleb. She looked at Honeymoon who was lying on her feet. It was hard to separate from the dog, too, but it would be selfish to drag him along. "This time you stay here with Evelyn."

Chapter Seventeen

ou're going back?" Incredulous, Regina asked at breakfast.

"It's for school, Mom. Our professor is meeting us there."

"I never wanted you to go to that school."

Caleb sighed.

"You didn't?" asked Freya. "How come?"

"It's a silly school," said Regina, as if that were explanation enough. Freya was bewildered by Regina's judgement, but Caleb cut off further inquiry.

"We need to get gas on the way. We should go." His college decision, to go there instead of an Ivy as both his parents had, well his dad went to Stanford but close enough, was an act of rebellion more than a considered choice.

"Don't get killed," said Regina. "I wouldn't forgive you."

This time Jake had been more specific about time and place and they found him quickly, with Coraline, and Lion Boy, and several others. Jojo hadn't shown up yesterday and she wasn't here today either. Coraline mentioned that she wasn't surprised—Jojo was basically just a bougie bitch. This made Freya flinch. She didn't like personal insults, even against someone who could be conceived of as a rival. And there were certain words that got to her especially. Bitch and cunt, but also non-swear words like shrivel and perpendicular.

The crowd was again enormous. This time the police presence was as well. In their riot gear they looked like something out of Star Wars. But then so did the anarchists from Eugene, who were also dressed in black like Shadow Stormtroopers.

Again the human river flowed through downtown. The chants raged like rapids. Now that the police were there in force, they themselves became the focus. "Defund the police!" Over and over. "What do we want? Pigs out. When do we want it? Now!" Over and over and over again. Sometimes they would say, "What do we want? Pigs dead." The ladies in the pink hats and the aging men with scraggly hair didn't join in; they were ambivalent, but to the youth, Black, white, Asian, Native, it was as serious as death. "Hands Up Don't Shoot!" They had had it with the world being a fucking miasma of pain and injustice. Freya watched Caleb shouting along, so fiercely that she trembled. She knew his heart was pure. He was a dog. Was she simply a coward, afraid of radical change, afraid to take the measures radical change required?

Though the crowd's mood was definitely harsh and edging toward hysteria again, the march was initially non-violent. But at some point late in the day, after the old and middle-aged had gone home to make dinner and watch the news and Jeopardy, the unbridled thrill of destruction began again for the young. This time, though, it was met by bull horn warnings to disperse, flashbangs and tear gas. Fool me once, thought the police. The crowd surged in a murmuration, a flock of starlings. Though Caleb and Freya were some distance from the breaking windows, the toxic gas released by the cops stung their eyes like Windex on their glassy corneas. Jake pulled extra water out of a backpack. "We'll come better prepared tomorrow. Pour this into your eyes, and follow me." He was genuinely worried about his flock of kids, and led them away from the cloud.

Once they were at a safe distance from the action and the poisonous air, Jake gathered the students around him. He discussed with them the violent power of the State so on display before them. Freya was thinking she wasn't made for this. She couldn't stop weeping. The noise and the breaking glass undid her, not just the tear gas. She felt a deep humiliation, familiar but secreted away since childhood. She wasn't like the others. She wanted to be in her room with her embroidery hoop and her miniature tea set to fete the fairies. But the frightening truth was that she couldn't take Caleb there. If she wanted him she had to stay in his world. She began to tremble uncontrollably and then started to heave. Her diaphragm was going insane, trying to expel her terror. She wretched out some water— there was nothing else in her stomach. Caleb had his hand on her back protectively. Coraline held her hair away from her face. Surprisingly avuncular, Jake huddled nearby, worried.

"You'd better get her home," he told Caleb. They all thought it was the tear gas.

"How far do you guys have to go?' asked Lion Boy, a.k.a. Trey.

"Our car is up at the other end by the Center," Caleb told him.

"Well I'll drive you to your car. I parked near here. C'mon."

Freya lowered her COVID mask again to heave her insides out one last time for good measure, and then let Caleb and Trey pull her through the crowd to where Trey had left his car a few streets over amidst the garbage and abandoned tarps of a freeway-side homeless encampment. They put Freya in the front passenger seat and buckled themselves in. Before starting the car, Trey let out a deep sigh.

"Right?" said Caleb. "It's intense."

Trey turned the key in the ignition and instantly his sound system blared. J.I.D. rapping loud and hard about the cold, the wet, the money, the energy. Freya shuddered and Trey clicked the music off. Still he didn't make a move to pull out from the curb. Just sighed again. Almost like he was holding back a sob.

From the back seat Caleb asked if he was OK.

"Yeah. I'm just . . ." He still didn't put the car in drive. "I'm just fucked up. It's like . . ."

Freya looked at him. She still thought of him as a lion, though he had cut his afro mane to a lower height so it wasn't as literal now. She watched his jaw muscles, just visible below his COVID mask, clench and release. Caleb reached a hand onto his shoulder. Trey nodded his head up and down a couple times, acknowledging the attention.

"I probably never told you," he admitted. "But my cousin, my cousin Eddy, he was shot by a cop."

"Whoa." That was Caleb.

"So I guess it's all just hitting me hard. You know." He slapped his heart twice with his palm.

"No doubt." Caleb squeezed his friend's shoulder but then took his hand back. "Can you tell us . . . like, what happened?"

Trey shrugged.

"I mean, you don't have to."

"It's OK. I'm just kinda having PTSD."

Freya suggested he take some deep breaths. This had been suggested to her many times when her own emotions scared others. Trey ignored her and plunged in. "It was in Atlanta. He's from Atlanta. That's where my auntie still lives." He pronounced aunt the British way, instead of like ant. "He was in the Seven Eleven. Just pouring his Icee. There was an armed robbery. Police came and started shooting. Wrong place, wrong time, wrong skin color, ya know."

"Fuck . . ." said Caleb.

"What did he look like?" asked Freya. "I want to see him better."

Trey had his elbows on his knees, his forehead squeezed against his palms. "He was kinda short, like five-foot-seven? Stout. Muscular. Dark skinned. Darker than me."

"How old was he, and how old were you?" Freya asked.

"He was sixteen. I was fourteen."

"What were his eyebrows like?"

Caleb thought of stopping Freya's questioning, but he knew it would be patronizing to her, and besides Trey didn't seem to mind.

"His eyebrows . . . I don't remember his eyebrows. I don't remember." And then he started crying. Sirens twined in atonal harmonies a few blocks away. Some black-clad rebels came rushing down the street, followed by a scattering of civilian protestors flurrying like dried leaves in a squall.

"Can we go?" Freya was not ready for more drama. "I need to go." The forces of antifa were whooping, white boys pretending to be Indians. She tried to imagine herself in the forest surrounded by friendly trees as the Lady had taught her to do long ago, but her heart was still pounding twice as fast as it should, and even Caleb noticed that she was white as a birch.

"I could drive if you wanted," he offered to Trey, who was roughly drying his tears with his sleeve. Trey responded by starting the car.

"I don't like the violence." Freya's voice made Trey jump. She was trembling again, looking like she might explode. Caleb now put his hand on her shoulder.

"Look at me." She twisted around in the seat but looked at his chest. "Into my eyes," he ordered. She raised her eyes to his. His eyes had little flickers of different autumn colors like a bouquet of chrysanthemums. She studied them, searching for a pattern. She discerned none. Caleb asked if she was OK.

"I don't think they should say that all cops are bastards."

"Freya. Trey just told us how they killed his cousin." He was warning her with his tone, to be sensitive, to not discuss it now, but she did not receive the message.

"Yeah, some of them are violent and racist. But not every single one. I mean, they're humans too."

"Shut your fucking face Freya. Fuck that. This is not 'all lives matter.' This is not some intellectual abstraction. This is Black people's lives. This is my cousin's life." Shocked by Lion Boy's outburst, she turned back around, facing front, and looked out the window.

"We can talk about it more later," Caleb said quietly and evenly. She was being stupid. They had crossed downtown in the car, going along the waterfront to avoid the remaining crowds straggling through the avenues. Past the arcades and fried clam restaurants and Aquarium. Caleb directed Trey up the hill past The Cheesecake Factory to the street where they had parked and they found their car. Freya couldn't wait to get into the safety of its familiar pine green body. Caleb got out more slowly, and stopped with the door open.

"Trey," he said. "You can call me anytime. To talk about anything. I'm so sorry about your cousin . . ."

Trey just nodded, and then he switched the music to top volume.

Before Caleb had even clicked in his seatbelt Freya was already relitigating her point. "I just don't think you can generalize like that. Of course there are some good people in the police force. They aren't a monolith. They aren't all murderers."

"But they're part of a murderation."

"That's not a word."

"Murderation. Like a flock of crows."

"That's a murder. It's called a murder."

"OK. Whatever. A murder. But, two things. One, think about the type of person who signs up for the police department in the first place. Or the military for that matter. It's not going to be somebody gentle, who believes in non-violence. Obviously. It's gonna be someone who tends towards an authoritarian point of view—that bad guys need to be dominated with violence and weapons."

"Some of them may just want to protect the helpless. As their slogan says, protect and serve."

"Well at best, that's a patronizing stance. A paternalistic sort of goodness. But point two. The system is corrupt at its core. It's been so racist for so long, it's kind of baked into the whole way they operate. Look at the statistics for who's incarcerated. The percentage of Black people and Latino people is outrageous."

"There could be sociological reasons people of color actually commit more crime. Like poverty and lack of other opportunities."

"Because the entire system is riddled with racism. Sick at the core. It's not just the police. It's the schools and the banks and business and politics. Real estate. It's an infection that permeates all our institutions."

"You sound just like Jake."

"Well Jake is right about some stuff. He can just be an arrogant asshole personally."

"I didn't know you thought that."

"Who fucks a student?"

"Yeah. I know." Freya suddenly felt like she had fire ants under her skin.

"You OK?"

"Fine." She rubbed her arms.

Out of nowhere, tenderness welled up inside him. "I love you, Freya."

She sighed deeply. "Thank you."

He chuckled a little. "You're welcome." She didn't know what was funny, but she was relieved to hear his love assured. She needed it. The fire ants were charging through her muscles, through her bloodstream.

"When we get home can we just go to bed and make love? I need to connect."

He looked at her face, anxious and pale. "Yeah," he said. "Yeah we can."

And so they did.

After, lying there beside him, Freya thought about what it meant to her. The miracle that God had made the vessel of her vagina and the perfectly fitting shape of his penis, and the merging of bodies that occurred both through evolutionary desire and through love. How two bodies merged into one. How this merging was both a magical itch and a magical excitement, with the miraculous potential to create new life, but in any case it was the dissolving of one body into another, and if there was really such a thing as a soul—this was what she needed to pin down—then surely it was the dissolving of one soul into another. She didn't need to take notes; she would remember this.

Chapter Eighteen

he demonstrations continued. Every day, into the evening. Protestors snaked through the streets, first downtown where they broke the big windows of Starbucks and Nordstrom and then toward the International District again to out-run the cops.

It got into a rhythm. By day peaceful marches. By night toe-to-toe with a line of riot policemen. Jake led his class crew up to the front lines, ostensibly to study the action. It was Caleb and Freya. Coraline of course. Jake and she weren't hiding their couple status anymore. Lion Boy and several others from their class.

After a week the protests moved from downtown up the hill to the neighborhood where many young people lived, many LGBTQ folks, one of the areas where before the pandemic a person might go to hear music and have a drink of coffee or microbrew. On the front lines, and they were literally lines because that's how the police arranged themselves, the most committed protestors pressed up against the enemy. That was, the aforesaid line of cops. The officers were churlish, perhaps not surprisingly, since the protestors pressed into their faces, telling them to kill themselves, flinging full water bottles at them like some kind of insurrection via Evian and Dasani bottles. When it got particularly intense the police loosed their flashbangs. Sometimes tear gas. Freya and Caleb wore bandanas over their COVID masks now and had goggles for when the toxins flowed.

Freya had stopped thinking so much about the right or wrong of it all. She had come down on the side of connection with Caleb über alles. The alternative was too painful. Just a single argument was proof of that. Their magical merging had become her home. Though she would never spit in the face of a police officer, she was willing to watch the others do it. She knew the protestors' anger was duly earned, if misdirected. The crowds',

Caleb's, small acts of violence were not truly harmful. The worst that would come of it was a bruise when a bottle found flesh. No one would die. And besides. Change was necessary, and it could catalyze change. The youth were rising up.

And really, they were too reactive, the police. She saw them spray a little girl, not more than ten years old, in the face with pepper spray. Yes it was intended for the man in front of her, who ducked at precisely the right (or wrong) moment. But how she had howled. The sound of her screams pierced Freya's body. Someone poured milk over the child's head and it dripped down her forehead, across her eyes, her cheeks, her COVID mask. Her father, she was with her father, screeched invectives at the cops and of course it was all filmed by a dozen phones. It went viral instantly, proof positive of police aggression and wanton brutality. Caleb and his new buddy Trey nearly went insane with anger.

They shouted, along with many others, in the faces of the police, as if hostility at a high volume might send the line of blue backwards, melt them into oblivion. More windows shattered. The entire neighborhood was written on like some unholy scroll. Black Lives Matter. Defund Now. FUCK THE POLICE. ALL COPS ARE BASTARDS.

And they proved it beyond a doubt to Caleb and Trey who had formed a close brotherhood in the last few days of resistance. (Freya tagged along and observed. She imagined herself some Clara Barton or Florence Nightingale, there to pick up pieces and provide sandwiches to the soldiers. She supposed it was a matter of testosterone that she couldn't bring herself to hate as harshly but she withheld any judgment against the others, even from herself. So when the incident happened all she felt was unmitigated horror.) The police used their bikes both as a barrier between themselves and the crowd, creating a fence of shields with them, and also as weapons as they pushed forward into the bodies in front of them to back up the crowd. The protestors were used to the back and forth. But this night, when Trey shouted into the face of one young recruit, "Kill yourself, Motherfuckin' Pig," the cop broke. He finally broke. He picked up his bike and struck Trey to the ground. And when Trey was on the ground, the policeman ran over him with the bike back and forth several times, before another officer pulled his lunatic colleague back. Caleb, Freya, a dozen others ran to Trey to make sure he was alive, breathing, unbloodied. They knelt over him. The cop was crying with rage, his bike retrieved by his fellows, his shoulders hunched in agony.

For Caleb it was an act of war. Hurting Trey made it tribal. The young people gathered up their friend and took him to urgent care to make sure there was no internal bleeding. He was OK, except for the bruises which he would wear as tire-striped war paint, shirtless and black and blue.

The protests continued. The government of the city ruled in a passive way. The City Council was more sympathetic with the rioters and resisters than with the authorities, though in fact they themselves were the authorities; they were the boss of the cops. Still, they receded, took no action. The mayor too deferred. The police precinct station, which was the focus of so much crowd venom, was abandoned and closed. The police officers withdrew. The kids had won, and they set up a village in the streets and the neighboring park. They painted happy slogans on the roadway in bright colors with donated house paint. They drank and smoked and partied, for victory was theirs.

It was like some modern-day Woodstock. Except the vibe was different. More militant maybe. Yes there were drugs and dancing, bonfires and shared food, but there was also an edge. Maybe those 60s kids took more psychedelics; that could account for it. Freya herself was ready to declare themselves champions and go back to the cloistered COVID life at home with Regina, Honeymoon, Evelyn, and of course Caleb. She didn't like living in the midst of an ongoing festival. She wanted to read philosophy books in the back garden, and applique patches on some of her clothes that had been eaten by moths. But Caleb was devoted to this new world order. It was a chance to create a civilization from scratch. No capitalism, no racism, no patriarchy. Someone had started a vegetable garden in the park, and people from all over the city were donating supplies to the new pioneers, because they wanted to support this City on the Hill, even if they weren't going to leave the comfort of their own eiderdown duvets and quartz top kitchen islands. The citizens of Seattle loved the idea of a free world, a paradise that could replace this sorry rat race. All over the city signs went up in yards: Black Lives Matter, and In This House We Believe with a list of positions that supported equity and reason. Badges of righteousness, on trend throughout the city's neighborhoods.

Caleb was among the committed leaders who kept the Capitol Hill

Autonomous Zone, or CHAZ as it was lovingly called (later CHOP, the Capitol Hill Occupied Protest), humming. Freya ended up bringing her embroidery and finding a spot in the sun where she could sit and turn her back on the goings on. Sometimes she would pause to spot her true love in the crowd, to watch him help put up a new tent or lean-to, shovel soil into the garden, share a blunt with a circle of comrades, distribute donated pizza to the villagers. She imagined a laser of energy traveling from her heart to his and back again, an unending circle that enlivened both of them. Contented, she turned back to the bodice she was decorating with violets.

One day she was sitting there reading when two guys approached and tried to get her to give them some attention. She politely declined, but they wouldn't let it go. She tried to bury her nose in *The Varieties of Religious Experience*. They called her a cold bitch. She got up and went to find Caleb. For the rest of the day she worked beside him. She didn't tell him about the guys harassing her, but she didn't feel fully safe anymore. The mood was shifting.

If Woodstock had lasted more than a weekend, would it have turned into Altamont? Altamont that was meant to be Woodstock West, but turned into a violent melee instead. And why was Altamont Altamont anyway? Was it a manifestation of human nature itself? At the CHAZ, the dark side was making an appearance, mostly at night. More and harder drugs, more alcohol, visible weapons. Some rough, rough types were attracted to the free food and weed and the young, open girls, tender boys. These interlopers were there for the pleasure, not to build a better society. And street gangs moved in to see how they could profit. Maybe greed and violence were not innate in humans; maybe they were. Or maybe these were learned behaviors responding to culture and circumstance. But in that world, then, in 2020, they were very present. A girl was raped in an alley. Gunshots rang out on more than one occasion. There were no police, of course, because it was an autonomous region. One had to imagine that the cops heard about the crimes from afar and felt some schadenfreude, thinking, *See how you like a world without us.*

Two people were killed, homicides, and finally the mayor realized she couldn't let it go on. Someone was going to hold her legally liable; the announcement was made that the CHAZ had to go. The villagers were given ample warning to dismantle their dwellings. Some of those who had homes to go home to may have been secretly relieved, but others were devastated. Caleb, who had been going to his mom's house every night with Freya but returning each day to build a new Utopia, was among the devastated. Helping to create the CHAZ had given his life meaning, true meaning, for the first time ever. Inspiration had elevated him to a formerly unknown plane, an opera aria, a new golden blood type shooting through his veins. And now that precious, precious meaning was being torn away.

On the day designated by the mayor the police came in force with shields, weapons and numbers. They drove out any malingerers, the homeless who had moved in with their tents, the drunken and the die-hard radicals. Caleb (with Freya at his side, eager to return to Regina's peaceful home) and Trey watched from a distance. The two young men were bitter. It was a fascist assault on a nascent heaven. Caleb and Trey didn't know yet how they would fight now, but they knew they couldn't be stopped. They had tasted victory.

Meanwhile, the police returned to the precinct building. The Park Department cleaned up all the mess in the park and turned the vegetable garden back into lawn.

Chapter Nineteen

rey moved into Caleb's old bedroom. Regina, who had always enjoyed having Caleb's sports teams and tribe of friends around, welcomed Trey into their pod as soon as he got a negative COVID test result. He had been living at an inexpensive motel usually inhabited by truckers since the virus closed the dorms. Now his savings were exhausted. His family was in Chicago, where they wanted him to return, since it looked like school might be remote indefinitely. But he had become accustomed to the freedom of escape from family strictures and the harsh city. Going back to parents and thus childhood and its limits was not an option. Especially not now.

For Caleb, his friendship with Trey was the entrée to manhood that he craved. He had an unconscious, visceral belief that Trey's experiences of racism and the streets made him a paragon of masculinity. By being tight with Trey, Caleb was masculine adjacent; it might rub off. His own privilege made Caleb feel spoiled and unmanly, like some pampered prince. Trey could initiate him into a different world. Caleb was excited to have him in the house.

This new-found brotherhood of her husband with Trey was disturbing to Freya. She felt a film growing between herself and Caleb. A fog that distracted him from seeing her with the focus he once did. It wasn't just a feeling she had. His priorities were shifting.

Two odd things happened. Saturday the guys said they were going out to play frisbee. They were gone for several hours. Meanwhile, Freya noticed their orange frisbee, their only frisbee as far as she knew, on the porch. When they returned, empty-handed, she pointed out their lack. Trey and Caleb exchanged a look. Some might have thought it conspiratorial or guilty, but Freya didn't have a suspicious mind, despite her sense of greater distance from her husband.

"Yeah," said Caleb. "We just walked around."

"You could have taken the dogs."

"Yeah. We weren't thinking."

What they were actually doing was scheming. Scheming how to express their horror at the world, how to tear it apart like an elaborate LEGO castle. Caleb loved to hear Trey's stories about life in Chicago, the ghetto as he re-imagined it through Trey's description. Caleb felt he was catching a whiff of the wind that surrounded the truly oppressed.

They walked over to the cemetery and sat down on someone's blocky gravestone. Caleb traced his finger, unthinking, along the letters of the dead person's name etched into the granite. **Meredith Mason 1899–1962**. The angles of the ems were satisfying to his touch. Trey was in the middle of a story about the high school he went to, and how even the Black teachers were racist. "Because they believed in the whole frickin' set-up. The books we read. Fuckin' *Lord of the Flies*. Memorizing the Periodic Table. What the fuck. What the fuck am I going to do with the Periodic Table. I can look it up on my phone. And the tests. The ACT and the SAT and you won't get to University if you don't score high. And you have to go across town to take them cause not enough kids in our school plan on going to college anyway. I mean, you believe in the system, you support the system, it's racist. Doesn't matter the color of your skin."

"It's hard not to be complicit. Just by virtue of living," agreed Caleb.

Trey emphasized his words like a preacher, cutting both hands through the air by his ears. "I don't want to comply."

"Yeah. No. Me neither."

"I wanna burn it the fuck down."

Caleb realized he had scraped the skin off the tip of his finger by rubbing it too hard on the stone. He sucked the blood off in his mouth. Blood was sweet and sour and metallic all at once.

"I wanna buy my mom a house in this neighborhood. Move her out here. It's like living in the country, but you're still in the city. You can hear the birds singing. That's crazy."

Caleb, once again reminded of just how lucky he was, since his mother already lived in an ample home in this leafy neighborhood, so safe and so sound, didn't know what to say. He was reaching. Reaching past his middle-class existence. "We need to take action. Parades and demonstrations are OK, but we need to start dismantling this motherfucker." He tried to say motherfucker like he said it all the time. He thought he pulled it off pretty well.

They daydreamed a while about what kind of action might make a dent. Obviously they weren't going to nuke the whole capitalist catastrophe that was the US, either literally or figuratively. But people were ready, people were angry, they could get the party started. They could lead by example. They could make the powers that be shiver in their shoes.

A few days later they went off alone again. They didn't take the dogs or the frisbee this time, either. "Just some guy-talk," Caleb explained.

"Guy talk?" Freya asked before they left. "Plotting to uphold the patriarchy?"

Caleb looked at her in wonder. "You told a joke."

"No I didn't."

"Freya. Trey just has some stuff he wants to talk over with me, OK?" And so off they went, leaving her behind to practice guitar and brood.

It wasn't that she needed undivided attention, exactly, but she, A) didn't want to be demoted to wifey and, B) she wanted magical connection. At all times and in all places. He seemed so excited by the radicalism and friendship he shared with Trey. Was she becoming just an ottoman? A place to drape his legs, while meanwhile his mind was churning elsewhere?

Their minds indeed churning, Caleb and Trey went to the library to do some research. Only a limited number of users were allowed in at a time, and they had to write down their names and contact info in case anyone got COVID and the Public Health Department needed to reach them. They used aliases and made-up emails. They were paranoid about seeking information on the internet; anything could be traced, especially if their plotting included any suspicious keywords. At the library they could go into the stacks which smelled of dust mites and leather, and no one would ever know what they discovered there. Information on DIY bombs. Explosive ingredients, fuses, timers. They didn't want to take photos of the diagrams and lists on their phones, so they carefully copied them into a composition notebook. It took hours. Afterwards they carefully returned the library books to their rightful places on the shelves, leaving no ghostly traces behind. They ignored the signs that told them to leave the books in bins for the librarians to shelve.

Freya and Regina ate dinner alone. Freya had made a stir-fry with tofu and broccoli over brown rice that smelled of soy sauce, garlic and ginger, and Regina was grateful, if not wowed. She knew it was good for her but missed the depth of flavor chicken or meat provided. She poked at it with her chopsticks, as she asked where the boys were. Freya said they were out bro-bonding. Regina crinkled up her face. "Like at a sports bar? A shooting range? What does that even mean?"

"I don't really know," said Freya.

Regina, who wasn't a particularly gentle person, especially where Freya was concerned, in this instance spoke kindly and without aggression. "Is there trouble in paradise?"

"Only that I feel forlorn and forsaken," admitted Freya.

This jolted Regina. She realized that she had come to rely on the sweet happiness that flowed between the two young lovers, a soothing drone in the background of their new shelter-in-place life. It assuaged any anxiety she might feel on Caleb's account. It was an ugly era, what with Covid, Trump and his nasty policies, and the climate hastening them all to their apparently inevitable doom. She had been resting in the assurance that her boy was happy. What if that happiness soured? Meanwhile Honeymoon and Evelyn were both staring up at the diners with moony eyes reserved especially for food quests.

"No," said Regina. "Stop begging."

Under the table Freya gave each of them a cube of tofu, making sure there were no onion bits attached.

When Trey and Caleb came home they smelled of beer and weed. Freya thought maybe Regina was right. Maybe they were watching football at a brewery. Was there a brewery open somewhere? Caleb pulled her up the stairs to their room, laughing at his own lust. "I missed you," he said, as he rushed her into the bedroom, onto the bed. They didn't speak, not more than exclamations and moans, as he eagerly undressed her, and himself, at least enough to fuck. It was like he'd never seen her delicate mounding breasts before with their bright pink nipples, her black fur pussy, her rosy vulva. His desire made her wet, and their excitement left them suspended together in a thrilling fairground ride of near-ecstasy, not quite achieved. Until it was, for Freya. She came and felt the release rippling through her body, but Caleb didn't come, and he kept moving inside of her. She came again, and again, and she felt like she was a pond, whose concentric waves overlapped each other, creating flowing patterns, arabesques, paisleys. Her watery pleasure, save some residual pulsing, ceased when Caleb said angrily, "Fuck," and pulled out of her.

"What?"

"It's chafed. It hurts."

He turned away from her onto his back. She didn't pick up on his sense of shame, his imagined lack of virility for this imagined failure. But she did have her own sense of the incomplete. Things needed to be finished in Aristotelian structure; beginning, middle and, in this case, end. She made sure her mouth was filled with saliva, to soothe the chafing, and took his penis gently in her mouth. He groaned, shutting his eyes. She felt it harden—it had started to go limp outside of her. She used her tongue, her lips. She could feel his veins snaking beneath the skin and taste her own body—salt and gardenia. It was hard to tell as his breath sped again, and his body tensed in a pure agony of desire, whether it was the rhythm of his hips guiding the actions of her mouth, or the other way around. They were in sync. And then Caleb erupted. He yelled in relief and joy. The semen was viscous and saline in Freya's mouth. Some women felt it a matter of pride to swallow—not so Freya. She spit it out on a nearby soiled sock. In the throes of his physical and mental bliss Caleb couldn't care less. When his breathing settled he turned to her on his side. "You're so beautiful," he said. "I love you." They slept with their arms around each other all night long.

Nonetheless, Freya had not forgotten how abandoned she had felt while Caleb was gone so long with Trey. The next morning she addressed it. "Dog Boy."

Something in her tone caused him to snap to attention sitting in his spot at the kitchen table. Regina was in her den, already doing lawyering work, and Trey had not yet emerged from his upstairs bedroom. They were drinking coffee and reading the newspaper, which Regina still had delivered to the house in paper form. Freya was good at the crossword puzzle and Caleb read all the political stories, national and local.

Noting that he was looking at her she went on, her own eyes on his chest. "I'm not feeling safe."

He smiled a bewildered smile, which she didn't see. When she didn't continue he prodded her to say more.

"I'm afraid you'll drift away from me."

"Freya. We were fucking like bunnies a few hours ago. Why would we drift away from each other?"

She clenched her fists around her long curls. "Trey."

"You're jealous of Trey? Are you kidding?"

"I'm not jealous. I just see your focus shifting."

He started rocking back and forth in his seat like a davening yeshiva boy. She waited.

"Yeah," he admitted.

She released her hair. She had been pulling on it, and it bounced up several inches.

He didn't want them to grow apart, either. He was feeling especially close to her right then after she had salvaged his dignity and pleasured him so completely the night before.

"There's something I'd tell you, but I'm afraid you wouldn't want to know. I'm afraid you'd tell."

"Tell whom? If I never had to talk again you know I wouldn't. I only talk out of necessity." She meant it at the moment. Conversation was hard and often fruitless. In any case, it would not be a challenge to keep silent, if charged to do so.

"We're planning something."

"You and Trey? What?"

"Revenge."

The word sent a chill through Freya.

They talked in low voices so that Regina wouldn't hear.

By the time Trey came down to the kitchen, bleary-eyed with sleep, Freya had learned of their plot, which Caleb had described as kidnapping. The bike cop who ran Trey over. She argued against it, it was dangerous, what about his gun, they could get killed, they could get locked up, they could harm another human in the process. Caleb assured her they would plan it better than that, that they would find him out of uniform, unarmed, that no animals or people would be harmed, that it was all to create a platform to get attention for their message, to ultimately change the world. Their ransom would be meaningful police reform.

Finally she was persuaded to go along, at least to get along. Once again it came down to the sense that if she were to diverge too radically from

Caleb she would die. Flesh of her flesh, certainly, and it would mutilate her to separate. There was no chance that she could simply agree to disagree. Her nature required one hundred percent adherence to a thing.

Caleb made pancakes.

As he poured syrup, warmed in the microwave, pure from Maine, paid for by Regina's law practice, Caleb told Trey, who had grown up with Mrs. Butterworth's and Kroeger's frozen waffles, that he had shared their plan with Freya.

Trey glanced over at Freya then licked his lips nervously. "OK."

But it was clear from his voice he wasn't sure it was OK. "She's gonna help us." Caleb was trying to reassure him and spare Freya's feelings simultaneously.

"I just... whatever..." Trey didn't want to insult Freya but he knew she was weird and working with her on something so hush-hush, and actually life risking, was iffy. Her commitment to the cause seemed fragile at best.

"Trey," said Freya, "You can trust me. I would never harm Caleb, nor you for that matter."

"She won't even eat an egg," pointed out Caleb, who had had to make the pancakes with egg substitute and soy butter. Trey wondered to himself how then she could possibly participate in their plan. He fervently hoped it would result in the red-headed bike cop's death. How powerful that would be. The whole country would hear and be set on edge. Did Freya not understand their purpose, or was she just pushing it out of her mind? Or maybe Caleb had lied to her or didn't understand the potential for violence himself. He watched Caleb kiss her, deep and long on the other side of the counter. Love was fucking strange.

But it turned out that Freya was useful. She could sit in the café across the street from the police station and in her careful way watch the comings and goings without drawing any attention to herself. She had a sketchpad where she kept track using a secret code she devised, and along with a few schoolbooks, her open laptop and a tall soy latte at the table she looked like any other college student trying to learn remotely. The boys wanted particularly to keep tabs on the bike cops, and especially Red. Freya drew on her screen a freehand chart of her own invention, illuminated with birds and butterflies. She drew cartoon caricatures of each of her marks, and timed their exits, their entrances. Tried to discern the patterns. Did they come on foot or drive into the underground garage? She came to recognize their personal cars, their bikes, their police vehicles. Her attention to detail was exact, as it always was. Her work was a gift for Caleb.

Because of COVID and an added exodus of disillusioned officers from the department after the summer of CHAZ, those who stayed were working many extra shifts. Really, it became evident, it was impossible to predict Red's schedule as it was so irregular. Just when they thought they'd pinned it down he'd come in unexpectedly for the night shift, or on a Tuesday, his day off. Caleb and Trey began to reimagine their plan. Their revenge need not be so specific to one particular bike cop. The point was, after all, to make a point. To clarify that there would be a new order and the old order would fall. Freya was recalled home to cease her intel activities. They regrouped.

Caleb and Trey decided to make a set of bombs and place them strategically around the newly reinhabited precinct station. The place was a symbol of all that was wrong with the world. Dominance, violence, racism. Existing to protect capitalism and capitalists over all else. Wearing stiff military style uniforms that enforced a uniform world of compliance and mediocrity through intimidation. A world Caleb and Trey refused to live in going forward. Like blood brothers, they committed together to forge their own path and live politically sinless, as much as was humanly possible.

They set themselves up in the basement workshop, where Caleb's father had left most of his tools when he moved out into a crisp downtown condominium with a view of Puget Sound. Regina never went into the shop—if she needed a hammer she sent Caleb because of the spiders who inhabited the dank recesses of the cellar. Conveniently for the revolution, she suffered from severe arachnophobia, so no danger of discovery from her. Strategically, the three young people went out and bought the necessary materials separately, choosing additional decoy products to allay suspicion, each going to a different store, paying in cash, relying on their pandemic masks to help disguise them from any cameras that might record the transactions.

Once the materials were assembled, Freya, hands accustomed to delicate work, was set to task constructing the product. As if it were a complicated sweater pattern, she was focused on completing her craft to perfection. The boys sometimes hovered, but she needed to focus and shooed them away. No music, no background noise. Cement walls, low ceiling, fluorescent light. She was making three bombs with internal clocks that would be triggered remotely from a burner phone. The fact that the boys were playing video games or making snacks felt normal to Regina. She was mostly working in her study on a case that required a lot of research and she hardly noticed Freya's frequent absences.

On the night, or rather very early morning they scheduled, each of the young people were to set one package down outside the station (assuring success even in case any one of them was apprehended or one of the bombs failed to detonate), and the explosives would go off simultaneously once they were at a safe distance. Windows would break, and possibly, just possibly, the structure of the building would be compromised. And it would have to be torn down. What the CHAZ occupation couldn't accomplish, their act of creative violence might. Two weeks into August Freya finished the bombs, and they planned to deploy them on the next Monday night, four days away, when it was least busy in the neighborhood and at the precinct, to minimize potential civilian casualties.

That night Freya and Caleb slept out in the backyard where they could look at the stars. On their backs they lay there, trying to pick out the constellations from the random glimmering sprinkle. It was easy to find the Dippers, small and large, and the Pleiades, but beyond that they weren't sure. So they began to invent their own, organizing clusters into images only they could see. Freya gasped when a meteor shot across the night and dissolved into nothingness as it entered Earth's atmosphere. She suddenly felt an enormous coldness in her chest, despite the fragrance of jasmine that filled the yard. A morbid sense of loss. She thought of Mei, hanging in the garage, the scent of auto oil greasing the air. She thought of the people dying miserable and lonely deaths from the epidemic. Tubes stuffed down their throats in hopes to siphon oxygen in. She began to pant—her body syncing to the bodies in the video footage she had seen, the old, the infirm, unable to breathe.

"Freya?" Alarmed, Caleb pulled her out of her nasty reverie.

"Oh," she said, remembering where she was, with whom she lay.

"You OK?"

"Yes." Her breath slowed down as she practiced counting as she inhaled, held, exhaled—regulating herself back to normal, the way the Lady had taught her so long ago. "Yes. I'm fine."

And really wasn't the sky salted with a million glistening suns? Weren't there likely planets revolving around some of them, filled with life one could only imagine. She wondered why space aliens were always pictured as having those strange turnip heads, with eyes positioned in their faces like humans. Why wouldn't they look completely other? Even the ocean was full of creatures who looked like they were from another universe entirely. Consider the octopus, the starfish, the anemone.

Caleb's breath had deepened beside her. She saw that he was asleep. *Dog Boy*, she thought. She could read him about as well as she could read Honeymoon, who was snoring at their feet. One could sense but could not know another being. So much was unspoken, unrevealed. Almost everything, really. She began to drift down into sleep herself, but came to abruptly, aware that she had been almost gone but was now awake again. The next time she descended she stayed. And began to dream. An explosion splintered the building, an old ornate building, and every fragment of stone and glass spun into space and became a star. She tried to comprehend the constellation that was forming, but there was no comprehending. No more than that of a dog's mind.

And then her father was there, as will happen in a dream. He said, "But where is your Torah portion, Freya?" He was holding the Torah scroll, wrapped in its ornately embroidered velvet mantle. Suddenly it exploded in his arms, and its bedazzled fragments too spun out into space. The scraps of parchment and fabric became stars, shaped like daisies, bejeweled like Tsarist brooches caked with emeralds and pearls.

When she woke she only remembered her father's voice asking her about her Torah portion. Hers, from her bat mitzvah, was a weird one. From Leviticus, it gave directions for how to purify oneself from a particular skin ailment. For her bat mitzvah speech she had approached it metaphorically—an ailment of the skin could be read as an issue of how one presents oneself to the world, the skin being the membrane between one's inner and outer self. Freya spoke about honesty and personal authenticity, and the ways one must be true to self in order to be true to the world. Her speech was received well by the congregation, and of course her parents swelled with pride. Afterwards there was a catered luncheon in the dining hall, but Freya had had enough of people and took a bowl of fruit to eat and a book to read behind the heavy burgundy stage curtain on the far side of the vast community room.

And now. Lying in the dawn beneath a sky tinged coral at the eastern horizon, beside her husband still in deep sleep, she found it difficult to swallow. She realized she had an ailment of the skin. Inner self and outer self were at odds. What had niggled at her conscience since Caleb admitted his plot over pancakes was now screaming at a volume she couldn't ignore: it was not possible to risk the life of the people inside the police station. It was simply impossible. There could be a teenager there, brought in for passing out drunk in the Seven Eleven parking lot, and slowly finding his way back to consciousness. There could be a night-shift receptionist who had a husband at home with emphysema, and adult children who needed her to watch their kids during the day. And even Red. Suddenly she saw him as a red setter dog, high strung, bound by his instincts and training. Limited by the many and varied limits that humans have. Dogs have. The three of them, she and Caleb and Trey, had no right to harm him.

Justice was God's job. God who could see with a God's eye view. God who knew all. God who could see inside the skin. If, of course, there was a God. She figured it was the same answer as the soul. Either there were both, or neither. But God or not, soul or not, there was right and there was wrong. That was Judaism. That was its truth.

Caleb woke up. He rolled over and stood. "I have to pee." He went behind a small grove of evergreens near the back fence.

When he came back Freya lifted herself onto her elbows. "We can't go through with it."

Groggy as he was, at first he couldn't grasp what she was saying. He became more alert slowly as she told him about her dream and how she realized what they were doing was wrong. She was sure it would convince him too, the message so obvious and powerful. She was chagrined when he let out a burst of stuttering laughter. Dry and unsmiling.

They went back and forth for an hour. Caleb fiercely argued that human beings needed to create their own destinies, not relying on some perhaps imaginary outside cosmic force to pursue justice. Freya said OK but then they ought to bring a civil suit against the police officer; perhaps Regina or his dad would take the case. Caleb insisted that there was no justice available in the current rigged system, and besides it wasn't about one rotten cop—the whole force needed to be disbanded. If she had cold feet she didn't need to come. She could take a pass. He and Trey would handle it.

"No," she said. "You can't do it. It's just not right."

"It is right. It's the rightest thing I've ever done. And we can do it. We will."

A distressed pink spread from her cheeks to her forehead, to her throat, her chest. "Caleb." She never called him Caleb to his face. She always called him Dog Boy. This alarmed him a little. "I can't let you."

Again a dry little laugh from him. "You can't stop me, Freya. I'm not some asshole pussy who backs away from a fight. Trey and I will do it. You stay behind. You stay behind in your little fantasy world." In that moment she knew she had lost because she didn't recognize him. He had never spoken to her with venom before. He had never insulted her before. She didn't know him. Maybe that's why she had changed his name.

He went into the house, leaving her there among the quilts on the grass.

For Freya, first a dizziness set in. It was not mild. When she tried to stand, the vertigo was so extreme, the world spinning around her, that she fell back to the ground. She had to lie on her back with her eyes shut to stop the whirlwind of trees, tool shed, clouds, house circling her like some crazed Kansas twister. The dogs sniffed at her, sensing that something was wrong. She didn't respond, she couldn't, so Honeymoon lay down beside her protectively. Evelyn, unnerved, went inside looking for human comfort.

When Dorothy and Toto woke up in Oz, the world and all its rules were changed, and this was how things felt to Freya. She could not look—opening her eyes made her feel unbearably ill—so who knew if there were munchkins afoot, or if a glittering Gilda waved a wand back and forth above her. In the before-times, before this morning's tornado, it had been her and Caleb, loyal to one another for eternity. It was the framework that held the world in place. But things were upended. Freya herself was the agent of the change, this change that was making her sick. Because she was saying it. That there was something even more deeply fundamental to the structure of life than their love, their marriage, and that this was morality. Her allegiance was shifting. Where would she turn for a handrail?

She took long slow breaths trying to ease her anxiety enough to think. She startled when she felt someone stroking her hair away from her forehead.

"Caleb?"

"No, it's Dad."

She exhaled with relief. His large hands felt familiar and comforting, like a bear's paw. Not everyone would find a bear comforting, given their claws, but Freya certainly did. Those hands had combed her hair for lice, soothed her childhood fevers, removed leeches from her legs. Her parents had not been terribly attentive, but her father's hands had been there at the crucial moments. Care more special for its rarity.

With him stroking her hair like that, she wasn't going anywhere.

"You've always been an all or nothing kid. But sometimes, things are not one hundred percent one way or another. There are layers of reality. Different considerations to weigh. Human actions are informed by ego, misinformation, tribal loyalties . . ."

"Are you saying nothing is certain?" Tears were dripping from the corners of her eyes, down her temples, into her black curls and onto the quilt.

"There may be things that are certain. But for a human, with our limitations, it is very difficult to know anything with certainty."

"But the Ten Commandments. Thou shalt not kill."

"Sometimes we kill and consider it righteous. The children of Israel were sent into war theoretically by God."

"Is God even good?"

"I don't know, Little One. I don't even know if there is a God."

"Are you saying that what Caleb is planning isn't wrong?"

"No, by my lights, it's wrong, but I know I have my biases and limitations. "

"How can we ever act, then?"

"We have an innate sense, imperfect, yes, but still a sense, of what is right and wrong. A moral intuition. We have to critique our choices, hold our instincts up against the facts, up against other's opinions, but still, that intuition is what we've got."

"Just our gut."

This was more spinning than her body could handle. Why had he even come? He was just making it worse. The nausea was unbearable. She groaned aloud.

And then he was gone. She felt his absence first, and then briefly opened her eyes to be sure. Gone.

She lay there for another hour or so. Honeymoon licked her face now and then, and Evelyn peered out from the doggy door to see if it was emotionally safe to come out. The sickness ebbed enough that Freya could get up and walk over to the hose spout hidden behind a rhododendron. She turned it on and let it gurgle out any bugs that might have taken refuge in its cave, then twisted it on, full force. Drinking from the arc of water that came out the metal lip of the green vinyl tube, she didn't see the prismatic colors let loose in a sunlit shower. She was still keeping her eyes closed when she could. In this way pain so very often erases beauty.

She didn't know what to do with herself. She knew she couldn't focus on a book or on embroidery. She didn't want to face Caleb until she understood her own intentions more fully. She tried to play back what her father had told her, to make sense of it and take it in. If she had to sum it up, which she was trying to do, he said that you couldn't really be sure of anything and the best you could do was follow your gut. OK. That gave her a theoretical compass point. Which meant she didn't have to continue to spin like a top without a stable center. She had to listen carefully to her gut. Except at the moment her gut was a molten spasm of lava.

Freya grabbed a trowel and a pair of gardening gloves and began to weed the flowerbeds. Their messiness bothered her. Messiness, as always, bothered her. It was all so messy. Her father insisted that messiness was the norm. This enraged her.

She stabbed the dirt and pulled out dandelions and buttercups by their roots, these plants the Trojan Horses of the garden. Their yellow blossoms were pretty, but if left to their own devices they would choke out every other growing thing. So she waged war. Her upper teeth gnashed into the lowers. Evelyn crept out from the house and watched from a safe distance while Honeymoon rested in the nearby shade.

It took several hours to clean up all the beds. She was hot and her body needed nutrition, though she rarely felt hunger. Certainly not when upset. Sometimes she set an alarm to remind herself to eat. She had heard Caleb and Trey leaving in Regina's car earlier, without checking in with her. Well, at least if she went into the kitchen she wouldn't run into them.

She went inside and drank raspberry lemonade. She could smell the berry in it before the taste of the juice hit her palette. It was perfectly tart and perfectly sweet. Did everything have to be a fucking metaphor? She hardly ever swore, but she was still angry that her father had charged her to accept multiple aspects of reality at once. Maybe she couldn't. Maybe she had reached her ceiling. She fixed a peanut butter and lettuce sandwich, and took her glass and plate back outside, the dogs at her heels as they always were at the possibility of food. She ate at the picnic table and then afterwards lay on top of it, staring into the blue heavens.

When she heard the boys coming home she dashed indoors and up the stairs to hide in the bedroom. At dusk she went to bed early, not to sleep but to avoid contact. She was curled away from the center of the bed when Caleb finally came up. He assumed she was asleep, though she wasn't, and he curled in the other direction. It wasn't that he had no doubts about their plot. It wasn't that he didn't mind being at odds with this sprite whom he loved so much. He doubted and he minded. But there was a part of him that fervently needed to proceed. He had much to prove to himself. It was about integrity and courage, and if he didn't have these, he couldn't respect himself, or expect others to respect him. It was the rite that would usher him into manhood. A bar mitzvah in the real world.

She turned on her side to face him. "You have to promise me you won't," she said.

"Can't."

"Dog Boy," she pleaded. "Someone could get killed."

"Get thee behind me Satan. Don't make me weak. I have to do what I have to do."

But then so did she.

Chapter Twenty

he next morning Freya arose early. She kissed Caleb (whoever he was) gently so he wouldn't awaken. The smell of him had softened her anger, though not her resolve. Honeymoon roused himself and followed her out of the room, but at the front door Freya took the dog's face in her hands. "Stay here. They're going to need you." She kissed him on his wet nose and he licked her face. Evelyn appeared behind Honeymoon, her rump wagged dramatically side-to-side by her tail. She came and licked Freya goodbye too.

Freya took a deep breath and, shutting the door behind her, faced the day. She reversed the Forester out of the long driveway, careful not to side swipe Regina's Volvo. She used the GPS on her phone to find the nearest Police Station. She drove like an automaton according to its directions through the neighborhoods. Every block or so she realized she was holding her breath and she reminded herself to inhale, to exhale. The end-of-August air smelled of dust and evergreens.

"Turn left in sixty feet," it said.

"Don't tell me what to do," replied Freya, but she did turn left in sixty feet.

"Your destination is on the right."

There was plenty of street parking in front of the station. She sat under a mammoth maple tree that had tiny hints of coming autumn red in the veins of its leaves. It made her think of the word turncoat. She was a turncoat. She could just go back and get into bed with Caleb. He was probably still asleep and wouldn't even register that she had been missing. She thought of the length of his legs and her hand measuring their length with a stroke. The golden scent of his flesh.

She opened the door and forced her feet forward. Shema Yisrael Adonai Eloheynu Adonai Echad. She repeated it to herself up the concrete pathway up to the heavy door. She gripped the metal cylinder handle and pulled it open. Remembering suddenly, she put on the mask that was stuffed into her pocket.

A Black woman in a blue uniform and Seahawks mask looked up bored from her seat at a desk behind bullet-proof glass. Freya cleared her throat. "I want to report a crime."

"Be my guest," said Officer Tanner, as her name tag, stitched in cursive, identified her.

"So there's going to be a bombing."

Officer Tanner's face suddenly lost its slack quality as she focused her attention on Freya's face. It was a hard time for the police, they weren't feeling much love from the community, and Tanner wasn't going to take such a threat lightly even if this girl looked like a ragamuffin, with her patched jeans and embroidered makeshift top. The cop listened carefully to Freya's first few sentences and then asked her to wait. She called in a colleague, and Freya was taken into an office, where she betrayed the man she loved. She told the police where and when the bomb was meant to be placed. And more importantly, where it was then as they spoke. And where Caleb was. She admitted that she had built the bomb. She assumed they would arrest her, and indeed, they did detain her. In the small room where they deposited her she sat on a molded plastic chair and looked up at the ceiling. The sound absorbent tiles were dotted and she wondered if there was any pattern to the positioning of the circles. A constellation or the graph of something or other. She couldn't perceive one. She started to hum. High pitched, a little like a whine. The cuticle on her thumb was bothering her and she lowered her mask long enough to tear it off with her teeth. Then it hurt. She put her mask back up.

Her phone vibrated. It was a text from Caleb. **Where r u?** She turned off her phone.

Her ears began to hurt. Like a knife was piercing them. *Good*, she thought. *I should die*, she thought. *I probably will die*, she thought. If their souls were ripped apart, which is what she was doing to them, then wouldn't she bleed to death? One summer day, a summer long ago, her family had visited friends out in horse country in Massachusetts. It was humid and hot and there was a pond in the field. Dragonflies and mosquitos skimmed its surface. Little Freya kicked off her white sandals with the magenta daisies on the straps and went wading. When she emerged from the mucky water her legs were densely adorned with leeches. She remembered screaming; though she loved animals in general she found these creatures horrifying, repugnant. The adults, Harold and Ruth and the couple they were visiting, also professors, came running from the screened-in porch where they were enjoying iced tea and chevre on crackers. They couldn't help giggling, and then apologizing, when they saw why Freya was yelling. The host showed Harold how to strip the slug-like creatures from Freya's skin. Her dad carefully peeled them off, using his fingernail to slide under the head, if you could call it a head, and pull like it was a band aid stuck on fast. He tossed the leeches into the muddy grass. Some of them left blood on her shins, calves, and feet in their wake. After he removed them all, he tenderly washed her skin up at the house, and bandaged the abrasions. She lay on a wicker couch upholstered with Marimekko poppies on the screened porch, as the adults returned to their talk of politics and books. They had given her a Ziploc plastic bag filled with ice to depress the inflammation.

She was the leech. Pulling herself from Caleb's soul. And flicking herself back into the muck beside the pond.

She was tempted to check her phone, turn it on and connect, but she controlled the impulse. It was a fearsome gravity that pulled her towards the orb of him.

They might be getting to Caleb's house by now. They might be arresting him. She imagined the knock on the door. The cuffs on his wrists. The look on Regina's face. Elsewhere a crack team dismantling the bomb. No one was hurt. Except her, destroyed, and Caleb too.

Two officers she hadn't seen yet came into the small detention room. They introduced themselves but she chose to think of them as Thing One and Thing Two, though they were polite and earnest. "We need your help."

"What help?"

"We can't get a warrant to search the house on your word alone. We need more to go on. Would you be willing to wear a wire?" She felt like she was falling off a cliff in slow motion and there was nothing to stop her hideous descent. They brought in a female officer to equip her for eavesdropping. The woman also coached her a little. Asked her what Freya would say when they asked where she had been. At first Freya was stunned by the question, but the lady cop asked about her habits, possible places she might have been if she hadn't come here. They arrived upon the idea that she had gone to a coffee shop to think. That she had turned off her phone to think.

Freya walked out into the bright sunshine, disoriented by the searing blue when it ought really to be a ghoulish gray. On her windshield she discovered a parking ticket—she had been in a two-hour space too long. It was $47. She wondered if there were a ticket one could be given for ruining everything in the entire world.

She drove back to Caleb's house. The door was locked, and Regina's car was not in the drive. Freya had no key—she hadn't needed her own since she and Caleb were always together. Inside Evelyn and Honeymoon knew it was her and yipped and scratched at the door. She sat on the two-person glider but didn't glide. She hadn't eaten anything that day, and little the day before. They gave her a bottle of water at the police station. She licked her lips. She tried to say the Shema again, but it wouldn't come out, which made her wonder if her own soul had actually died. Finally Caleb opened the door to see why the dogs were making such a racket.

"Why didn't you knock," he asked. She shrugged. "Where were you?"

"Coffee shop," she said.

"Why didn't you answer my texts?"

"Turned off my phone."

"Why?"

"To think." She followed him into the kitchen. Trey was in the living room watching TV. She sat on a stool at the island. "Is there coffee?"

"You want more coffee?" She didn't usually drink more than a cup.

"Yeah, I feel like coffee."

He put the water kettle on—Regina had a French press.

He looked at her. It wasn't unusual that she didn't meet his eyes. She was feeling the scratch of the microphone taped to her skin. "Are you still going through with it?" she asked.

"Yup."

"What if someone gets killed?"

"Unlikely."

"But possible."

"Well. All's fair in war. They shouldn't have killed George Floyd."

"*They* didn't. One man did."

"With his henchmen."

"Yes, they were inhumane. Inhuman. But we shouldn't be."

"It's human to fight for what's right."

"So you're still going to place the bombs and detonate them?"

It never occurred to him that she would betray him. It never occurred to him that she was trapping him. "Yes," he said, sealing his fate.

"OK. I'm going to go on a hike then. I'm going to take the dogs."

"Whatever." She was exhausting him. It took so much energy all the time to absorb her weirdness and translate it for everyone else. And her self-righteousness on top of it.

She didn't want to be there when the police came. She assumed they'd come immediately because of the danger factor. She didn't want the dogs to live through it either.

After she had driven a few blocks she pulled over and parked. She tore the spy paraphernalia off her chest. She was crying. She called the police officer who had coached her. The woman assured her they had what they needed; she had done well. Freya wished the ground would open and pull her down to the earth's core where she would burn like one condemned to hell. However, it didn't. Tant pis.

She decided she might as well tell the truth and really go for a hike. She drove east toward the Cascades. Over Lake Washington, dotted with brightly striped sails on its slate-colored waters, driving the highway which led to the mountain pass with its many trailheads. Her mind was not exactly blank, but it was filled with meaningless designs and sounds swirling without pattern.

She and the dogs, who were not allowed in the State Park even though she kept them on leash, trod through the pine and cedar forest at the start of the trail. It was a popular hike, and they had started late in the day, so they met other trekkers already returning to their cars. Some gave Freya and her contraband dogs the side-eye, but they didn't say anything about the canine trespass, so Freya was oblivious to their disapproval. Her pack ascended through switchbacks, the dogs open-mouthed and panting, coming out of the forest onto scree. Narrow waterfalls trickled down the sides of the mountain, and the dogs drank from the puddles that formed among the rocks, Freya ignoring the risk of giardia. Dehydration would be worse. The tiny puddles were peopled with tiny tiny green frogs the size of a fingernail. The girl and dogs climbed and climbed. Their reward was wildflowers and swarms of delicate periwinkle butterflies. They passed more descending hikers, again ignoring their shock at the rule breaker and her companions.

They began to glimpse snowy peaks, and after another set of switchbacks an alpine lake, their destination, came into view. It was ringed by meadows, and beyond the meadows, meringue-capped mountains. The air up there was thin and seemed to have a mind of its own. Freya knew perfectly well that God did not reside exclusively in the firmament of heaven, but she did feel His presence here in the shadow of the mighty mountains. She didn't know if she should turn away from the holy one; such was her shame at what she had done to Caleb. And Trey. And Regina too. Instead she led the dogs along the lip of the lake, until they were far from any other late-in-the-day hikers. She let them off their leashes and Evelyn dashed into the water, while Honeymoon waded in carefully up to his chest. Freya took off all her clothes and walked in. The floor was glacial silt, smooth and comforting to her feet, but the temperature of the water was also glacial. The only way to endure it was quickly, so she squished along up to her waist and then released into a breaststroke. It was far too cold to put her head under, and she lasted only half a minute before she had to make her way back to shore. Shivering, she lay on a sunny flat rock, with Honeymoon and Evelyn lying on either side of her. She remembered the similarly flat rocks, one thousand times smaller, Caleb had shown her to skip on their first real encounter, and thought of monsters skipping the boulder on which she lay. She realized she hadn't talked to her parents in days, except for that mysterious appearance of her father in the backyard. She wondered if she would tell them what she had done. What would horrify them more, the bomb plot or the betrayal? Lying with her bare body towards the azure sky, she begged for forgiveness, but felt none. The acute beauty that surrounded her was merciless.

She and the dogs made their way back down the trail. They were the last of the hikers, and it was quiet except for their steps and the percussive hoots of the hawks and jays. The dogs were too tired to sniff at the August-dry forest dirt, the salmon berry bushes that lined the path. They were happy when they finally saw the car.

They stopped at a country store made of horizontal logs just outside the State Park. She bought herself water, cashews, and fruit, and a box of kibble for the dogs. She let them out in the meadow next to the shop, and poured their food in the grass, where they could dig it out like mini Easter eggs. The first stars were visible in the darkening sky. When the dogs were done eating she gathered them back into the car. She drove until she came to the turnoff for a lonely service road, driving down it for a mile or so. She pulled off onto a wide shoulder under the cedars and parked. She put the backseats down, and fixed a bed. The remnants of dusk turned to deep night she and the dogs snuggled together. If they wondered why she was crying Honeymoon and Evelyn didn't ask.

Chapter Twenty-One

he next day the three of them returned to Caleb's house. She was assuming everything would be different—Caleb and Trey in police custody and God knows how Regina would greet her. But they were still there. Nothing had happened. She let the dogs out and they ran up to the front door yipping with excitement to be home.

Caleb came out onto the porch. The dogs nuzzled at him, and he patted their heads, but his sights were all on Freya. "Where the fuck were you?"

"I went hiking. It got late so we slept in the car."

"And it didn't occur to you to let me know where you were? You can do whatever you want with yourself, but you can't just take the dogs with you. I mean, Evelyn isn't even half yours."

Freya was toying with the idea of saying her phone had died, but she couldn't bring herself to compound her lies. It frightened her that she could see her own moral fiber fraying. She wanted only to repair it.

Regina came out the screen door and Evelyn jumped on her with glee as if to prove his point. "Where were you?" she asked.

"They were camping." Caleb answered her.

"We were terrified," said Regina.

"I wasn't terrified. I was pissed," said Caleb.

Just then though, everyone's attention was drawn to the arrival of two patrol cars, a SWAT team, and a bomb squad all converging on their street. Pulling up in front of their house. Freya's timing was really off. She hadn't accounted for warrants and red tape.

"What the . . ." said Caleb as he escaped inside.

"Stay right where you are," yelled a policeman. He pulled out a bullhorn, and shouted again, this time with reverb. "Stay where you are." Freya remained by the Forester in the driveway, with one policewoman hovering, while Regina, agog, was on the porch. Several cops ran through both side yards to cover the back of the house.

"What the hell is this," she yelled at them. "What do you think you're doing? You have the wrong address."

The officer with the bullhorn shouted again. "Everyone come out of the house. Come out of the house immediately."

Another policeman explained to Regina, "We have warrants for Caleb Becker and Trey Jackson and Freya Rubenstein. And to search your house. Please back away from the door."

Regina screamed into the house. "Caleb, come out now. Trey!" She turned to the nearest policeman. "Please don't hurt them. They didn't do anything."

"Then you don't need to worry." Regina was not particularly anti-police, but she did know their forbearance was not guaranteed.

"I'm a lawyer," she yelled helplessly.

Freya was shaking so hard she had to lean against the car door to keep from collapsing. The dogs were somewhere in the house, cowering no doubt. The female officer came to her, asked her name, and apologized as she hand-cuffed her narrow wrists. Freya's guilt was so great, she didn't even question her own arrest. She had built the bomb, after all.

After a very long minute both Caleb and Trey came out of the house.

"Put your hands up," yelled the bullhorn cop.

"Put your hands up," urged Regina. Caleb and Trey put their hands up. The police swarmed them, three officers on each scared boy, pulling their arms roughly behind their backs and cuffing them.

"Where are you taking them?" demanded Regina. "What are they charged with?"

"We have to take you too."

"What the hell?" asked Regina, as a young cop politely asked her to put her hands behind her back.

"Everyone in the house has to come with us," the uniformed kid, who was about Caleb and Trey's age, explained apologetically.

As they pushed the boys into separate squad cars Trey hissed at Freya. "Fucking snitch."

Freya tried to catch Caleb's eye as he took his seat but he didn't look her way. His face was hard.

The police ushered Regina and Freya into a third and fourth squad car.

Neighbors lined the sidewalks, watching in silent horror.

Freya had drawn a precise plan of the basement, so the cops knew where to look for the bombs. They would be using a robot to dismantle the explosives, and it would take all day.

"I need to go back in," said Regina, from the backseat of the cruiser. "I need my purse. I need a cigarette." She was so stressed she was on the verge of tears.

An older veteran, stocky and red-faced, ordered a rookie to go grab her handbag. Meanwhile he took a Pall Mall pack from his own pocket and asked if she'd like him to light it for her. She grudgingly let him place it between her lips through the open window. He clicked his lighter and she inhaled. She coughed a little because it wasn't her brand; it was unfiltered and rough on her throat. But it was a relief anyway. The smoke was a friend that inhabited her body. She exhaled through her nose, instead of her usual puckered mouth, having no hands available. After a couple more puffs the cop asked if she'd had enough and she nodded. He took the cigarette from her lips and stamped it out on the driveway. The rookie brought her retrieved purse. The older cop got into the passenger seat, with the young one driving. The abandoned butt on the pavement nagged at Regina. They took off.

Regina didn't really know what was going on, but she had not missed what Trey said to Freya. The blotchy faced older veteran told her that her son and his friends were accused of making bombs, with plans to deploy. As they rolled through her familiar, now surreal neighborhood, she pondered whether or not it could possibly be true that they were plotting such a thing. She didn't think so. But maybe. But no. But then why did Trey say that to Freya?

All four squad cars headed downtown to the jail. The curious neighbors who had come out like figures on a cuckoo clock retreated back into their houses, shaking their heads. What on earth could have been going on right under their noses. They felt but did not say—it must have had something to do with that Black boy. Probably some kind of drug thing.

In his car as they rode through first the leaf canopied neighborhood streets, and then the larger urban roadways, Caleb felt his heart beating aggressively. Yeah he was scared. He had some idea about the amount of trouble he was in. Secretly he felt an element of relief that their plan was foiled, and even more secret was his shame about his own cowardice and lack of commitment. When he thought about Freya—and anyone with half a brain had to assume she had outed them, he couldn't ignore that—he felt raw. Raw like a wound scraped down to the sinew, the flesh exploding with pain. He thought the grueling pain was anger.

Once in jail, both Regina and Caleb separately used their call to contact Dan, who arrived in thirty minutes. After a brief interrogation, Regina was released, and she and her ex walked down the fentanyl-drenched sidewalks of downtown Seattle to the parking garage. The two lawyers put their heads together and came up with the best attorney they could think of, and soon they were off in Dan's car to see about bail for Caleb and to set his defense in motion.

Meanwhile, the cops explained to Freya that they had only brought her in to maintain her anonymity as an informer. Little did they know that ship had sailed, simply from logical deduction by her co-conspirators. When they released her, she was at a loss. She supposed she should head back to the house to check on the dogs. Who knew what had become of them, left alone to their own devices after the police raid.

She waited on the downtown sidewalk at a bus stop surrounded by a homeless encampment. A man, grimy from the streets, asked her for a smoke, for money, for sex. She told him she had nothing. He screamed at her, flailing his arms. "Take off your mask," he screeched. "Smile." The bus came. The doors gruffed open and she made a quick escape into the cavernous maw of the Metro. Like the sidewalks, it smelled of urine and sweet wine.

It was a long ride on the bus, and her brain was not functioning well. The motion of the big vehicle, its jerky stops and starts, played out as a visual graph on the screen of her mind, and she couldn't focus on anything else. The pictures out the window and inside the bus with her fellow passengers were reduced to two dimensions and plotted on a diagram. It re-awoke her vertigo. When she finally got off, walking through the tree-lined streets grounded her a bit, seeing the first signs of autumn's fire in the leaves, but she was still not tracking reality well. It didn't help that when she arrived at the house some of the police were still there, finishing up with their robotic bomb squad work. She sat on the house's front path at a distance from the porch, until they finally left. And she was all alone.

She had no key, so she went into the backyard and lay on her back by Wren's grave. The dogs came out the doggy door and stretched out on either side of her, seeking assurance after what was such a peculiar and startling day for them. She could do no more than pat them distractedly.

When the sun abandoned the backyard, she moved to the glider on the front porch. After a couple hours, Dan dropped Regina off on the sidewalk and drove off. Regina slowly trudged up the front path. When she reached the porch she gasped when she realized Freya was sitting there. Freya looked ghoulish as a ghost, her always pale skin drained completely of pigment. Her black hair hanging down like the girl from *The Grudge*. "What are you doing here?" asked Regina.

"I don't have a key."

"Where's Evelyn?"

"In the backyard. With Honeymoon. Or maybe in the house . . . I'm not sure." On cue Evelyn started barking. Regina unlocked the heavy wooden door and went straight to the back sliding doors and called the dogs into the house. She poured kibble into their dishes. Freya lingered in the doorway between the dining room and kitchen.

"I don't know if I want you in the house." Regina still couldn't look at her. In the meantime she had spoken to Caleb, Trey, the lawyer they brought in. Everyone was pretty sure what Freya had done. "You could have come to me instead of the police. I could have stopped them."

This Freya doubted, but she said, "OK." The last thing she wanted to do was argue with Regina who was scratching Evelyn's cheeks. Finally the woman faced the girl. "Go get your things."

Being punished felt appropriate to Freya. She climbed the stairs and quickly packed her clothes and belongings. It took a few trips down and back up to load the Subaru. When she was all packed, she returned inside. Regina was in the kitchen fixing herself dinner. Freya went in to grab Honeymoon's food and water dish—it was one of those two-in-one arrangements. "Oh no you don't," said Regina. "You aren't taking the dog."

Honeymoon had heard noise around his dish and came into the kitchen with high hopes for an extra meal. Evelyn followed. "But Honeymoon—" protested Freya.

"No!" said Regina. "Honeymoon will be here when Caleb comes home, and you won't be. You'll be God knows where, but you won't be here. And

I'm changing that stupid fucking name."

Freya shrunk visibly. Regina relented just a tiny bit.

"Are you all packed?"

"Yes."

"OK then."

"Thank you for your hospitality and, everything . . ."

A disdainful "Hah" from Regina saw Freya out of the kitchen. Regina didn't follow. Freya kissed both dogs at the door again, lingering over Honeymoon and whispering to him, telling him he would be OK and please take care of Caleb.

Regina was all alone in the house, except for the dogs, of course. A little lost, she went up into the kids' room to put things in order and change the sheets. She picked up a pair of jeans and some dirty socks that Caleb had left on the floor and put them in the pile for the laundry with the used linens. On the night table she found a scrap of paper in Freya's writing.

To Research:

Connection between personality and the soul

Is the soul unique throughout eternity or does it meld back into Godliness to re-emerge as an individual in the next life? What is the constant—if there is one?

Or is it all just chemicals and projection

Chapter Twenty-Two

n the car Freya considered where she ought to go. Really she had nowhere. She decided to go to the zoo, thinking she might find some wisdom there from the wild animals or at least some solace. She felt ill, like she'd been hyperventilating for hours. Maybe she had. She certainly hadn't eaten. The zoo parking lot was expensive so she parked in the neighborhood and walked a couple blocks, past the family houses, and then past the zoo's rose garden with its thousand species of bloom. She paid for entrance the way she paid for everything—with the credit card her parents gave her. The ticket taker reminded her she needed to wear a mask. She almost jumped. It was the first time she had forgotten since the pandemic began. There was one in her pocket, and she put it on guiltily. Guilt was apparently her new baseline.

She followed the pawprints painted on the cement leading to the jaguar exhibit. She loved the way the huge muscular cat swam in the pool the public could see through the glass window that served as his exterior wall. She stood before him as he stroked through the crystal blue water. She wanted him to look at her, but he didn't. She'd have to find a tamer animal for communion. What would it be like to have his power? Had he known despair? Certainly animals experienced emotions—dogs were festivals of feeling. She listed the emotions she knew they felt: love, contentment, anger, fear, jealousy, joy, dislike, grief, anxiety, hurt. Some of these were very complex, but did they experience despair? Or self-loathing? A jaguar taken from the rainforest to live in a cramped though picturesque habitat of limited square footage—he had reason to feel despair. But did he? He seemed to exist in a state of proud petulance. They had removed all the elephants from this zoo precisely because captivity depressed them and caused them to ail. The sad pachyderms had been sent to a refuge where they could roam freely and thrive. What would happen to Dog Boy in a cage? She couldn't think about it now.

She made her way to the Living Northwest Trail. She liked the otters and the black bear there, whose ponds were also behind a plate of glass to view their swimming habits. The pathway was a slight incline upwards as the habitat switched from the viny rainforest, where she had last been watching the orangutans, to familiar evergreens native to the area. As she made the gentle climb she spotted one of the elusive gray wolves who lived among the tall grasses of the faux tundra. She stopped to watch him, and he, likewise, stopped to watch her. Slowly the wolf slinked closer. He looked straight into her eyes. Freya had no trouble maintaining eye contact with animals. They stared at each other like it was some sort of game of who will blink first. Neither did. "What are you trying to tell me?" This was only a murmur. From Freya, not the wolf.

She thought, telepathically, he was saying everything would be all right, but she rejected his assessment. *How would you even know*, she wondered.

That night she slept on a side street in the car. A few neighbors walked by on the sidewalk and saw her there, but homelessness had become such a regular sight in Seattle that they didn't even think about it twice. They assumed she would be gone the next day, and if she set up camp there or littered, or worse, shit on the parking strip, only then would they call the authorities in to clear her out.

When morning light buzzed her awake, the hopelessness of her plight fell upon her heavily. She could not leave the Seattle area, because the State would be needing her, it was part of the deal she made, but she had nowhere to go. Mei was dead and anyone else from school would hate her for what she did. And they never liked her to begin with anyway. She needed to find somewhere to pee. She went to a Starbucks, went to the bathroom, and then bought a soy latte. She drove to a park and went for a walk with her coffee. Longingly she remembered her attic room in Cambridge. Its pale northern light. Her books and dolls and stuffed animals. The safety. It occurred to her to call her parents.

"Hi Sweetheart. Daddy isn't here. How are you?"

Freya explained to her what had happened, including her own making of the bomb, to which her mother said, "Jesus, Freya, what were you thinking?" Ruth ordered her home, but Freya explained she was required to stay in the region. Ruth asked if she and Harold should come there.

"You don't have to. I'm sure you have work."

"You need someplace to stay. Find an Airbnb for now. You have money?"

"The credit card."

"OK. Text me when you've found a place and we'll talk later when your father gets home."

Freya opened up the app and scrolled through the housing options. One apartment had chairs with large floral patterns and a garden in back guests shared with the landlord and goats. Goats. She filled out the form, and by the late afternoon she was communing with Coco and Delilah who both had beards and otherworldly gray eyes with enormous rectangular pupils. They too seemed to tell her that things would be OK, and again she had to push back. Maybe in their world. Unless of course they wanted to consider climate change. She tried not to think about it in their presence, so as not to worry them. There was certainly nothing they could do to ameliorate the melting of the Arctic ice. The lady, Phoebes (rhymed with Thebes), who rented out her daylight basement apartment was older, friendly, dressed in overalls replete with gardening tools in her pockets, like some character on a children's show. No one was traveling because of COVID, so she was happy to have Freya there. She needed the income to supplement her Social Security. The girl's kindness to the goats endeared her to Phoebes who offered Freya a reduced rate for a month or longer, if the pandemic lasted. Since the elderly woman couldn't see her friends, it was nice to have someone around. She would only interact with Freya outside, masked, six feet apart, but still it was nice. Phoebes didn't even go to the grocery store—she got her food delivered—so another human being, even one who didn't make eye contact and talked about as much as the goats did—was a blessing. Freya saw that Phoebes was a ewe.

Once Freya was settled she called her police connection and left a message letting them know where she was, and then she called her parents. Only her dad was home, but he cheered her on, and told her that she had done the right thing, she was a hero, which struck her as absurd. She was no hero. First she had built a bomb, and then she had betrayed her own husband. But her father had always chosen to see her in the best light. It was easiest. "But Dad, were you here a few days ago, in the yard?"

"What?"

"Never mind."

When they hung up she went out into the garden again and gave Delilah and Coco each a green apple from a bag she had bought at the fruit stand. The police lady called her back. Freya wanted to know what would happen to Caleb now.

"They'll set bail at a hearing in the next day or two, and his family or someone may pay it though it will be steep, in which case he'll get out until the trial. And then there will be a trial, and he'll be found guilty or not. And if guilty the judge will sentence him. Of course we'll keep you in the loop and the prosecutor will meet with you before you testify."

Freya was silent. The police officer cleared her throat. Still nothing from Freya. "Are you OK, Honey?"

"Yes." Freya forgot her manners and hung up.

She discovered online that visitations to the jail were suspended due to COVID protocols. Of course Caleb had no phone with him. She had to await his call. She kept her phone charged. In the meantime she wrote him a letter.

My darling.

The wolf at the zoo and Delilah and Coco the horned goats in the garden where I am staying insist that all will be fine in the end. As far as your legal troubles, I think this is true. Even if you spend a year or more in prison, it will not be so bad, and you'll still be so young when you are freed. Meanwhile there you can read and read and read. Probably take remote classes. So it won't be so bad, and it will end almost before it begins.

As far as we are concerned. I am choking. There is no air for me to breathe if I am not breathing you. I don't know if I will live, honestly. I read of the old folks dying of the virus, intubated, gasping, their lungs failing them. This is me now. All my internal organs are crushed.

Only if you call me and we speak and I know you love me still, love me as much as ever, as I love you, will I survive. I will mail this letter now. Call me instantly.

Your wife,

Freya.

He did not call.

After ignoring Freya's incessant voicemail messages for days, Regina finally picked up her phone. She explained to Freya that she was dead to her, to Caleb, to Trey. She need not call anymore, and Caleb would never be speaking to her again. His choice, by the way, not Regina's.

Later that day her heart briefly flooded with hope when the postman brought a letter with her name and current address in Caleb's hand. She opened the envelope hoping for communion, hoping Regina was utterly wrong, but when she unfolded the piece of paper inside all it said was, "I divorce you. I divorce you. I divorce you."

PART THREE

Off the Rails

Chapter Twenty-Three

As Mei had modeled, suicide was a possibility, but it was too violent for Freya. On the other hand, a passive dissolution of body was conceivable. She stopped eating for several more days. In the bath her ribs showed through her skin like whale bones bleaching on a beach. Phoebes noticed and lured Freya into helping her milk the goats. Freya, vegan, had always considered milking a cruelty done to captive female dairy animals, but Phoebes insisted that Coco and Delilah liked it. Indeed, they came maa-ing when their udders were full and seemed content as Phoebes tugged at them and their herb-smelling milk squirted into the bucket. Phoebes took the pungent liquid to the kitchen where she pureed it with fresh blackberries and clover honey. She urged Freya to taste it. Freya, having starved herself for half a week, might have been tempted by most anything, but the sensationally lovely pink of this concoction, goat milk and the red juice of the black berries, was what won the day. She sipped one glass, and then another. Though it had been over a decade since dairy had passed her lips, her body welcomed it. She felt the nutrition in her bloodstream and her muscles. Phoebes watched with satisfaction from her COVID-safe distance as color literally returned to Freya's whiter than white skin. A tinge of pink, as though the blackberries were dyeing her from the inside.

Phoebes clapped her plump hands, punctuating a sudden thought. "I want to do a reading for you!" She went to the cupboard and pulled out a Tarot deck. "Sit down, sit down." Freya obediently sat at the kitchen table. All the windows were open, as was the door, protecting them both from possible infection thanks to the breeze, sweet with cool marine air. Plus, now that the smoothie was consumed both had put their masks back on. Freya didn't know much about Tarot, but she had feelings. Witches and vines and hideous gargoyles. She thought it was probably forbidden by Torah as magic was in general (unless specifically OK'd by God, as when

Moses' rod turned into a snake or parted the Red Sea). But as the old woman stood over at the counter, shuffling the suspect cards, Freya felt it would be rude to refuse and imply that Phoebes was somehow not holy enough. Freya tortured herself about rudeness since she couldn't really tell what was rude and what wasn't. She had to untangle it with logic, which didn't always suffice. Now she preferred to err on the side of caution.

Phoebes approached the table gingerly, and keeping an arm's length, put the deck on the edge of the table, opposite Freya. "Cut." Phoebes retreated again to a safer distance. Freya did as requested and placed the cards back on the table. Phoebes stepped forward again just long enough to lay the top three cards out face up. She held her breath to avoid virus. Then from her safer place across the kitchen, she looked at them pensively. "Hmmm." Freya looked at them, too, but their medieval style designs meant nothing to her. She could read their captions, even upside down. Two of Cups. Hermit. Fool. "Hmmm," said Phoebes.

Freya found herself alarmed. "What?"

"Well. Past. Present. Future. The Hermit is your present. He's telling you now is the time to reflect, to spend time alone, to come to grips with who you are and where you might be going."

"OK." That seemed harmless enough, and probably right. Of course wasn't it one of those things you could say to anyone at any time and it would apply? Like the generalizations in an astrology column in the newspaper, or a fortune cookie. Is there ever a time one shouldn't reflect? Maybe the spend time alone part—sometimes it might be the right time for some people to go on spring break to Acapulco and let loose, but that would never be Freya.

Phoebes studied the cards from afar. Picking up on the energy. "The Two of Cups is your past. It's reversed here."

"Upside down?"

Phoebes nods, and muses. "Were you in love?"

"I *am* in love."

"But there was a betrayal? They betrayed you? Or you betrayed them?"

"I suppose I betrayed him."

Phoebes raised an eyebrow. "Well, we all make mistakes."

"The sad part is it wasn't a mistake. I would have to do it again. And yet I want to die."

"Oh no no no no no. Don't ever say that. Don't manifest that. You're young and the whole world is at your feet." Phoebes looked at Freya for a long minute, while Freya looked at her lap. "Let's look at your future. The Fool."

"That sounds about right."

"It doesn't mean what you think. The Fool's advice is to recognize where you are on your path. Maybe you tripped and fell. Well, own it. Get up and dust yourself off." She tried to hold her tongue, but she couldn't. "Did you sleep with someone else?"

"What? No!"

"OK. I'll mind my own business." This was offered as a tacit request for more information.

Freya didn't read the question in Phoebes' tone and accepted her at her word. She didn't respond at all, leaving the older woman stewing in curiosity. But Phoebes held herself to professional standards when it came to Tarot, so she pried no further. "Only to say, you must study the situation and learn from it, or it's a waste of everybody's time and, it sounds like, pain."

She continued watching Freya. She was growing very fond of this nymph of a girl, and maternal juices were flowing. "What else can I feed you?"

"Nothing thanks. I need to go lie down for a while now."

Though the September sun was shining through the daylight basement windows, she curled into the overly soft mush of her rental mattress, hugging the comforter around her. "I am a larva," she whispered to herself. She wasn't thinking of butterflies. She was thinking of Kafka. She was thinking she might transform into a cockroach.

Where is a safe place to let my mind wander, she asked herself. She thought of school, which felt so very far away now. She thought of her quest to uncover the reality or unreality of the soul. Did this so-called soul have a physical existence, on the atomic level say? Or were there other planes of non-material existence, the astral plane, where an entire alternate world functioned? If something was non-material, could you actually even say it exists? Well, she argued, emotions exist beyond their physical manifestations. Ideas. Imagination. She came down on the side of non-material existence, at least as a possibility. Not to say that ideas, emotions, or imagination didn't have a neurobiological origin, but from there they flew out into the world, and they existed on their own. The same way that stories were more than printed words on a page.

And then another thought came to her. What if one's soul, disembodied, could travel? Could meet up with another? What if her soul could communicate, no, more than communicate, mingle, with Caleb's soul? Wherever he was. Out on bail. Or still in jail. What if she could be with him on that mysterious plane where spirits dwell?

She got out of bed and began to google at the little desk by the window. She wove through Kabbalah and esoterica. Hours later, by then it was dark. Through seers and mediums. Mediums near me. On their websites they described their talents. Not that many of them claimed to be able to communicate with other spirits, the spirits of the dead, though there were two. She emailed both of them, asking if it were possible to connect to a living spirit from a physical distance.

Freya knew it was unlikely the mediums would respond immediately, so she crawled back into the bed, its structure so lenient it gave in even to her slight weight, engulfing her. She managed to reach for her book and read by the light of the bedside lamp until words started to double on the page. The book slipped onto her chest and she slept. Undoubtedly she dreamt, but deep, deep in her subconscious. She would not retrieve it.

One of the mediums never did respond to her missive, perhaps dead from COVID or otherwise occupied. But Number Two, Hitty Galbon, who lived about an hour north in Mt. Vernon where there was an annual tulip festival, where tulips striped the landscape with magentas and orange, and tourists took selfies in the fields hoping the beauty of the flowers rubbed off. When Freya awakened she found an email response from Hitty. The medium suggested a Skype or Zoom call; she wasn't giving in-person sessions because her daughter had severe asthma and couldn't afford to get sick. That was long before kids could be vaccinated, or adults for that matter. Hitty couldn't promise she would be able to connect Freya with a living spirit, but she was willing to try—she was always looking to expand her range—and she wouldn't charge if they were unsuccessful. Freya wrote back that she wanted to schedule a session.

As it turned out the following Saturday looked auspicious to Hitty because of the phase of the moon and the alignment of the planets, and they agreed to Zoom at 10 p.m., once the lunar light was shining. By then Freya had shed her worries about Judaic restrictions, realizing she broke a million prescribed rules every day, so why be concerned about these particular ones regarding magic and the metaphysical universe? There were rules about which sock to put on first. She didn't really think God, if there was God, cared about these minutiae. Metaphysics of course was different; it could interfere in Godly territory, cross up the spiritual circuits possibly. But despite this worry, she trod on hungrily.

At the appointed hour, with her laptop plugged in and turned on, Freya sat at the table by the window. She could see the moon, bluish, like veins under skin, and was optimistic. Hitty's image appeared on the screen. Her frizzy curls obscured her face until she pulled them back into a scrunchy. Her eyes were earnest and sad, as if she bore within her a great weight. Freya wondered if seeing so much, what normal people see, and then also the world beyond, was exhausting.

"I call him Dog Boy," Freya explained after they had exchanged greetings. "His brain has rejected me, but I know his soul would never. I need to reach him. Soul to soul." Obviously at this point she was believing in the soul, or at least that there might be a soul, and hers and his might be able to communicate. She was, after all, desperately unhappy.

Hitty instructed her to put her palm to the screen, so they were hand to hand through the electronosphere. Hitty shut her worried eyes and tried to connect. "Breathe deeply," she instructed. "Focus." So Freya shut her eyes and slowed her inhales and exhales until they were wind tunnels where spirit might roam. Her heart quickened.

"Caleb," she whispered.

"You can put your hand down but keep breathing deeply and keep him in your mind."

They sat for five minutes, then ten. Hitty asked if he liked rap music, and Freya said yes. "I can hear that, anyway," said the medium. "Stay focused." Another ten minutes passed in silence, except for the breezy sound of their breath in and out, synchronized now.

"He's pushing back too hard. He doesn't want to open."

"Please keep trying."

"No. It's not right. He has a right to privacy. I can't invade. But I won't charge you since we didn't break through."

Freya was stunned by disappointment. "OK." She took Hitty at her word about the cost, though someone else might have thought the medium deserved payment for her obvious efforts. "Can you tell me something, though?"

"Yes?"

"When you do connect. What exactly are you connecting with?"

"I'm not sure what you're asking."

"Well, for instance, do you hear voices? And if you hear a voice, how is it projected? From where? From whom?"

"Oh. I see. Well, you know how you see images in your mind's eye? Like a movie playing inside your forehead? Sometimes I see things there. And sometimes I hear things, voices, or sometimes crying, or songs, or screams, in my mind's ears. That's mostly it. Sometimes I feel a touch, like a breeze on my skin, but that has only happened two or three times."

"So it could just be your imagination."

"I see and hear things I know nothing about, but that my clients recognize. I see people's grandparents and lovers I've never seen before wearing clothes or jewelry that my clients remember well. I hear words that mean nothing to me but answer questions for them."

Freya let out a quiet involuntary whimper.

"I'm sorry I couldn't help you," said Hitty.

"That's OK," said Freya, and she clicked the Leave Meeting bar, erasing Hitty from the screen. By then it was midnight. She could hear the creaking of Phoebes' bed in the room above her as the old woman changed position on her mattress. The moon and its light had disappeared, orbiting beyond the window's frame.

Her room opened onto the back garden. She went out and listened to the night. She thought she heard an owl's hoot, and there was rustling in the laurel hedge. Raccoons no doubt. Phoebes had warned they had sharp teeth and mean tempers, though Freya thought she might be able to tame them, given a chance. They traipsed through the yard on a nightly basis. Their route included the chicken coop, which was carefully secured against them, and the garbage can, likewise snapped shut and battened down with a brick to prohibit their rummaging. Freya thought about what she had gleaned from Hitty, while the raccoons scuttled about in the bushes. Hitty had hit a wall, yes, but what exactly was the wall? Was it the edge of Dog Boy's soul? He had hung out the No Entry sign. What territory exactly did he protect? The entire transaction, unsuccessful though it was, where had it occurred? She was beginning to think it undeniable that there was a space, a spiritual space, where meetings of souls occurred, where ideas lingered, where imagination roamed. She knew some called this the astral plane. Was it simply invisible to the naked eye, but made of molecules, like air? Or was it made of some other undetectable substance? A substance yet to be discovered by science? And the soul—was it made of this invisible substance? She had reasoned before that if the soul were a real thing, and not just a projection, then so was God. Was God too made out of this mystic substance? Had she just finally convinced herself that God was real?

Well then, she thought, she would try to pray.

Dear God, she said. She imagined God like the air around her, present, invisible, necessary. Dear God. Please soften Dog Boy toward me. Help him to forgive me. Bring him back to me. I don't know how else I can go on.

Amen.

Chapter Twenty-Four

he trial was scheduled for winter, just before Christmas. Throughout the autumn which came washing through in warm colors and cool breezes, Freya stayed in the daylight basement apartment at Phoebe's house. She helped with the goats and chickens and the kitchen garden as if life were a normal thing, though it wasn't. Not only was the entire world still held hostage by the virus—everyone masked, everyone apart from one another, everyone hibernating back in their houses with the colder weather—but for Freya her ongoing separation from Caleb was an illness that consumed her. She didn't try to go back to school. Her parents accepted the choice, thinking remote school was just not for their daughter. They were college professors, after all, and saw how many students, especially the lower classmen, struggled to learn on Zoom. It was fine with them that she postponed until classes were in person again. But they had it all wrong. Remote school was no problem for Freya, who loved to be remote and completely to herself, as herself. That wasn't it. Consumed as she was, though, by her loss, she could not focus on assignments. Better to spin goat hair into yarn and embroider her pain into her red cloak. She had added black thread to its design.

In September she wandered around the neighborhood, uncharacteristically oblivious to the chrysanthemums and asters in their star-shaped glory as she trekked. On one meandering walk, she discovered a tiny brick library set well back from the road, hidden by a thicket of trees, with an ancient wooden sign at the sidewalk the only advertisement of its presence. THEOSOPHICAL LIBRARY ALL WELCOME, it said, the letters carved and gilded with gold that was scratched and worn. When she wound her way along a mossy path to the front door she found it less universally welcoming, mandating that one person could come in at a time, wearing a mask. A string of bells rang on the inside of the door as

Freya slowly opened it. A powerful blast of sandalwood scent hit her nose as she poked her head inside. A tiny woman, shriveled as a toe soaked too long in a hot tub, looked up from a desk, quickly pulling on her own mask.

"May I come in?" asked Freya. She had run out of books, and even though she didn't know what Theosophy was, she was willing to see if there was anything in this library within a convenient walking distance from her house that she might want to read.

"Of course, dear. There's no one else here."

Freya thought that might be true, or maybe the place was full of ghosts; it felt like it. All the book spines were leather and looked ancient, and there was simply something spooky in the air.

"I haven't seen you here before." The woman's voice was wobbly. She may have been a hundred and twenty years old, with a shock of white hair sticking up in an unintentional mohawk and a velvet shawl around hunched narrow shoulders.

"That's because I've never been here before." Not one to enjoy small talk, Freya swiftly lost herself in the narrow stacks. Sections had labels in a gothic font engraved in leather. The paranormal, karma and reincarnation, the astral plane, chakras/kundalini—every other sort of esoteric arena. Despite the fact that she had recently been exploring some of these very ideas, Freya was getting the creeps. The overpowering incense, the dust, the dark books, the little librarian who looked more like a bird skeleton than a human, combined to make her shiver and she turned to make a getaway. But then a book caught her eye. *The Contours of the Soul*. She pulled it down and read the first paragraph.

"What is the soul?" it asked.

"Yes," she whispered. "Yes, what is the soul?" She read on: "That inner spirit which we recognize intuitively, that which Carl Jung called the Self, is this a real entity, or is it a construct of our imaginations?"

Exactly, she nodded to the author. *That's exactly what I want to know! Yes!*

"And by 'real' what do we actually mean? Do we mean something physical, something perceivable by the five senses? This question leads us to two further important lines of inquiry. First, are the five senses all we have access to? In later chapters we will study this more closely and look at possible evidence of extrasensory perception. Second, could there be physical realms which our scientific instruments have yet to discover? There was a time before the microscope, a time before we had physical evidence of the molecule and the atom. Might there one day be instruments of a new sort that can recognize the reality of an entirely different, more subtle plane?"

Freya emerged from the stacks and hurried to the checkout desk, eliciting an alarmed "Oh" from the bony, raven-like lady in her purple shawl.

"I need to check this out." Freya's urgency alarmed the old woman.

"Do you have a card?"

"No, I told you. I've never been here before. How do I get a card?"

The woman pulled open a drawer and handed Freya a form. "Do you need a pen?"

Freya took the form to a wing chair in the corner. The librarian watched her from across the small room. She sniffled inside her mask, and squinted her eyes, getting a keener view of the girl. The young rarely entered the Theosophical Library these days, gleaning whatever information they wanted from the internet now, and Freya's glossy black hair, smooth ivory skin and rose-colored cheeks burst in like spring to a world that had been all winter for years now. Winter had its own beauty and the raven was skeptical about a new season poking her nose into this kingdom of ice and proximity to death. Still, as the sign outside said, anyone was welcome to delve into the wisdom of the volumes housed here. Maybe the girl would be an avatar for the next generation. Her aura was strong.

"Your aura is very strong," said the old woman, who Freya had decided looked most like Baba Yaga from the story books.

"What do you mean?"

"You're emitting a deep indigo aura."

Freya felt uncomfortable and wanted to make a quick exit. But she was also curious. The woman was making a hand-written library card for her with a shaky hand as Freya looked down at her own hands, her feet, to see if she saw any waves of color, but no. Was Baba Yaga senile, or could she perhaps perceive things unavailable to the average bear?

"It means you are a spiritual seeker. Are you a spiritual seeker?"

"Spiritual ... well ... I'm doing research ..."

The crone nodded and handed Freya both her new card and the book.

"It's due in two weeks. I may not live that long, but someone will be here."

Freya was taken aback. "Are you sick?"

"No dear. Just ancient and ready to move on. Looking forward to the next adventure. Any day now." The old woman's eyes crinkled, so Freya supposed she was smiling behind her mask. She didn't know what to make of it, so left, feeling both eerie and awkward.

As she walked along the woman's last words, any day now, rattled in her brain, shaking loose a song from her mother's record collection, a Joan Baez album, a Bob Dylan song. The words I SHALL BE RELEASED emblazoned themselves on a banner, like a knight's banner, bright on the screen of her forehead: I SHALL BE RELEASED. She heard Joan's honeyed voice.

It was not in Freya's nature to laugh at people, including herself. She didn't ever reflect on her thoughts or actions and think *What the Hell*. She took events of the mind seriously, literally. She wondered if it meant she herself was going to be released, and if so, from what? Or perhaps it referred to Caleb. Maybe Caleb would be released. After all, he and Trey didn't actually do any harm in the end.

COVID precautions prevented Freya's parents from flying out to support her at the trial, but Phoebes went with her. Freya had no intention of watching the whole business, but it was part of her agreement with the police that she would testify. They were trying the two young men together, since their crime was identical, and they didn't want to have one trial for the Black boy and another for the white—too much of a potentially hot potato politically. Best to treat them as the same person.

Because of the virus the judge was in a separate room and so were the witnesses and lawyers. Screens filled the courtroom, and when Freya was called in, there was almost no one else there, a court recorder, a security guard. The overhead monitors made it feel like she was facing the gods of Olympus. She settled into the leather witness chair while a heavily masked tech guy made sure the camera and microphone were functioning properly.

The prosecutor led Freya through her testimony chronologically and thoroughly. It was easy for Freya to answer her questions because her memory was accurate, and she was habitually honest. She did not prevaricate to make herself look better. When it came time for the defense attorney to cross examine, it was the same. The truth and nothing but the truth. Caleb (and Trey) could see her on screen of course, as they were Americans with the right to face their accusers. Caleb was starting to see her with more objectivity, or at least more distance. How odd she was, sitting there, a creature unlike any other, so carefully speaking the truth that would destroy his life. He didn't doubt for a minute her feelings for him. He struggled to understand how she could separate truth and love so surgically. He struggled to understand how he could have failed to see this coldness when he lay beside her.

Freya was devastated not to be physically in the same room as Caleb. Much as she was relieved not to face Trey or Regina and their hate, she had counted on seeing Dog Boy. She knew his loyalty would be aroused once he felt her near him. And now she was denied that access. She could not visit him, she could not see him in court and she wondered if she would ever see him again. The judge released her, and that was that.

Phoebes took her to Molly Moon's for ice cream. Customers had to stand outside the shop and order at a window. There were footprint stickers on the sidewalk to keep people in line 6 feet apart. A lot of anxiety-provoking reminders of peril in order to get a frozen treat, but there they were. Freya, who was convinced to eat dairy by proximity to Phoebe's happy goats and hens, had not had cow's milk ice cream since she was a little girl. Phoebes insisted she choose two scoop flavors, so she did. She licked the first, the coffee, and its creamy sweetness transported her to a place beside herself. The pleasure derailed her from her misery over Dog Boy. The lack thereof. Him. She understood now why some people got fat, because one could eat ice cream and be happy for a moment. She and Phoebes ate their cones as they walked back to the car, and then sat inside Phoebe's old Civic to finish. The best part was the crunchy cone chewed with the last remnants of her second scoop, rocky road. But as soon as she had swallowed that last bit, there was a sick taste in her mouth, a sort of bitter hangover, and her heart sank even further than before, when she had left the courthouse. Phoebe sensed the atmospheric change (though she could not see auras like the Theosophy lady) and asked if Freya was OK. Freya just claimed exhaustion, and a desire to crawl into bed and, she didn't say die, she said read.

She did lie down beneath the duvet on the mushy mattress, and took out the book about the soul, but it felt so abstract when she tried to focus. Like she was trying to catch air in her fists. She gave up and turned from her side to her back, staring up at the ceiling. Tears leaked from the corners of her eyes. She thought of calling her mother and father but fingered her clitoris to soothe herself instead. Imagining it was Caleb's tongue on her. Until she felt that almost painful itch that required so much attention. She rubbed more intensely. Still crying, she came, and then fell into a troubled sleep.

Chapter Twenty-Five

aleb and Trey were convicted and sentenced to five years in prison. The judge who sentenced them was a woman, in her forties, with a gentle voice and a pretty face. It seemed inconceivable to Caleb that someone such as she could ruin their young lives in this way. He didn't yet feel remorse for what they had done, except insofar as it had got him to where he was. He was still feeling put upon by the oppressive system, and his sentence, which he considered excessive, supported his feelings. He did not know that the years in a cell would change him. He didn't realize that he would have time to reflect on every single thing, and to read history, biographies, political philosophy. That his vision of humanity and its cruelty would change his perspective on strategies for change. He did not know that he would come to see the evolution of mankind as a flow chart of everlasting famine, drought, war, migration, colonization, and genocide. Even revolutions were just a part of the fluid and harsh change that continually washed over the globe. And he would come to see the individual as a drop of water, ultimately powerless, useless, his only purpose to survive, help his family survive, his neighbors, maybe his tribe. Years in prison would teach him that his goals were merely short-term health and happiness for himself and his own. The occasional generous act to his neighbors. Nothing else was under his influence, certainly not in his control. All a person could do in this ocean of woe was to tread water.

Of course that was much later. At first he was focused on his outrage. The fluorescent lighting of the institution. The salty smell of the meals—salt seemed the only seasoning on the menu. Trey was not on Caleb's bloc, so he didn't run into him. He met others though, made allies, and managed to outsmart and avoid the most dangerous fellow inmates. He led with his sense of humor, which proved something of an iron dome. He went to the gym to work out and got more buff than he had ever been.

His muscles began to bulge. He witnessed plenty of violence and brutality among the prisoners, and between guards and prisoners. It was a primitive society. As much as possible he kept to himself and read.

Every letter that Freya sent to Caleb was returned. She didn't know what to do. Time was torture. It passed and stabbed her as it fled. Moment after moment was another landscape of searing pain. Phoebes watched with great concern, read Freya's Tarot cards again, and ferreted out Freya's loss not only of Dog Boy but of dog Honeymoon. Phoebes cursed Regina for her cruelty in keeping the pet from the girl who loved him so. She landed on the idea of getting a puppy for Freya. Though Freya was skeptical that anything could help her she allowed Phoebes to drag her to the Humane Society. Like the smaller facility where she had found Wren, here there were two long rows of cages with a corridor in between. The floors were cement. The dogs responded to their captivity in varied ways; some barked for attention pressed up against the bars that contained them, some hovered towards the back of their cages in fear, and some had fallen into a state of ennui, sprawled hopelessly on the concrete. The majority were pit bulls, canine flotsam. Freya and Phoebes walked down one side. Freya made eye contact with each dog who would allow it. She was deeply moved by them, their differences, their apparent personalities, their vulnerability. She longed to kiss and cuddle each of them.

As they walked up the opposite side of the dog prison they came to a section alive with puppies. Waves of love flowed around and through them as they tumbled over one another. Freya unconsciously grabbed onto Phoebes' hand, overcome by emotion. "If you get one this young, you'll have to house train it," Phoebes pointed out, but she wasn't going to object. She wanted Freya to be happy. And she knew how to train a dog— she'd done it many times over the course of her life. As long as Freya took the nighttime potty trips outdoors she was OK with newspapers spread on the kitchen floor for a bit. And the nipping—of course they might get a chewer. She'd have to hide her shoes.

There it was. A small gray pit with sapphire eyes. She was sleek and perfectly formed. She held Freya's gaze, and as if mesmerized, she untangled herself from her puppy crew and made her clumsy way towards the human. Freya poked her fingers through the cage and Celeste (for that would be her name) softly nuzzled her nose against her knuckles. There was not a moment of question that this was a match. Not for Celeste, not for Freya, not for Phoebes. They filled out the requisite paperwork, bought the necessary equipment, paid the adoption fee, and took the puppy home. Sitting in the passenger seat Celeste wiggled into the pocket of Freya's lap, gave out a sigh, and fell asleep. Freya realized she had been freezing ever since she first went to the police months ago now, shivering all the way down to her core, and she finally felt a small part of her body warming. As if Celeste were a miniature wood stove. Freya put her palms around the dog's sweet head and the buzzing in her nerves stopped.

Life had purpose again, narrow, yes, but forward moving. All the girl focused on was caring for and training her baby dog. Celeste was smart. She learned eagerly because it was their shared mission. The dog wanted to please the girl and vice versa. Freya dared to imagine a future, perhaps as a dog trainer, or a doggy daycare owner. Her parents might scoff at such a humble life, but she could glimpse a little contentment in it. The beating heart of the puppy, lying on her chest, was proof enough of the soul's existence. This reminded her she needed to return the book she borrowed from the Theosophical Library. She needn't grasp at the ephemeral evidence of another plane of reality when evidence existed so clearly in the sweet meaty smell of Celeste's breath.

She decided to walk to the little hidden library and give the puppy her first leash training. Celeste's stride was short, thanks to the minimal height of her legs, so it was slow going. Freya carried the soul book under her left arm and held the leash with the other. She marveled at the dog's curiosity and perseverance. On and on they went, a mile that must have seemed a thousand to the small creature. When they arrived at the Theosophical Library Freya tied Celeste's leash around a slim trunk. "Be good. I'll be right back." The dog watched her go into the building and, exhausted by their marathon walk, lay down to rest.

The bell jingled as Freya entered and the exotic smell of incense-heavy air hit her. She wondered if it damaged lungs to breathe that in for hours at a time. The old woman wasn't at the desk today—it was a thin youth with a long black beard and longer hair. His glasses frames were round black plastic above his black mask, and he had a Harry Potter vibe. She was almost surprised he wasn't wearing a cloak studded with stars. "I came to return this book," she said, placing it before him on the desk.

"Did you like it?" he asked as he picked it up and read the cover. He had an accent. Maybe it was Irish.

"I lost interest."

He looked at her more closely. "Why?"

Some might be taken aback by his prying, but to Freya this seemed a natural conversation. "I'm not sure. Timing maybe. I liked it at first, but then . . ." She was thinking of Caleb and the trial and the nausea she had felt for months. ". . . I really just lost my ability to focus. I decided to drop out of college too."

"That's a big decision. But maybe you're meant to learn elsewhere for the time being. Everything happens for a reason."

She laughed, a soft little guffaw, from behind her grapevine embroidered mask. "Do you really believe that? That everything has an intentional cause?"

He peered at her even more closely. "Of course I do. It isn't an anarchic universe."

"No, there are natural laws, like gravity and inertia. But EVERYTHING?"

"The way I see it, if there is an ultimate intelligence, what some people call God, then yes, everything. Karma is working itself out at all times in every way."

"Punishment?"

"Karma isn't punishment. It's a learning system to promote evolution. Maybe that can feel like punishment, if you need a harsh lesson. But we're always moving towards Enlightenment, guided by an intelligent hand. Why do you think you came in here today?"

"To return my book."

It was his turn to guffaw gently. His mask was black, printed with golden stars.

"To have this conversation. To meet me. Both of us can grow through this meeting."

"How?"

"Broaden our experience. Share understanding. Challenge one another."

She had to admit to herself that he had already given her some new ideas to ponder, but what had she done for him? "I don't see me offering you anything."

"Maybe not yet. But if you give me your phone number, we can go for dinner, I will take you, and then I'm sure you can absolutely blow my mind."

It hadn't occurred to her that she would ever have any sort of relationship with any sort of male companion again, and she could literally feel her blood pressure rising. It wasn't comfortable. And yet she was intrigued by the surprise of it. So she gave him her number and he put it into his phone. She told him her name was Freya.

"The Norse goddess of beauty and fertility," he said. And then added quickly: "Don't worry, I'm not flirting."

Flirting was not a behavior that Freya really understood, because it was so indirect and sly, neither characteristics she practiced nor recognized easily in others. He could hardly take his eyes off her. She didn't know this about his eyes since she barely glanced at his face. She remembered to ask him his name.

"Thor," he said. "No. Just kidding. I'm Arthur." Thor who was the lover of the mythological Freya. This was obviously, to almost anyone with a knowledge of mythology, flirting, but still Freya didn't catch on.

"OK, Arthur. Well, I've got to go." She pointed vaguely toward the door. "My puppy. . ."

Outside Celeste was overjoyed to see Freya again as if they had been separated for lifetimes. The little dog jumped up on Freya's shins and licked her knees. When she started to walk, Celeste balked. Freya pulled on the leash, but the dog sat stalwart, unmoving. "C'mon, Girl." But no. There was no movement. Celeste was still light enough to drag, but Freya would never risk choking her or scraping her against the pathway. "Did I walk your little legs too far today?" She scooped the dog up and carried her onward. Cheek-to-cheek they walked.

Freya had a revelation. Or rather she felt a revelation which she didn't articulate verbally. Celeste had a personality and a will and the capacity to love. If this was not a soul, what was? Earlier she had decided that if there were a soul, there must be a God. And as Arthur pointed out, that meant there was intentional intelligence and that things occurred purposefully. She tabled for now the questions this raised about why this God would allow the innocent to suffer. She didn't want to suggest to them, the suffering innocent, that they had a lot to learn and this was their lesson. That hardly seemed nice. For now it was enough that she held a furball and that God, whatever it was, was running the show. It meant there was a future and she only had to lean into it.

Chapter Twenty-Six

ime passed: it was early spring, when the air that had been foggy with winter began to turn a sweet yellow green as the trees budded. Freya was feeding tender emerald-colored grass to the hens when she heard her phone ring. She rushed inside to answer it before it went to message. There was a time she only answered numbers she recognized, and then only if she was in the mood, but now she answered every call from every telemarketer in the hopes that it might be Caleb. Who knew from whence he would call.

"Hello?" Breathlessly.

"Hi, it's Arthur." It had been a while. It took her a moment to remember who Arthur was, though the Irish accent helped to place him. The wizard from the library.

After a back and forth of chitchat, initiated by Arthur, of course, Freya told him that when they initially met she forgot to mention she was married. This took him aback.

"Really? But you're so young."

"Did you know that you can be married as early as twelve in some states if you have parental consent?"

"Did you get married at twelve?"

"No. I didn't have parental consent, but I find that interesting."

"I find that creepy."

"That's what makes it interesting. I am an aficionado of creepy."

"Man. Are you sure you're not available for a date? 'Cause creepy is so cool."

Given even the notion of another option, Freya was absolutely sure she would never love anyone but Caleb. Marriage was forever. It was a covenant, and she would not break it, no matter what. Caleb would come around eventually. It was written, spoken, carved in her flesh. She got off the phone with Arthur. She felt no loss knowing she would never speak to him again.

Just then Phoebes rang the dinner bell. They were no longer keeping their distance from each other; Phoebes trusted that Freya did not have the virus and that she took the appropriate precautions to keep them both safe. So they ate dinner together. Phoebes didn't know why, but she sensed that Freya's mood was lighter than it had been in all the time since she came to live there. Her cheeks had color and she actually looked pretty rather than gray and sickly. A rainy day finally seeing a sunburst. Celeste sat on Freya's feet. They ate quiche made from the hens' eggs and newly thriving garden spinach. They discussed veganism versus vegetarianism, and agreed that as long as dairy products came from family farms that really cared for the animals it was OK to eat eggs and milk and cheese. They agreed that they would go get real butter croissants for breakfast the next day, as Phoebes insisted there was nothing better. And then they listed all the foods that were in contention: really ripe berries (which led to a list of many fruits when eaten at their peaks), chocolate, salad fresh from the garden, crusty bread. Phoebes said that triple fat cheese had to be on the list, and Freya agreed she would try it sometime soon. And they remembered ice cream.

After dinner Freya insisted she would do the dishes. As she thrust her hands into the invitingly warm and soapy water, she noted that she had made a big moral shift by abandoning veganism. That a moral shift was possible was shocking to her. And quite disturbing, really. If morality was not written in stone, like the engraved tablets God purportedly gave to Moses, it was possible some of her other beliefs, assumed till now to be immutable, could be examined and changed. She felt the seas shifting, leaving her adrift. She didn't want to think about it too hard right now, the possibility that maybe she hadn't needed to go to the police to stop Caleb, or that maybe a promise of eternal love wasn't true? She finished the dishes and went downstairs to her room to read, to fill her brain with something a little less thorny. Thankfully the book was engrossing, if a little sad. She was reading *Franny and Zooey* and she thought she could have been Franny, with her spiritual questions and fragility. Except Freya had Celeste the puppy. Phoebes the ewe. Her mother, the donkey. Her dad, the sun bear. A menagerie of love. She tried to be grateful, despite her missing Dog.

It was getting dark and Phoebes had gone to bed. In the backyard Celeste was barking and barking, without cease. Freya called to her, but the puppy wouldn't come. She was barking at something, and even Freya's beloved voice could not distract her. Freya slipped on some sneakers and went out her French doors into the yard. From their pen the goats maa-ed at her, and the chickens came running, their wings akimbo, to the front of their coop, hoping for some juicy grass or pansy petals. She ignored them for now because of Celeste's frantic rooff rooff roofing.

Celeste was staring into the thick laurel hedge at the back of the property, protecting them all from some intruder. "What is it, Girl?" Freya made her way toward her dog. This ignored part of the garden was overgrown, the thick spring grass thigh high, and filled with dandelions and other happy weeds that Phoebes would let the goats out of their pen to clear some afternoon soon. The little seeds at the top of the grasses popped and leapt as Freya swished through them.

Even when Freya arrived at her side Celeste continued barking. The dog was so excited that she levitated off all four feet with each yelp. Freya parted the fat glossy leaves of the laurel to see what she could see. She pulled back abruptly when she realized that it was a raccoon, sitting on a black branch, staring at her with its smart eyes, its sharp teeth visible in what appeared to be a smiling mouth. "I see," she said to Celeste. "Nothing to be done about it, unless you can annoy it to death with your barking. It's clearly not afraid of you. Or me." She backed away, and as she did she accidentally bonked her head against the limb of a budding plum tree that overhung the untamed hedge. A paper wasp nest, pale brown, a pinata shaped like a lantern, dislodged from the impact of her contact and fell to the ground, cracking. While she was regaining her balance, from the inside of the nest an apparently infinite number of angry wasps emerged, as if the gates of hell had opened wide and let loose its demons. They knew who had destroyed their castle and they were out to avenge their kingdom. They stung their enemy and stung her, a buzzzing, buzzzzing, cruel army. There must have been thirty stings.

Once when she was small, Freya had been running barefoot in the daisy speckled grass when she was stung by a bumblebee. Her foot had swollen up like a pink balloon, but her mother had given her Benadryl and removed the stinger. Ruth soothed the angry spot with ice and calamine, read the little girl a story, and all was well. But not so this time.

Freya was shocked by the pain itself, each sting a sharp burning into her cheeks, arms, legs, and then up inside her nightgown, her stomach, her back. She swatted at them and tried to free them by waving her skirt, to no avail. Immediately her throat began to swell and so did her tongue. Her normally white skin turned a rosy red, polka dotted all over with even redder hives. She fell to her knees, unable to take a full breath. She knew she should do something to save herself but her mind was foggy and unable to grasp at any plan of action. The wasps, meanwhile, continued to sting. Forty stings. Fifty. Feeling nauseous, Freya fell onto her side and vomited, soaking her hair with partially digested quiche. She rolled onto her back away from the puddle of puke. She looked up into the night sky in its last stages of dark blue before turning black, and then she shut her eyes.

Even as it was happening, she knew, it could just be a surge of chemicals, meant to protect her from the pain of the stings or the terror of dying. It could be. But it was so strong and so present that she soon just released herself into the experience. She heard the angels singing.

Despite closed eyes she was awash in spring green, willow green light beckoning her into an arbor made of color. The world smelled of lilac. And then it was roses. All the finest fragrances, wafting by one after another. Nutmeg and then anise. And there was grass recently mown. And then flowers again. Orange blossoms. She looked for them inside her lids but could not see them.

In the arena made of light she held her grandmother's hand—she knew it was hers, though she didn't see her. Nerfma, she had called her, because of the dry spongy texture of her skin. Around Freya only soft, sparkling waves of color, as if she were inside the rainbow itself. Swimming in the softness of it. And then. Suddenly a nova—it exploded and all the colors and smells and sensation turned into starlight as her grandmother kissed her cheek.

Celeste moved onto Freya's stomach and mewled. She cried actual tears, like pearls. There they lay, the two of them, throughout the night.

The next morning Phoebes came out to feed the animals. She was pulling out the pail to milk the goats, when she heard the puppy whining from the unkempt back forty, as she called it. "Celeste?" The dog, usually so eager for attention, did not come, but cried louder. Concerned, Phoebes went to explore.

She found Freya like Sleeping Beauty, lying in the high grass. Her skin was no longer red, but a white white, verging on pale blue. From this Phoebes recognized that the girl was dead. She checked her pulse, just to be sure. Her wrist was icy, and there was no heartbeat. Phoebes saw the wasp nest, now empty, and marveled that insects could be so powerful. People romanticized nature, even Freya had romanticized nature, but it was no idyll. Phoebes picked up the dog and carried her into the house. She called 911 and the firemen came, and the police came, and the body was taken away.

Pre-empting the officials, thinking that she would wish the same if she were the parents, Phoebes dialed the emergency number that Freya had left on her application for the Airbnb. She heaved a huge sigh and sent a raspberry through her lips in preparation.

"Hello?" It was Ruth on the other end of the phone.

"Hello. My name is Phoebes Shepherd, and I have been hosting Freya Rubenstein in my household."

"Yes. This is her mother. Is everything OK?"

"Well that's why I'm calling. Everything isn't OK."

Phoebes shared the news of Freya's death and her assumption that she died from an allergic reaction to wasp stings, which is what the EMTs had confirmed. Ruth hung up the phone in shock and went to find Harold in his study. She never bothered him there, so her knock and entry were in and of themselves alarming. The expression on her face nearly stopped his heart. "What?" he said, fearing the worst though he couldn't yet imagine what it was.

No one ever described Ruth as gentle, but she gently put a hand on his shoulder, and told him ever so gently that Freya had died. Those who have not known the grief of outliving a child cannot imagine how very sad they were, and how the sadness never went away.

As far as Caleb was concerned, when Regina told him the news via phone in the federal penitentiary, his anger was still so strong that his first response was relief. Good riddance to bad rubbish. Now he wouldn't have to jump through the hoops of getting a legal divorce. It was only later, lying on his cot in the middle of the night, that he wept.

In fact, he was inconsolable. Somewhere inside him he knew that she was the purest and most precious person he would ever know. Losing her to death was worse than losing his freedom to prison. His captivity was temporary, as he reminded himself daily, sometimes hourly. Freya was gone forever. So he wept. He fell asleep crying.

Epilogue

That very same night there was a meeting of the crones. Present were the elderly librarian from the Theosophical Society who had recently passed onto the next life, and Phoebes from the Airbnb where Freya died. And Mimi Katz, who was a little younger than the rest, but was there because she knew how to run a meeting and could offer that kind of necessary leadership. Rachel, Freya's grandmother, flew in like a great blue heron. They were all very sorry about Freya's death; they agreed that she was full of the sap of life and to see it squeezed out so soon was a little tragic, though of course death came eventually to everyone. The library lady, whose name was Yarrow, had not yet run into the girl on the Other Side, though she looked forward to it. Of course, she and Rachel believed in the afterlife, as they had empirical evidence.

Freya with her long tangles of hair and posey petal skin reminded all the women of their youths. This raised a chorus of sighs. Long ago memories of boys, or in Phoebes' case, girls, with smooth long limbs braided with their own.

Mimi had a talking stick. She explained to the circle of women that only the holder thereof could speak, and that she would then pass it round to the next participant once she had had her say. She passed to her left, and this was Phoebes.

"What are we talking about?" asked Phoebes.

Mimi reached out her hand to take back the stick so she could respond. "Well, anything you want, really, but I suppose whatever Freya brings up for you." Mimi handed the stick, which was decorated with glued-on feathers and sequins, back to Phoebes.

"Well. One thing is I can't get the image of her dead body in my backyard out of my mind. I let the goats back into that section of the yard, and they've eaten it down to the ground. I had let it grow wild and that's how the wasp nest was able to hang there undetected." Phoebes started sobbing. "It's my fault."

Yarrow motioned to have the stick passed to her, but when she went to grab it, it fell to the ground, because of her insubstantial being. "I forgot," she said, looking at the bejeweled staff at her feet. She hadn't been dead long.

Mimi picked it up. "I'll hold it for you. You go ahead."

"I want to say this to you, Phoebes. It is not your fault. The ways of the universe are mysterious but sure. Things happen in their time, and we may be the conduit for occurrences, but we are not their authors."

"Nonsense," said Rachel, Freya's salty grandma, trying to grab the talking stick. But she too was only ghostly matter and couldn't hold a material item.

"Go ahead, Rachel," said Mimi, who was starting to think the talking stick, which worked so well in Advisory Class, was a little clumsy in this setting. She had created an icon to pass around in online school, but that wouldn't really work here either. This was new territory. Meanwhile Rachel was talking.

"That's new age crap. Jews know we are responsible for our own actions." She whinnied like a horse. "Conduit my foot."

Mimi murmured, "I'm Jewish too."

"With a name like Katz, of course you are," said Rachel. "The thing about a Jew is you don't pretend you don't have choices. You have free will." She turned to Phoebes. "That said, accidents happen. You didn't kill my granddaughter. Those friggin' wasps did."

"It's something that bothers me," admitted Mimi, picking up the talking stick from the floor. The others turned to her. "Why does God allow a beautiful child like that to die too soon?"

"Even God is subject to the laws of physics," said Rachel. "You bang into a wasp nest, He's not going to reach down out of Heaven and catch it before it falls."

"Why the hell not?" asked Mimi.

Yarrow smiled. "When you pass over to the other side you will see that the dualities you imagine, good and evil, happiness and sadness, pleasure and pain—they're all an illusion. They are perceptions but not reality."

Mimi was outraged. "Pain is fucking real. Cut the crap." She was thinking of her students who suffered in front of her. She was thinking of victims of famine, war, climate catastrophe. Of young Mei and the several others who had committed suicide on her watch. "In real time, in real physical time, there is pain and it is sometimes unbearable."

Yarrow smiled an enraging grin at Mimi. "Life is but a dream," said Yarrow smugly. Mimi couldn't control herself. She threw the talking stick directly at her, but it went through Yarrow's ghostly body and hit the wall.

"I'm sorry," said Mimi. "I just can't stand it if you minimize suffering."

"I hear you," said Phoebes.

"Life is but a dream," repeated Yarrow.

Mimi glanced over at Rachel, who was shaking her head. "No," said Rachel. "No it isn't."

The next morning before dawn Caleb was woken by someone touching him on the arm. But he looked and there was no one there. But there was someone there. He sat up on his cot. "Freya?"

The only response was gentle puffs of air against his face. Like someone was blowing on him, teasing him. He traced his finger across his lips, feeling the kiss of... what? Nothing. "Is that you?" He spoke aloud to the emptiness.

He remembered their séance by moonlight in the bedroom, reaching out to Mei. That seemed years ago now, though it wasn't really so far in the past. He sat up straight, pulling his legs into the closest semblance of lotus pose that he could muster with his tight boy hips. He breathed carefully. He was conscious of the coolness in his nostrils as he breathed in, and then the heated breath as it came out again.

And then there it was. His cell filled entirely with a floral fragrance; perhaps it was freesia. It couldn't be anything but Freya's soul. The slightest smile came to his face. If she was there with him, then everything would be all right.

Breathe in. Breathe out.

Freya.

Acknowledgments

hank you to all my teachers, students, friends and family. If consciousness is created by experience, then you, along with the books I've read and the beauty I've seen and heard, are the sources of mine. Special gratitude to my longtime writing group, Heidi Raykeil, John Brockhaus, Wendy Rasmussen, and Annie Fergerson, and early readers Lya Badgley, Howard Lovy, Shira Richman, Elise Richman, Kresha Richman Warnock, and Martha Baer.

Thanks to Kayla Higgins and David Warnock for expertise on courts and policing. And thanks for the wonderful crew at Rootstock Publishing: GOAT Samantha Kolber, editor Erin Stalcup, and book designer Eddie Vincent.

About the Author

A native of Seattle, Meg Richman studied painting in college but transitioned to film in graduate school. She worked as a screenwriter in Hollywood for ten years where she wrote the original treatment for Tim Burton's *The Corpse Bride*, a draft of *Up at the Villa* for Sydney Pollack's company, and the pilot for Aaron Spelling's series *Malibu Shores*. The film she wrote and directed, *Under Heaven*, was a jury selection at the Sundance Film Festival and a nominee for an Independent Spirit Award for Joely Richardson's performance.

Motherhood brought her home to the Pacific Northwest where she became a teacher for thirteen years, first at Interagency Academy and then at Franklin High School. She currently writes fiction and has stories published in *Louisiana Literature, Isele Magazine*, and *Judith Magazine*. *Freya the Deer* is her debut novel.

She and her son live with their enormous dog in an old farmhouse in a diverse urban neighborhood, surrounded by the sounds of city sirens and birdsong.

🍃 We Grow Our Books in Montpelier, Vermont

Learn more about our titles in Fiction, Nonfiction, Poetry and Children's Literature at the QR code below or visit www.rootstockpublishing.com.

www.ingramcontent.com/pod-product-compliance
Lightning Source LLC
LaVergne TN
LVHW041632060526
838200LV00040B/1554

*9 7 8 1 5 7 8 6 9 2 1 5 6 *